WATTERS · LEYH · PIETSCH · SATUYO · LAIHO

LUMBERJANES™

A BIRD'S-EYE VIEW

BOOM!
BOX™

Ross Richie...CEO & Founder
Matt Gagnon.......................................Editor-in-Chief
Filip Sablik.............President of Publishing & Marketing
Stephen Christy.................President of Development
Lance Kreiter................VP of Licensing & Merchandising
Phil Barbaro.......................................VP of Finance
Arune Singh.......................................VP of Marketing
Bryce Carlson...................................Managing Editor
Mel Caylo...Marketing Manager
Scott Newman.....................Production Design Manager
Kate Henning.............................Operations Manager
Sierra Hahn...Senior Editor
Dafna Pleban....................Editor, Talent Development
Shannon Watters..Editor
Eric Harburn..Editor
Whitney Leopard......................................Editor

Jasmine Amiri..Editor
Chris Rosa.......................................Associate Editor
Alex Galer..Associate Editor
Cameron Chittock.........................Associate Editor
Matthew Levine.............................Assistant Editor
Sophie Philips-Roberts.....................Assistant Editor
Jillian Crab......................................Production Designer
Michelle Ankley.............................Production Designer
Kara Leopard.................................Production Designer
Grace Park.............................Production Design Assistant
Elizabeth Loughridge................Accounting Coordinator
Stephanie Hocutt.....................Social Media Coordinator
José Meza...Event Coordinator
Holly Aitchison.................................Operations Assistant
Megan Christopher.........................Operations Assistant
Morgan Perry.....................Direct Market Representative

BOOM! BOX™

LUMBERJANES Volume Seven, December 2017. Published by BOOM! Box, a division of Boom Entertainment, Inc. Lumberjanes is ™ & © 2017 Shannon Watters, Grace Ellis, Noelle Stevenson & Brooke Allen. Originally published in single magazine form as LUMBERJANES No. 25-28. ™ & © 2016 Shannon Watters, Grace Ellis, Noelle Stevenson & Brooke Allen. All rights reserved. BOOM! Box™ and the BOOM! Box logo are trademarks of Boom Entertainment, Inc., registered in various countries and categories. All characters, events, and institutions depicted herein are fictional. Any similarity between any of the names, characters, persons, events, and/or institutions in this publication to actual names, characters, and persons, whether living or dead, events, and/or institutions is unintended and purely coincidental. BOOM! Box does not read or accept unsolicited submissions of ideas, stories, or artwork.

BOOM! Studios, 5670 Wilshire Boulevard, Suite 450, Los Angeles, CA 90036-5679. Printed in China. First Printing.

ISBN: 978-1-68415-045-8, eISBN: 978-1-61398-722-3

THIS LUMBERJANES FIELD MANUAL BELONGS TO:

NAME:_____

TROOP:_____

DATE INVESTED:_____

FIELD MANUAL TABLE OF CONTENTS

LUMBERJANES
FIELD MANUAL

For the Intermediate Program

Tenth Edition • July 1984

Prepared for the

Miss Qiunzella Thiskwin
Penniquiqul Thistle Crumpet's

CAMP FOR  HARDCORE LADY-TYPES

"Friendship to the Max!"

A MESSAGE FROM THE LUMBERJANES HIGH COUNCIL

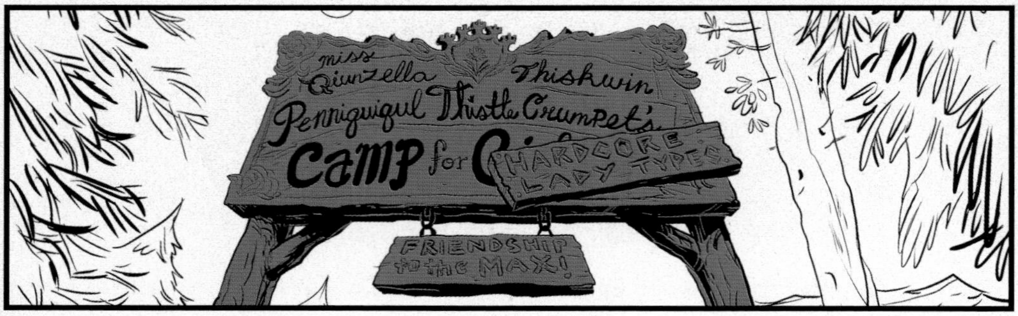
miss
Quinzella
Thiskwin
Penniquiqul Thistle Crumpet's
Camp for
HARDCORE LADY TYPES
FRIENDSHIP to the MAX!

At our camp, we hope to teach you Lumberjane scouts to cultivate an appreciation for nature and the world around you. There is, after all, so much to see and experience when one's mind is not only open, but eager and excited to learn. We hope that in your time here you will come to see the beauty in all things, from the wriggling tails of tadpoles, to the brilliant colors of a sunset, to the way the new fronds of a fern unfurl in the early morning, coated with dew and hungry for sunlight.

But, just as much as we want you to come to appreciate animals both wild and tame, and as much as we hope that you will learn to nurture the plants of the forest and field, so too do we dearly hope that you will learn to care for and cultivate yourself.

It can be easy to forget, particularly when faced with the wonders of the world, and even more so when one is young and eager to explore, but you, too, are a precious growing thing. You, too, are constantly changing in incredible and implacable ways. And just as we hope that you will learn to see the beauty and intricacy in a spider's web, we hope that you will also see how everything that you are, and everything that you might one day become, is something amazing and worth holding dear.

Allow yourself those soft and quiet moments of thought, whether they come to you through writing in a diary, or through creating things, or through drinking hot chocolate and allowing the steam to warm your face or fog your glasses. Try your best to forgive yourself for past mistakes, but also be brave enough to try new things and to open yourself up to make new mistakes and bigger mistakes.

Dive headfirst into the lake and climb mountains… but also remember to take a satisfied sigh from the top of that mountain and to look to yourselves, young scouts. You've climbed both farther and further than you ever had before this summer. Take a moment to catch your breath and feel proud of yourself, and know that you are capable of so much, if you only give yourself the room and permission to keep growing and changing.

THE LUMBERJANES PLEDGE

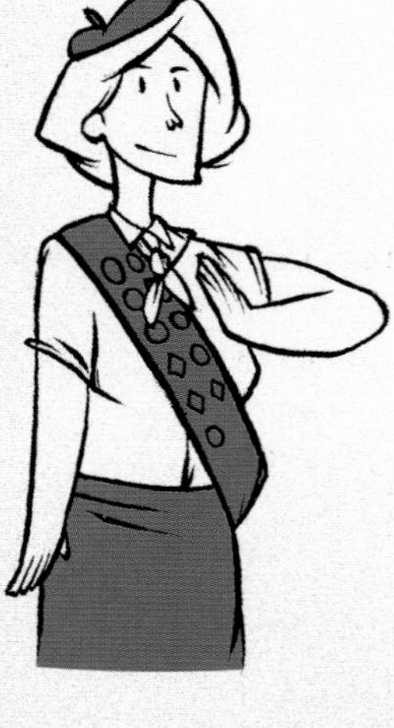

I solemnly swear to do my best
Every day, and in all that I do,
To be brave and strong,
To be truthful and compassionate,
To be interesting and interested,
To pay attention and question
The world around me,
To think of others first,
To always help and protect my friends,
[redacted]
And to make the world a better place
For Lumberjane scouts
And for everyone else.

THEN THERE'S A LINE ABOUT GOD, OR WHATEVER

LUMBERJANES™

A BIRD'S-EYE VIEW

Written by
Shannon Watters
& Kat Leyh

Chapter 25 Illustrated by
Carey Pietsch

Chapters 26-27 Illustrated by
Ayme Sotuyo

Colors by
Maarta Laiho

Letters by
Aubrey Aiese

Cover by
Noelle Stevenson

Badge Designs
Kelsey Dieterich
Designer
Marie Krupina
Assistant Editor
Sophie Philips-Roberts
Editors
Dafna Pleban & Whitney Leopard
Special thanks to **Kelsey Pate** for giving the Lumberjanes their name.

Created by **Shannon Watters, Grace Ellis, Noelle Stevenson & Brooke Allen**

LUMBERJANES FIELD MANUAL

CHAPTER TWENTY-FIVE

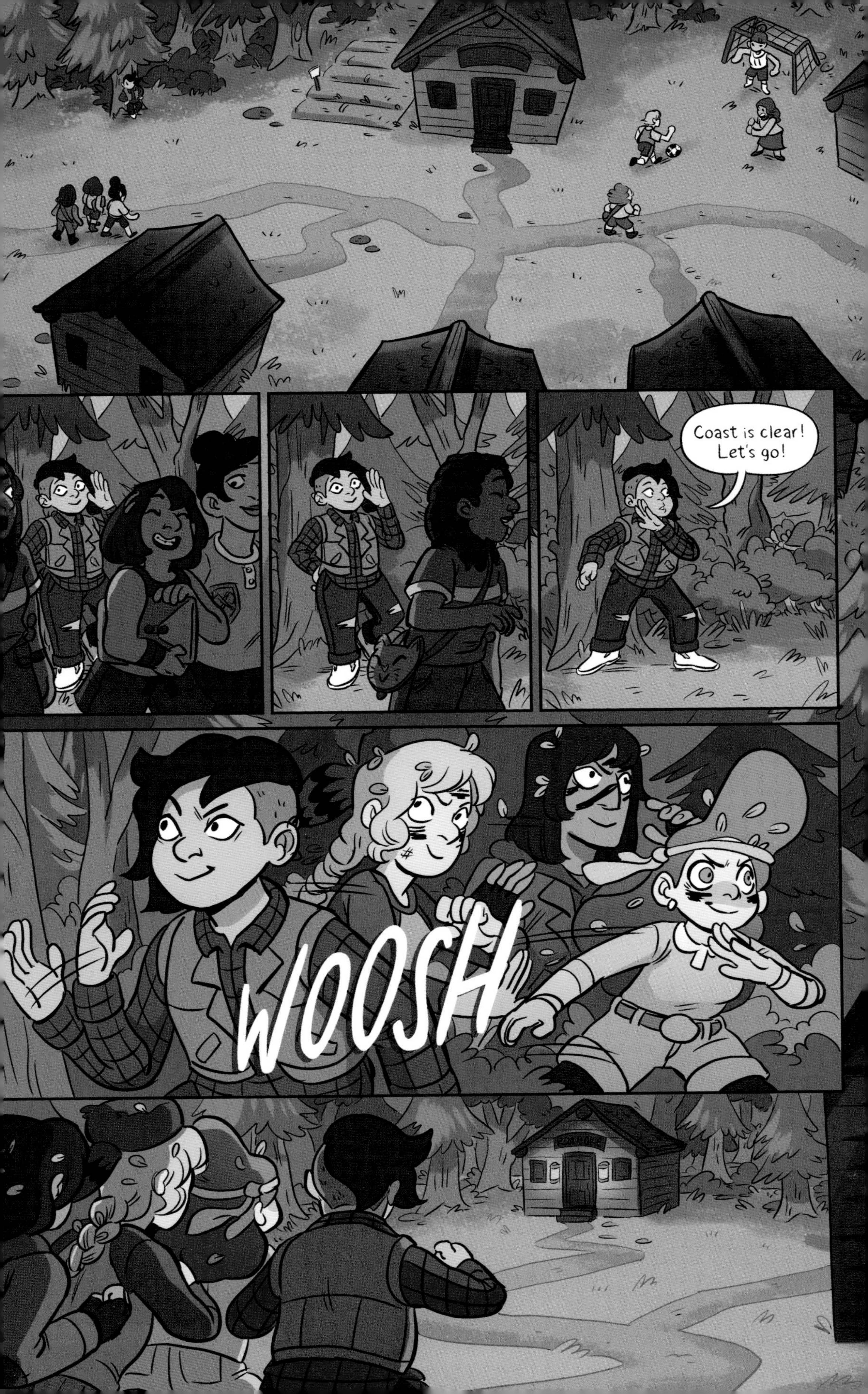
Coast is clear! Let's go!
WOOSH

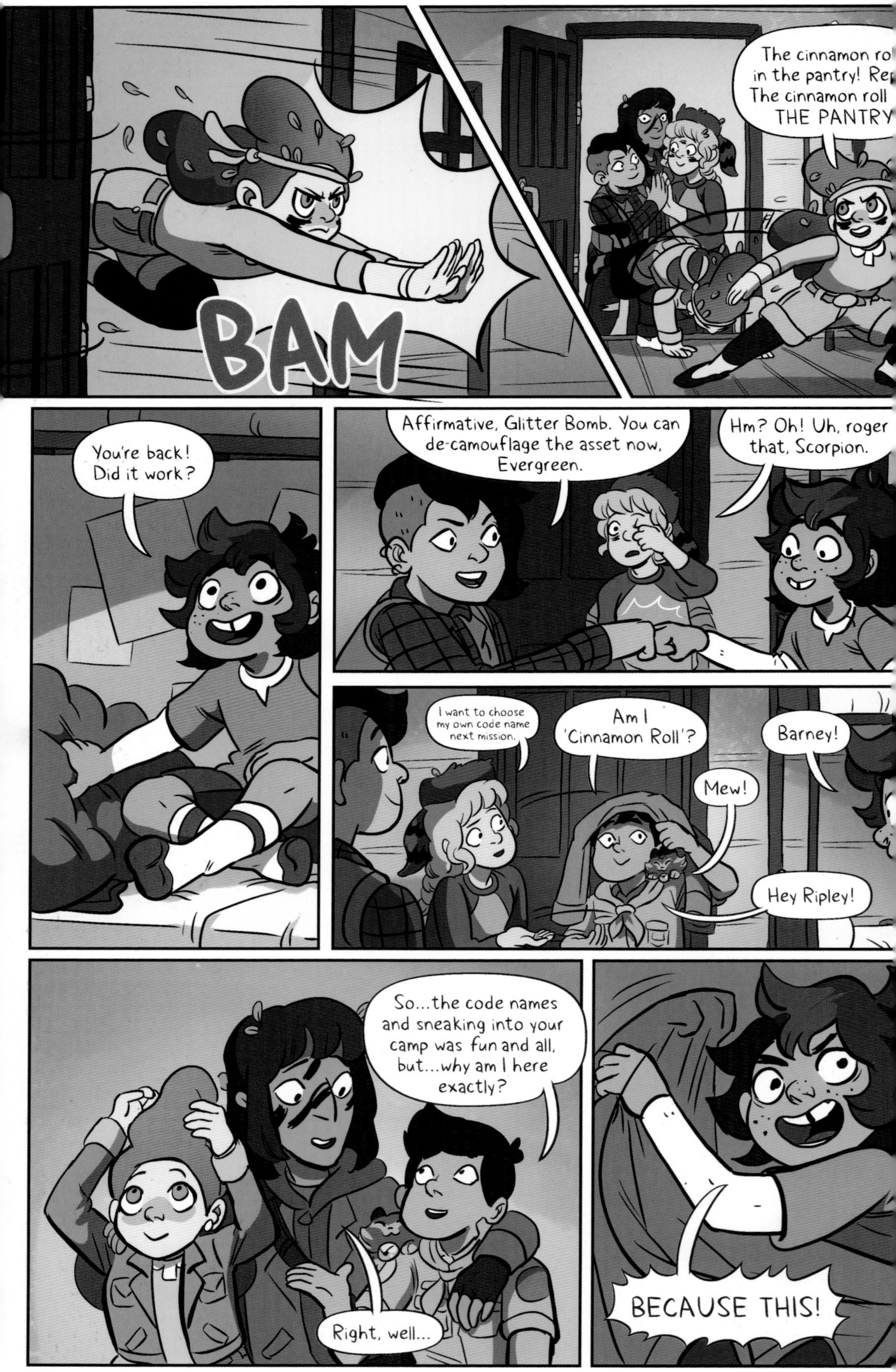
BAM
The cinnamon ro
in the pantry! Re
The cinnamon roll
THE PANTRY
You're back! Did it work?
Affirmative, Glitter Bomb. You can de-camouflage the asset now, Evergreen.
Hm? Oh! Uh, roger that, Scorpion.
I want to choose my own code name next mission.
Am I 'Cinnamon Roll'?
Barney!
Mew!
Hey Ripley!
So...the code names and sneaking into your camp was fun and all, but...why am I here exactly?
Right, well...
BECAUSE THIS!

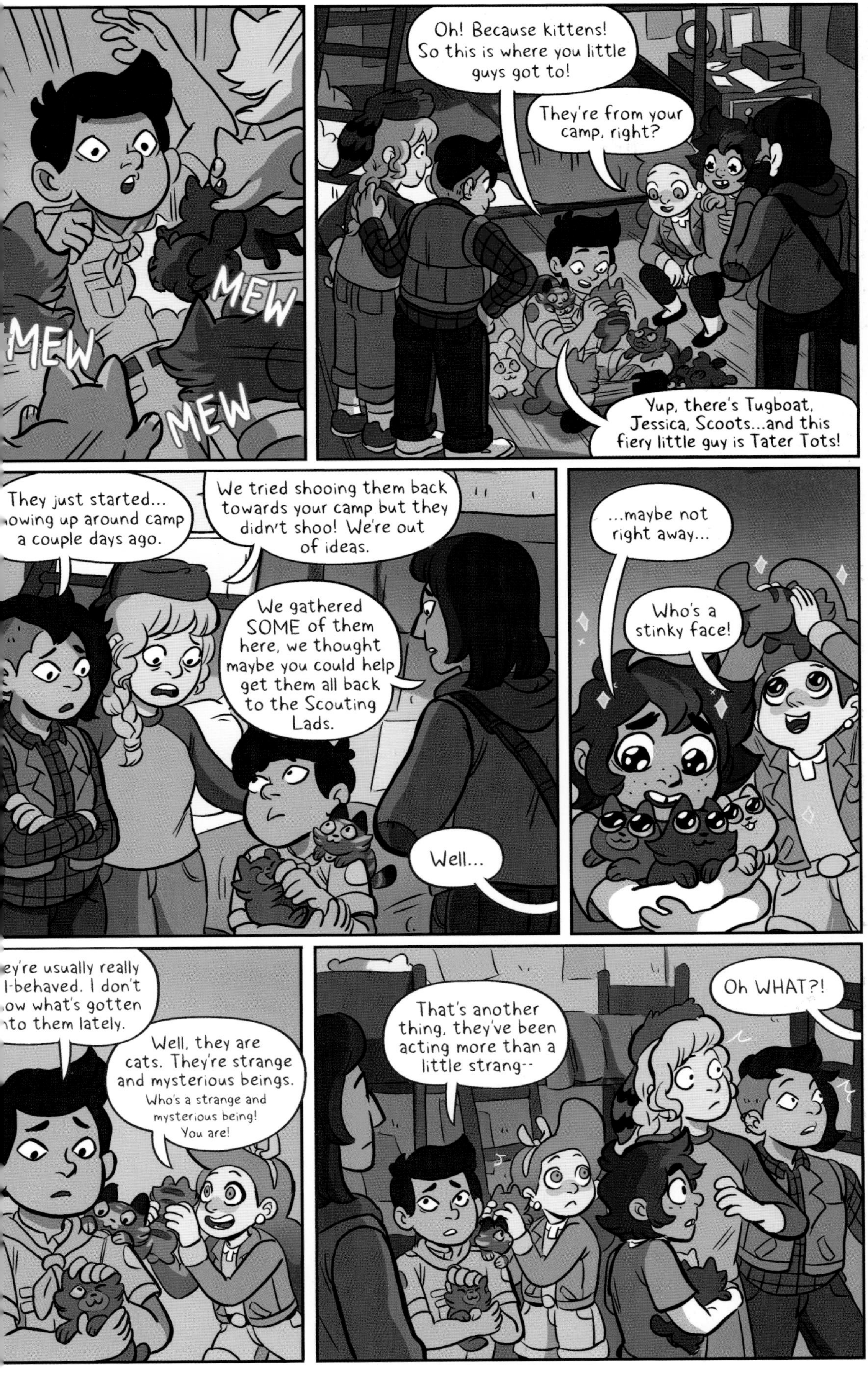
MEW
MEW
MEW
Oh! Because kittens! So this is where you little guys got to!
They're from your camp, right?
Yup, there's Tugboat, Jessica, Scoots...and this fiery little guy is Tater Tots!
They just started... owing up around camp a couple days ago.
We tried shooing them back towards your camp but they didn't shoo! We're out of ideas.
We gathered SOME of them here, we thought maybe you could help get them all back to the Scouting Lads.
Well...
...maybe not right away...
Who's a stinky face!
ey're usually really l-behaved. I don't ow what's gotten nto them lately.
Well, they are cats. They're strange and mysterious beings.
Who's a strange and mysterious being! You are!
That's another thing, they've been acting more than a little strang--
Oh WHAT?!

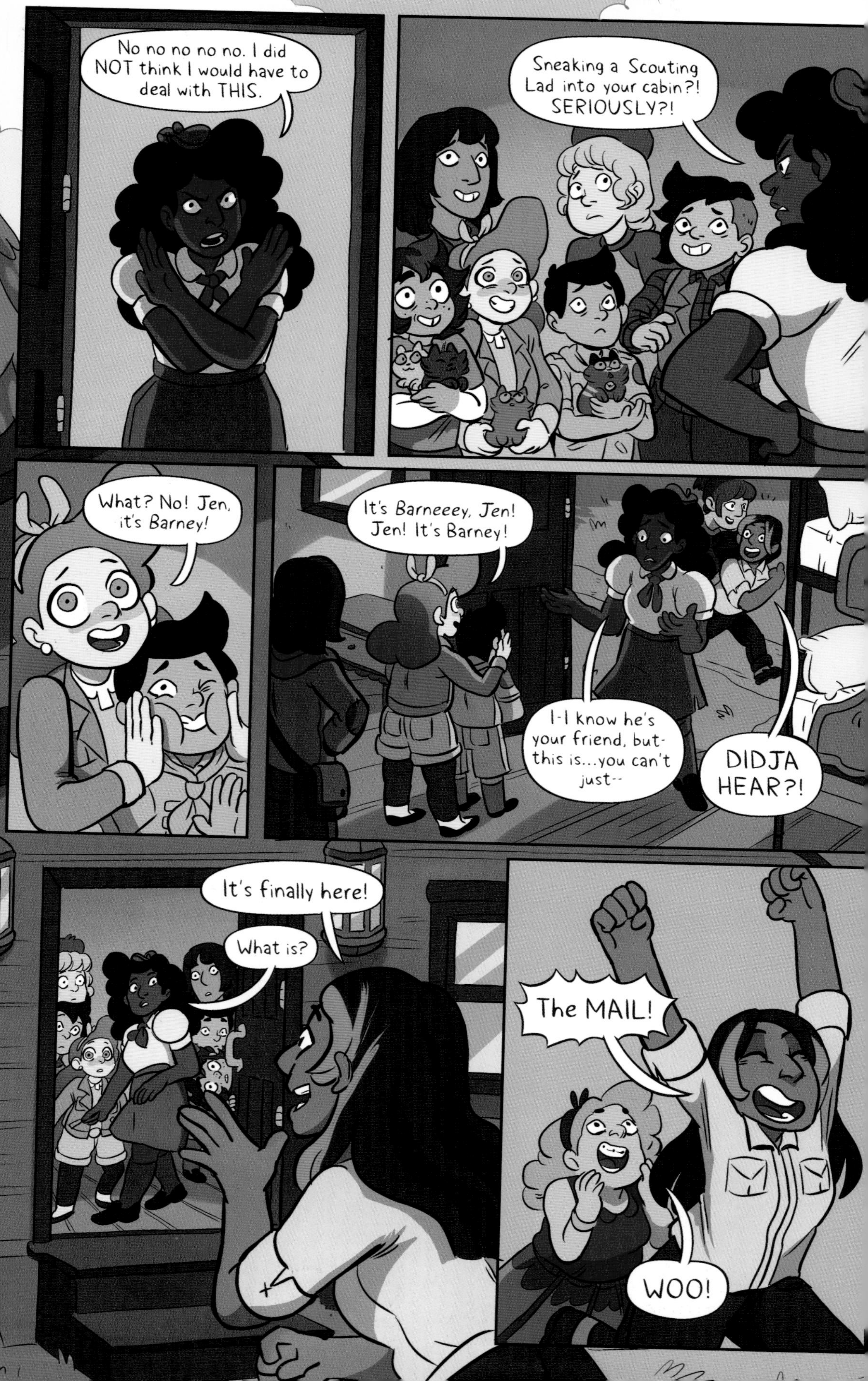
No no no no no. I did NOT think I would have to deal with THIS.
Sneaking a Scouting Lad into your cabin?! SERIOUSLY?!
What? No! Jen, it's Barney!
It's Barneeey, Jen! Jen! It's Barney!
I-I know he's your friend, but-this is...you can't just--
DIDJA HEAR?!
It's finally here!
What is?
The MAIL!
WOO!

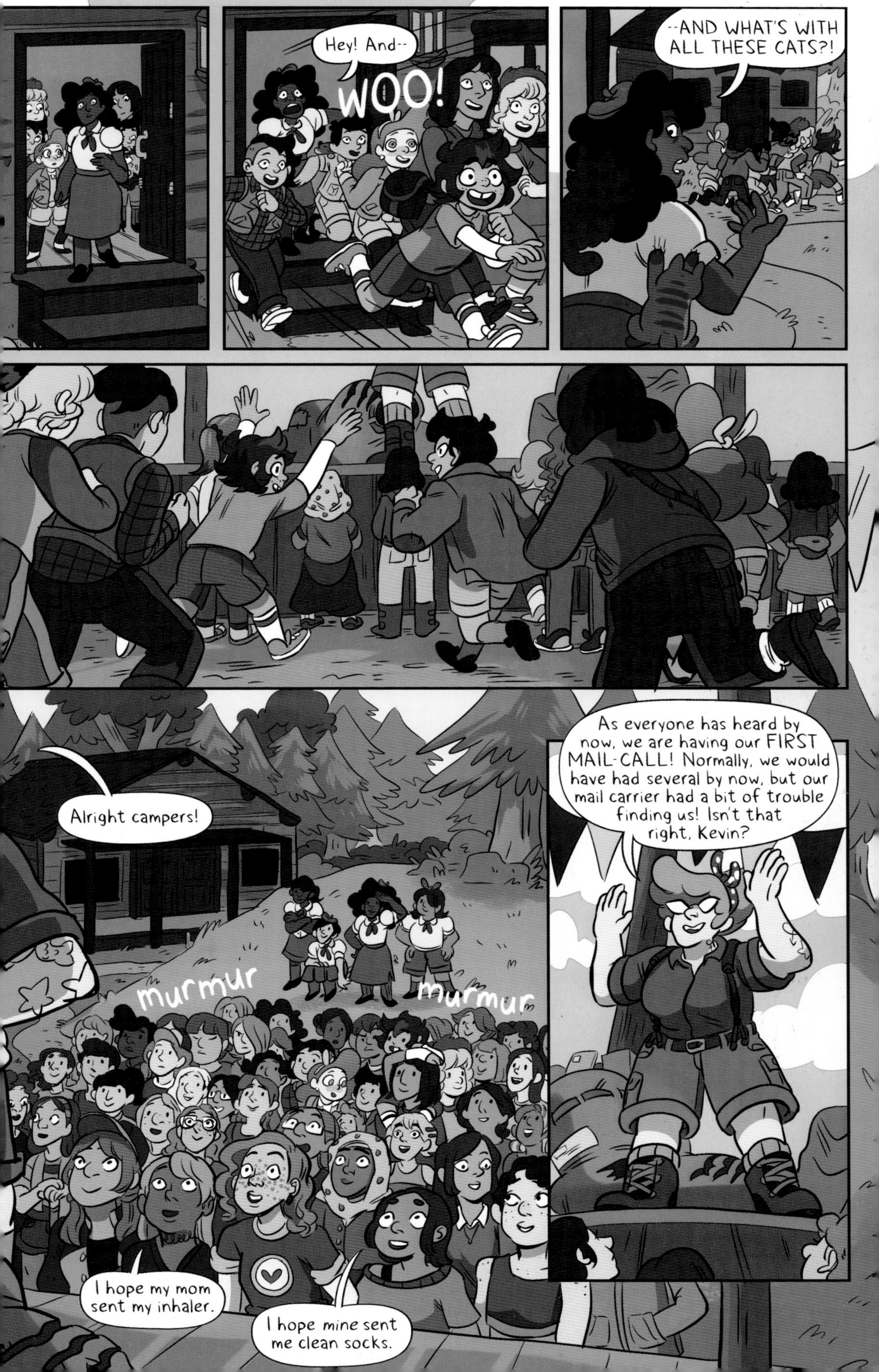
Hey! And--
WOO!
--AND WHAT'S WITH ALL THESE CATS?!
Alright campers!
As everyone has heard by now, we are having our FIRST MAIL-CALL! Normally, we would have had several by now, but our mail carrier had a bit of trouble finding us! Isn't that right, Kevin?
murmur
murmur
I hope my mom sent my inhaler.
I hope mine sent me clean socks.

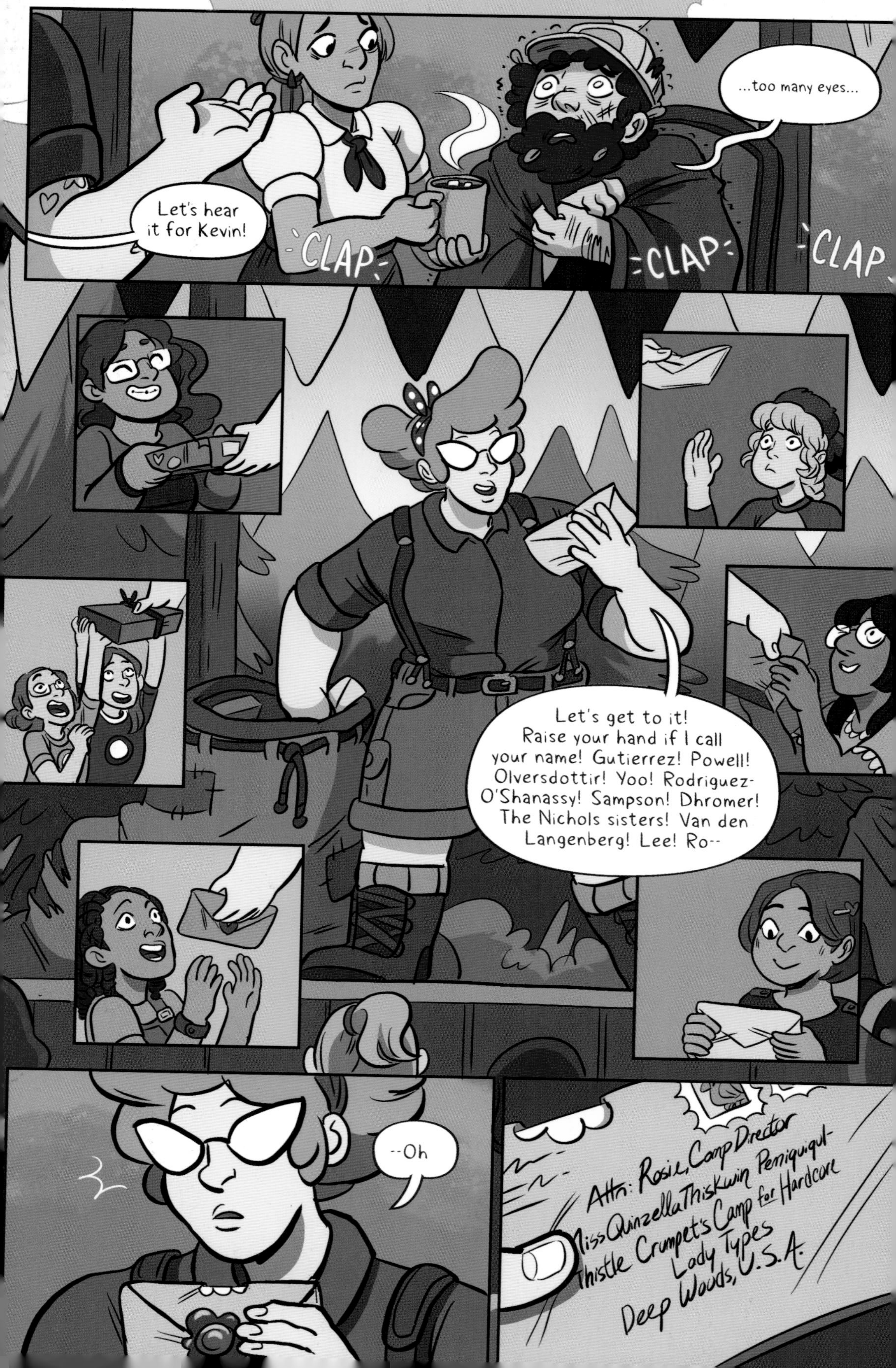
...too many eyes...
Let's hear it for Kevin!
CLAP
CLAP
CLAP
Let's get to it! Raise your hand if I call your name! Gutierrez! Powell! Olversdottir! Yoo! Rodriguez-O'Shanassy! Sampson! Dhromer! The Nichols sisters! Van den Langenberg! Lee! Ro--
--Oh
Attn: Rosie, Camp Director
Miss Quinzella Thiskwin Penniquiqul-Thistle Crumpet's Camp for Hardcore Lady Types
Deep Woods, U.S.A.

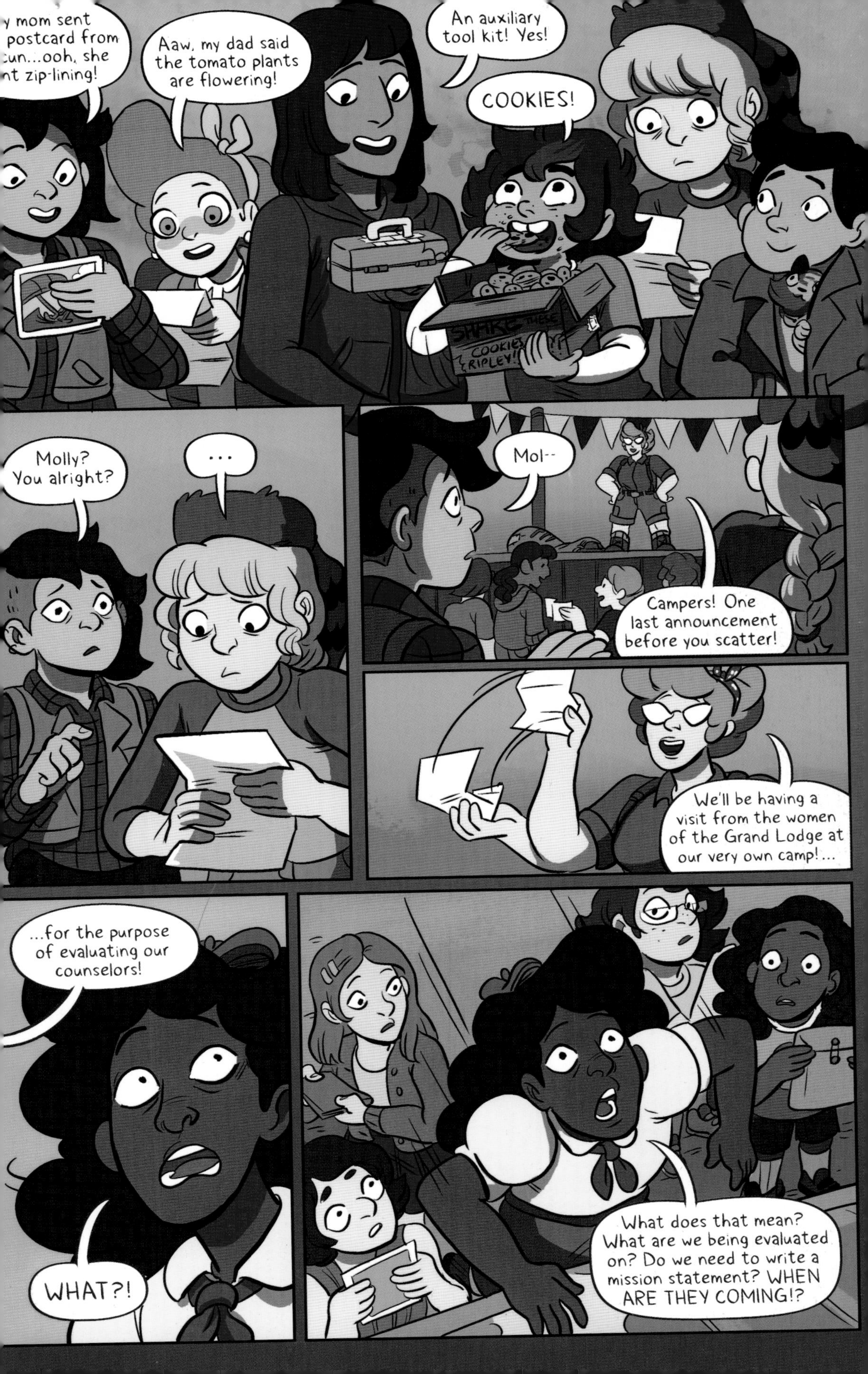
y mom sent
postcard from
cun...ooh, she
nt zip-lining!
Aaw, my dad said the tomato plants are flowering!
An auxiliary tool kit! Yes!
COOKIES!
SHAKE THESE COOKIES RIPLEY!
Molly? You alright?
...
Mol--
Campers! One last announcement before you scatter!
We'll be having a visit from the women of the Grand Lodge at our very own camp!...
...for the purpose of evaluating our counselors!
WHAT?!
What does that mean? What are we being evaluated on? Do we need to write a mission statement? WHEN ARE THEY COMING!?

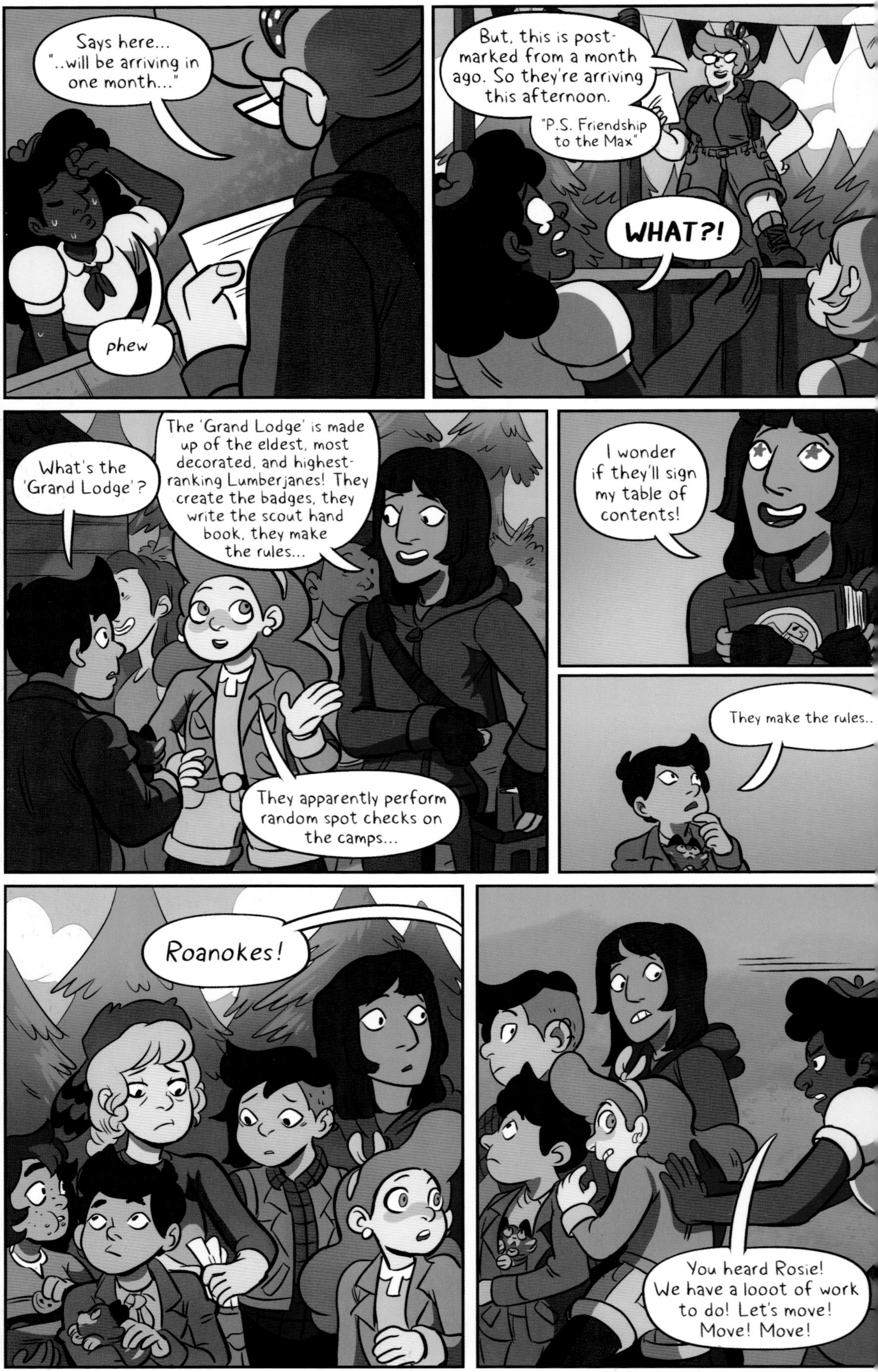
Says here... "..will be arriving in one month..."
phew
But, this is post-marked from a month ago. So they're arriving this afternoon.
"P.S. Friendship to the Max"
WHAT?!
What's the 'Grand Lodge'?
The 'Grand Lodge' is made up of the eldest, most decorated, and highest-ranking Lumberjanes! They create the badges, they write the scout hand book, they make the rules...
They apparently perform random spot checks on the camps...
I wonder if they'll sign my table of contents!
They make the rules..
Roanokes!
You heard Rosie! We have a looot of work to do! Let's move! Move! Move!

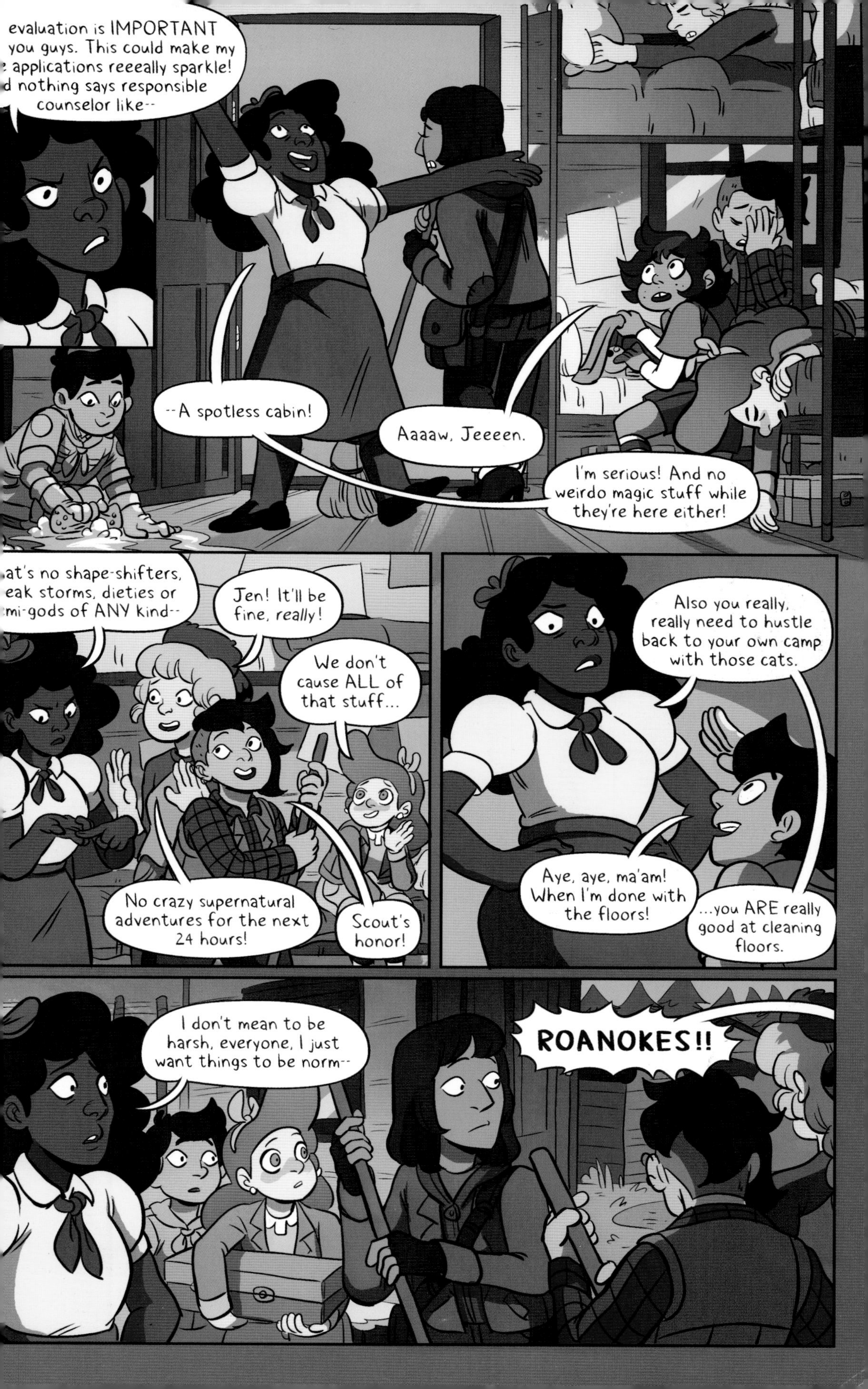
evaluation is IMPORTANT you guys. This could make my applications reeeally sparkle! nothing says responsible counselor like--
--A spotless cabin!
Aaaaw, Jeeeen.
I'm serious! And no weirdo magic stuff while they're here either!
at's no shape-shifters, eak storms, dieties or mi-gods of ANY kind--
Jen! It'll be fine, *really*!
We don't cause ALL of that stuff...
No crazy supernatural adventures for the next 24 hours!
Scout's honor!
Also you really, really need to hustle back to your own camp with those cats.
Aye, aye, ma'am! When I'm done with the floors!
...you ARE really good at cleaning floors.
I don't mean to be harsh, everyone, I just want things to be norm--
ROANOKES!!

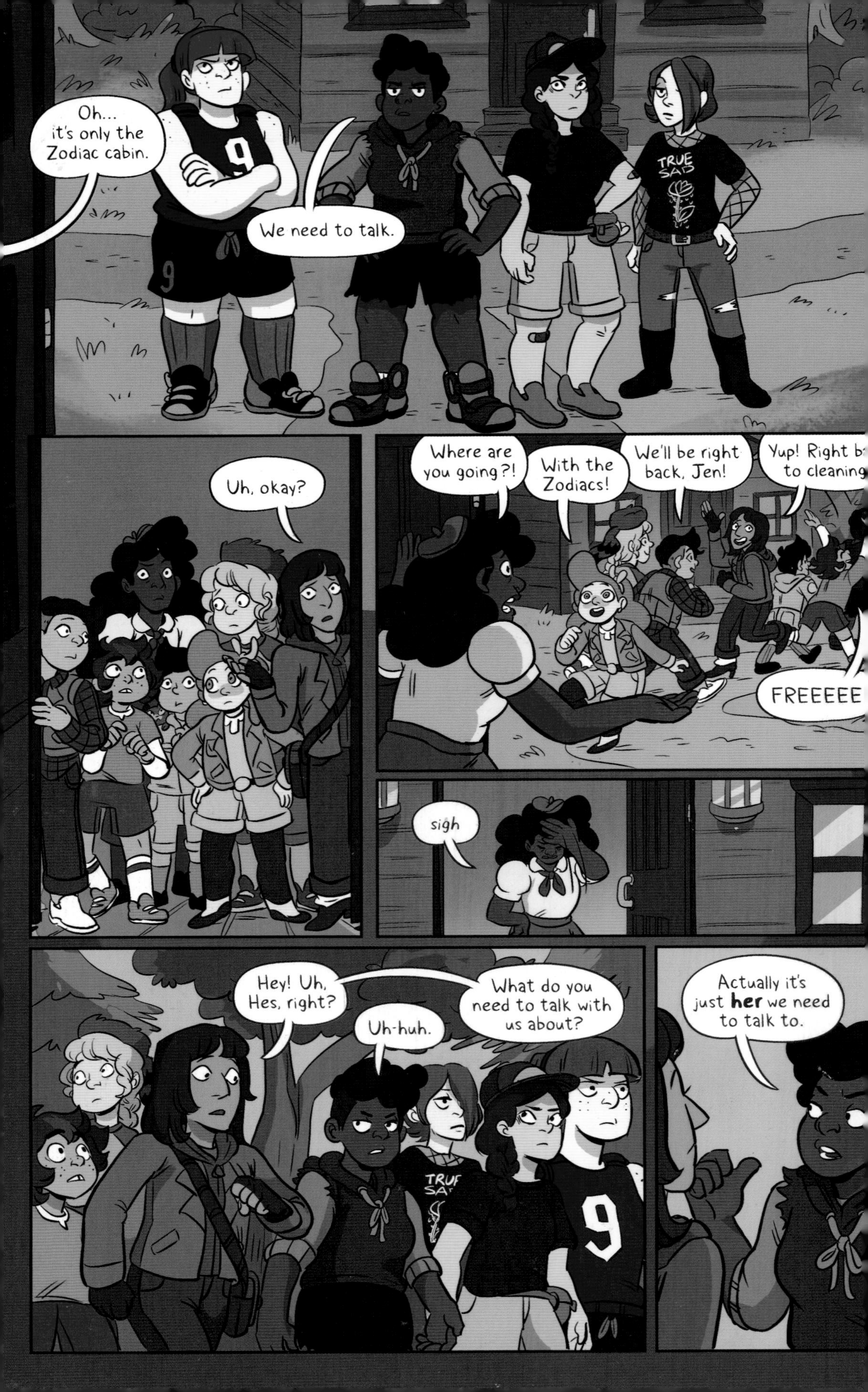

Oh... it's only the Zodiac cabin.
We need to talk.
Uh, okay?
Where are you going?!
With the Zodiacs!
We'll be right back, Jen!
Yup! Right b
to cleaning
FREEEEEE
sigh
Hey! Uh, Hes, right?
Uh-huh.
What do you need to talk with us about?
Actually it's just **her** we need to talk to.

Huh?

Ripley? Why?

Remember when you were briefly a god a couple weeks ago?

And created all those kittens?

Yeah!

Well NOW they're HERE. Making seven shades of mess! We need you to deal with them, since you made them!

That's all? We already know they're here.

Yeah, we're on top of it, that's why Barney's here!

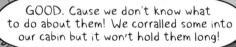

GOOD. Cause we don't know what to do about them! We corralled some into our cabin but it won't hold them long!

I can't go back in there...

Be strong, Emily.

What's so bad about a few teeny little kittens?

ZODIAC

...they've been going through some...

I was about to tell you guys earlier...

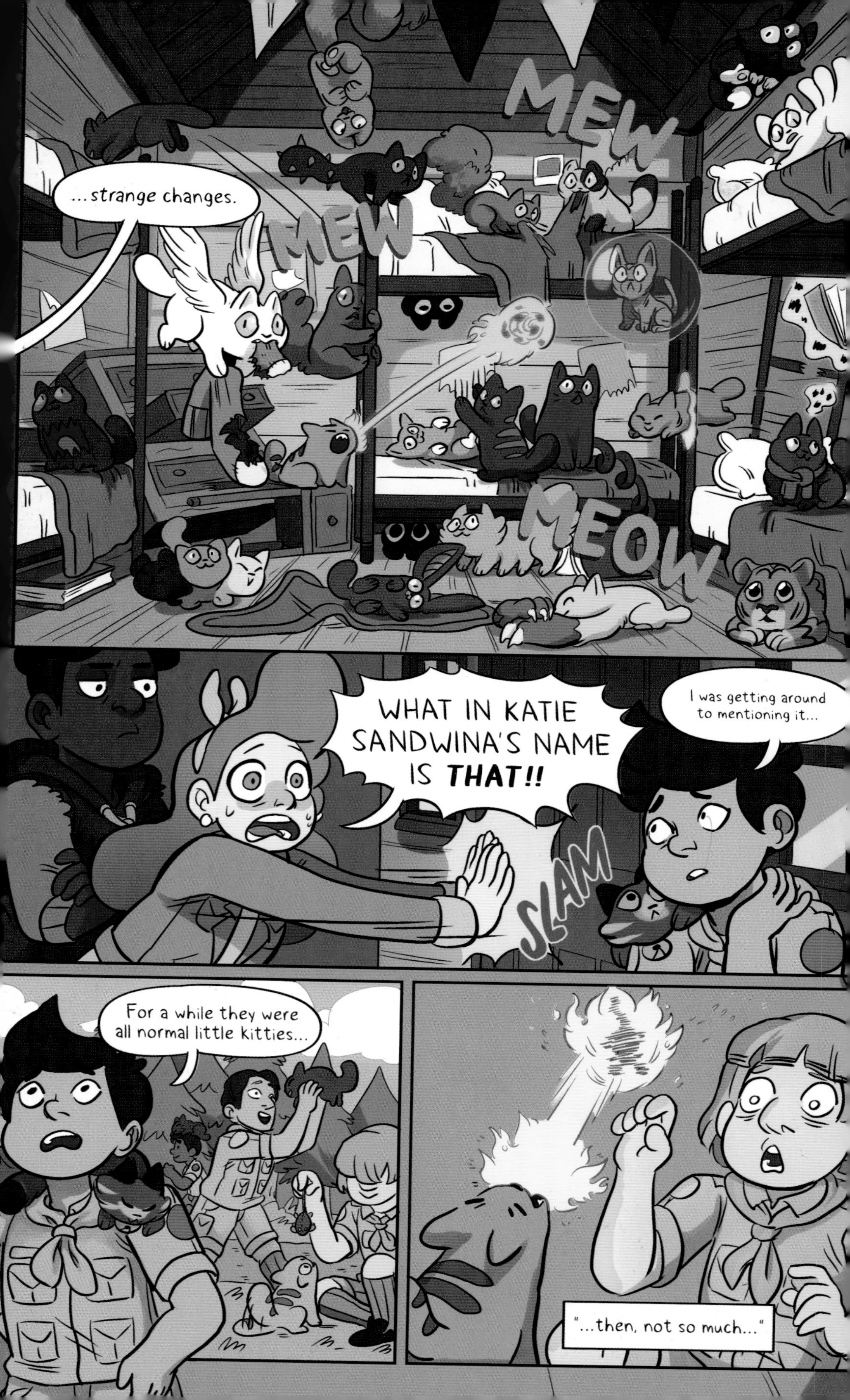

...strange changes.
MEW
MEW
MEOW
WHAT IN KATIE SANDWINA'S NAME IS **THAT!!**
I was getting around to mentioning it...
SLAM
For a while they were all normal little kitties...
"...then, not so much..."

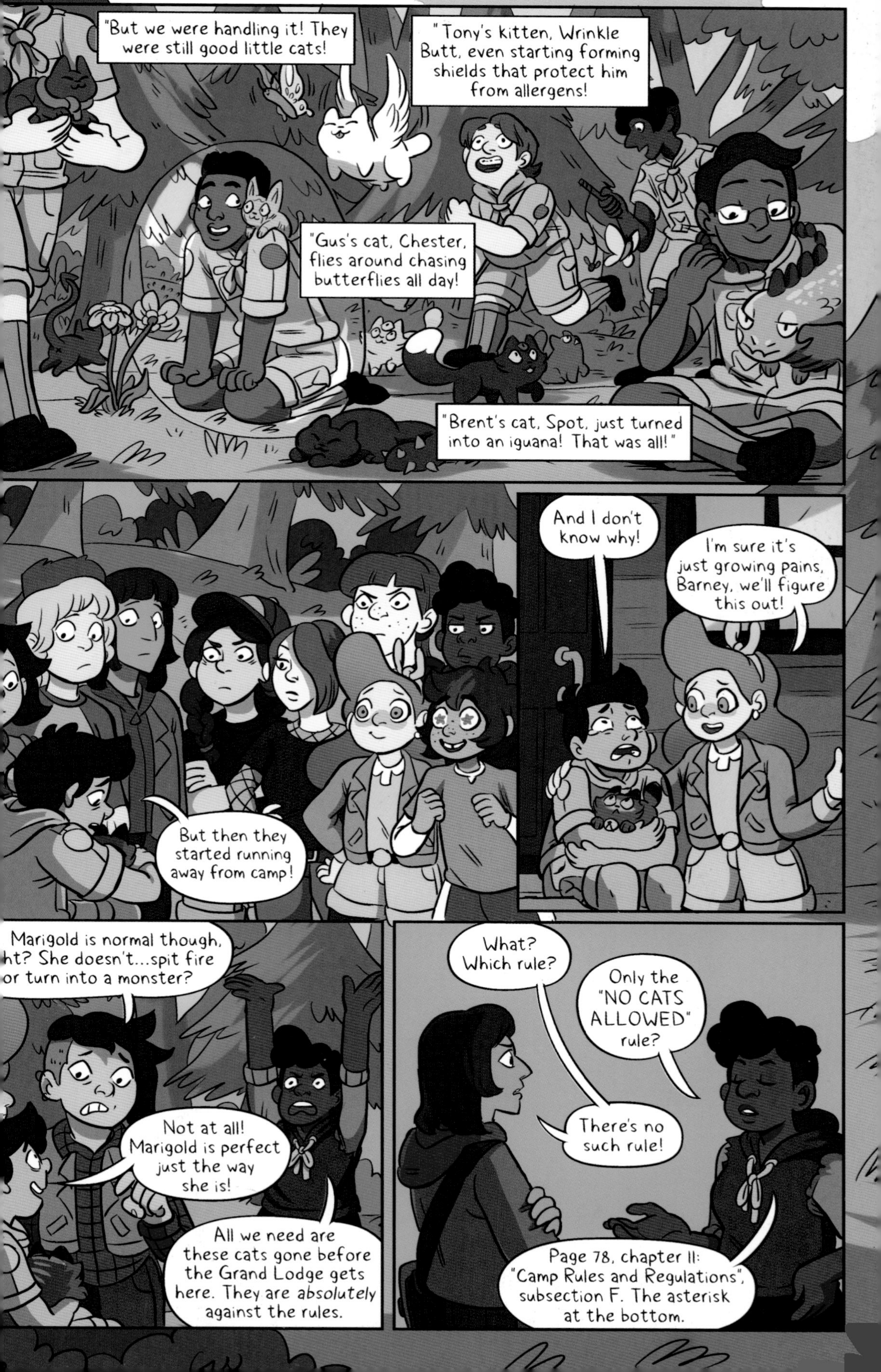
"But we were handling it! They were still good little cats!
"Tony's kitten, Wrinkle Butt, even starting forming shields that protect him from allergens!
"Gus's cat, Chester, flies around chasing butterflies all day!
"Brent's cat, Spot, just turned into an iguana! That was all!"
But then they started running away from camp!
And I don't know why!
I'm sure it's just growing pains, Barney, we'll figure this out!
Marigold is normal though, ht? She doesn't...spit fire or turn into a monster?
Not at all! Marigold is perfect just the way she is!
All we need are these cats gone before the Grand Lodge gets here. They are *absolutely* against the rules.
What? Which rule?
Only the "NO CATS ALLOWED" rule?
There's no such rule!
Page 78, chapter 11: "Camp Rules and Regulations", subsection F. The asterisk at the bottom.

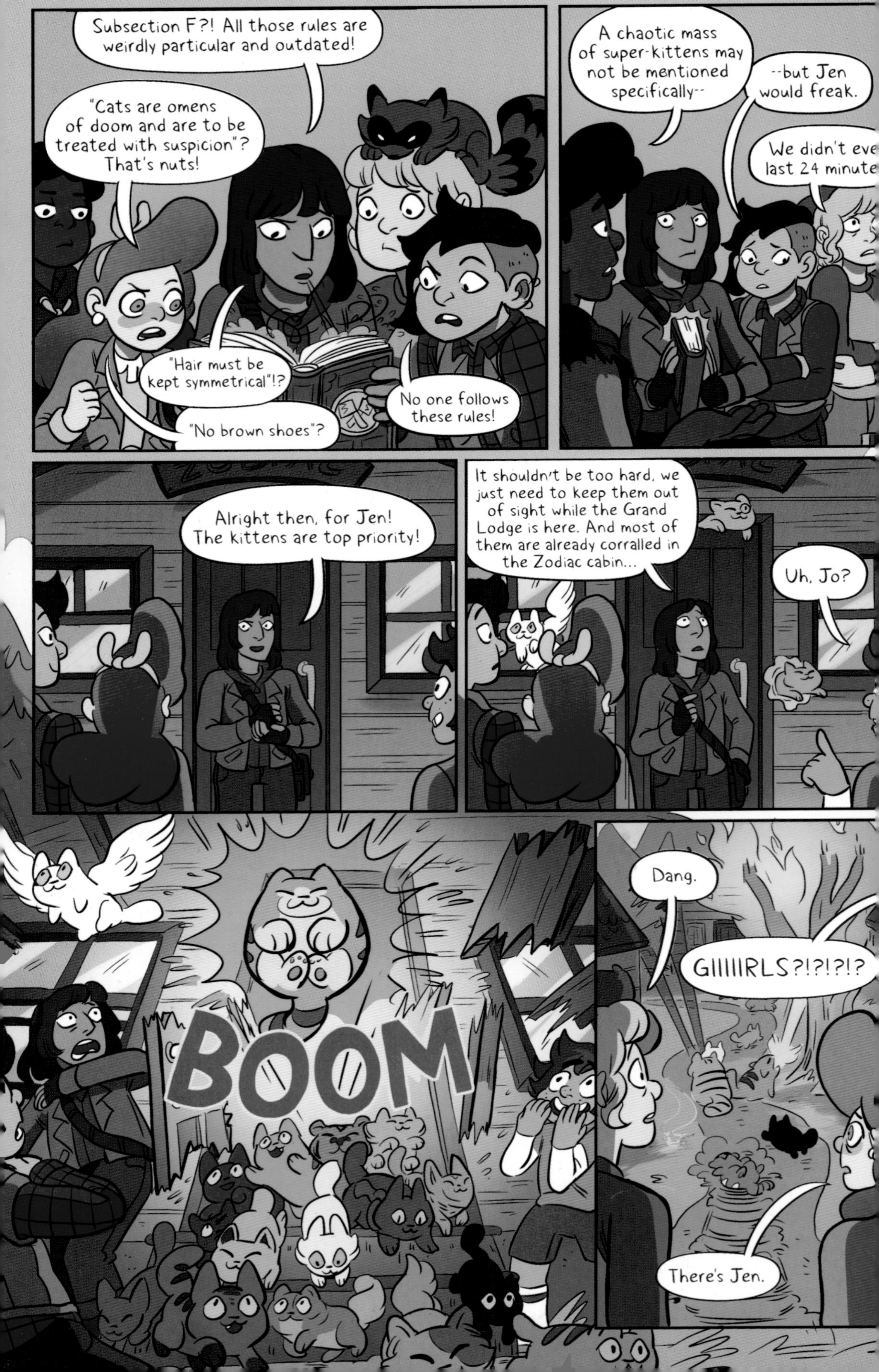
Subsection F?! All those rules are weirdly particular and outdated!
"Cats are omens of doom and are to be treated with suspicion"? That's nuts!
"Hair must be kept symmetrical"!?
"No brown shoes"?
No one follows these rules!
A chaotic mass of super-kittens may not be mentioned specifically--
--but Jen would freak.
We didn't eve last 24 minute
Alright then, for Jen! The kittens are top priority!
It shouldn't be too hard, we just need to keep them out of sight while the Grand Lodge is here. And most of them are already corralled in the Zodiac cabin...
Uh, Jo?
BOOM
Dang.
GIIIIIRLS?!?!?!?
There's Jen.

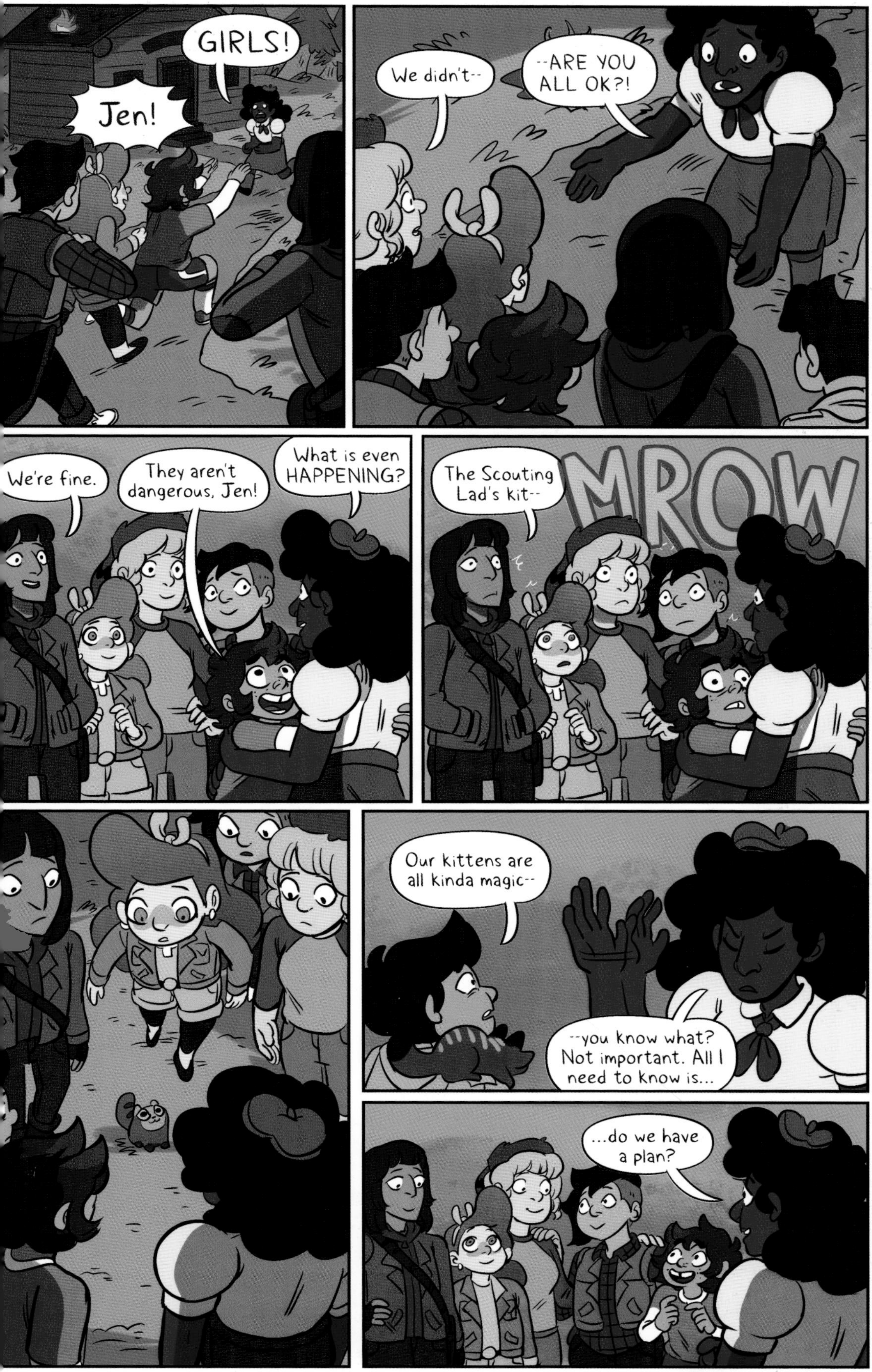
GIRLS!
Jen!
We didn't--
--ARE YOU ALL OK?!
We're fine.
They aren't dangerous, Jen!
What is even HAPPENING?
The Scouting Lad's kit--
MROW
Our kittens are all kinda magic--
--you know what? Not important. All I need to know is...
...do we have a plan?

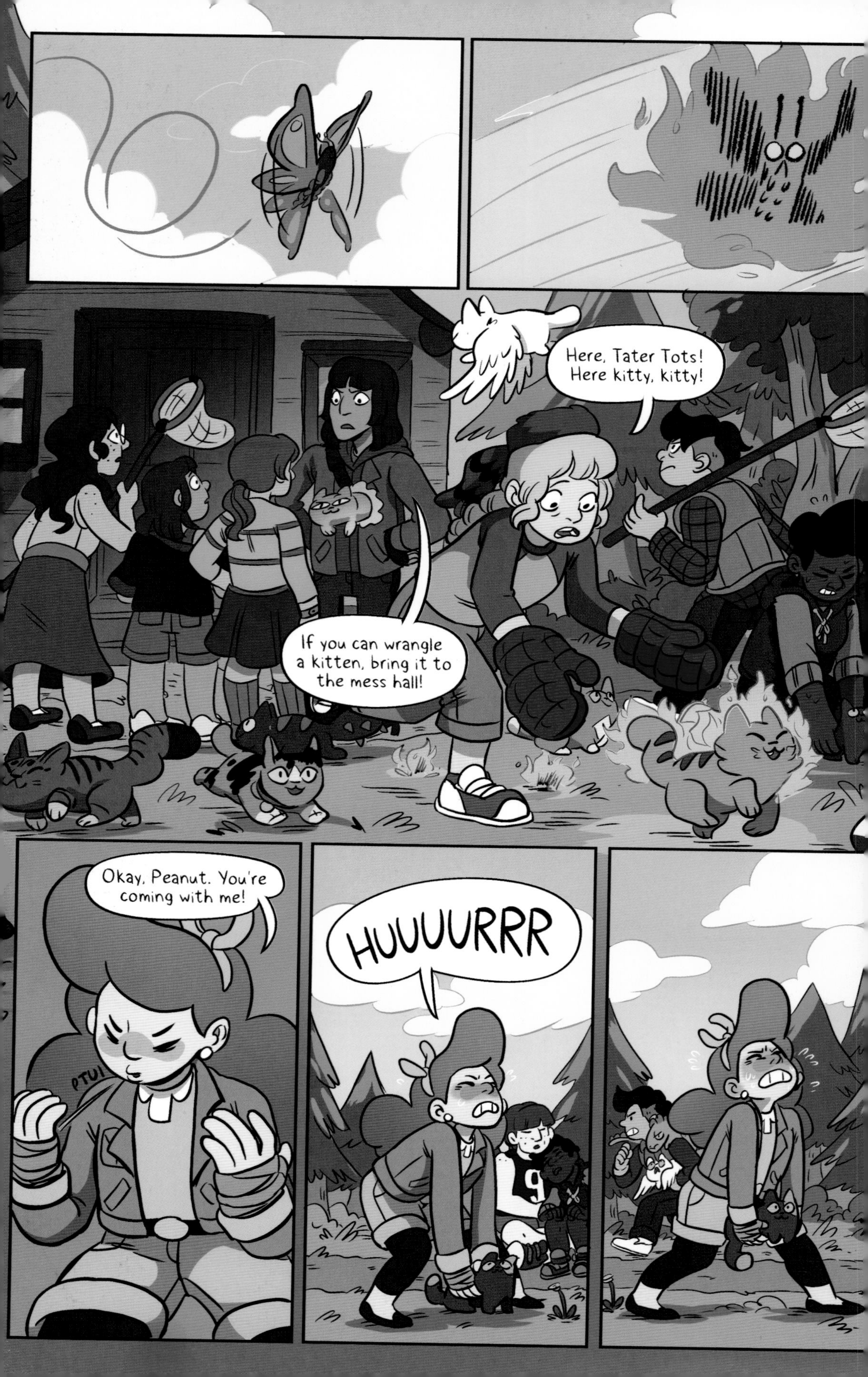

Here, Tater Tots!
Here kitty, kitty!
If you can wrangle a kitten, bring it to the mess hall!
Okay, Peanut. You're coming with me!
PTUI
HUUUURRR

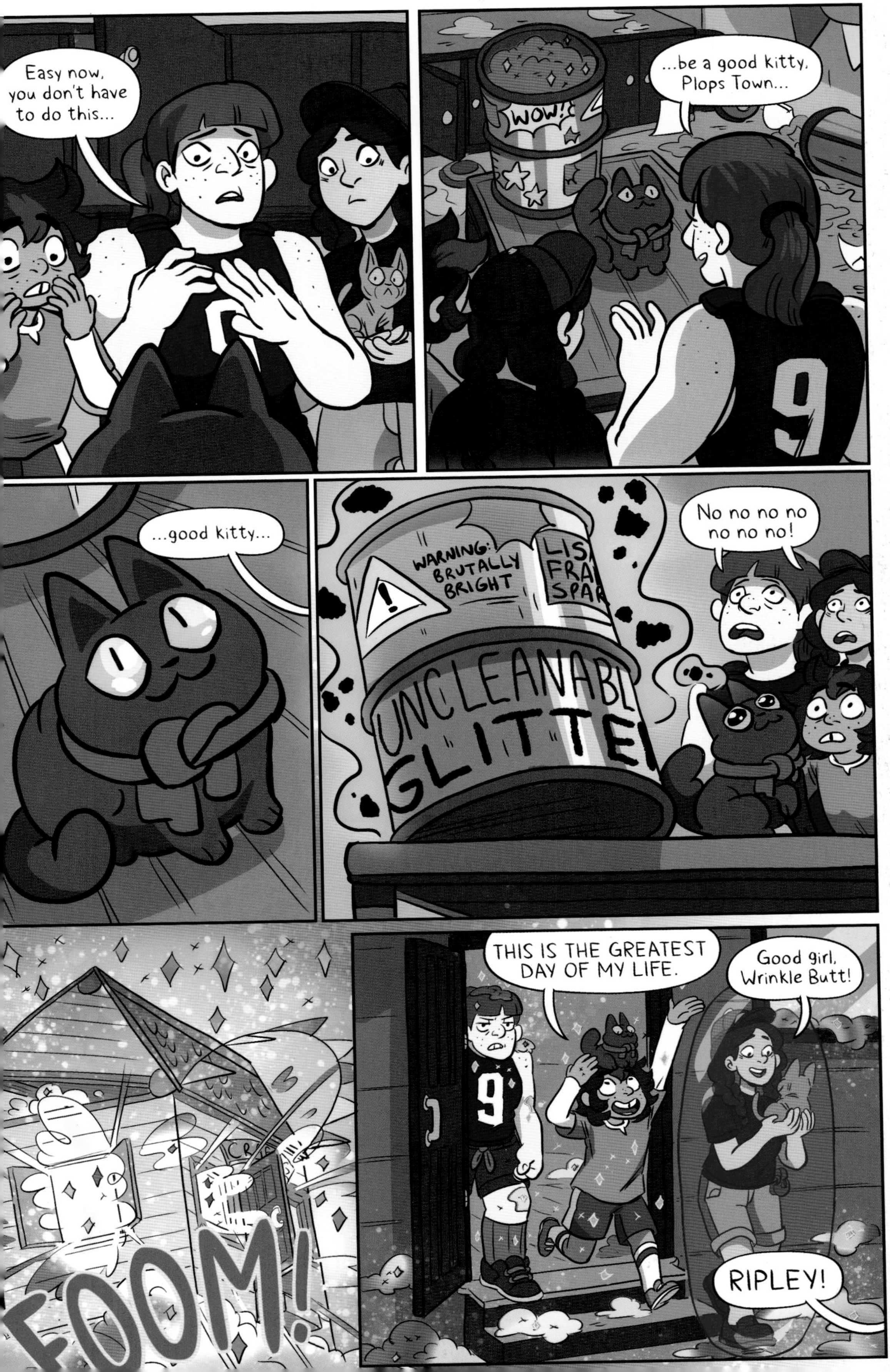
Easy now, you don't have to do this...
...be a good kitty, Plops Town...
WOW!
...good kitty...
WARNING: BRUTALLY BRIGHT
UNCLEANABL
GLITTE
No no no no no no no!
FOOM!
THIS IS THE GREATEST DAY OF MY LIFE.
Good girl, Wrinkle Butt!
RIPLEY!

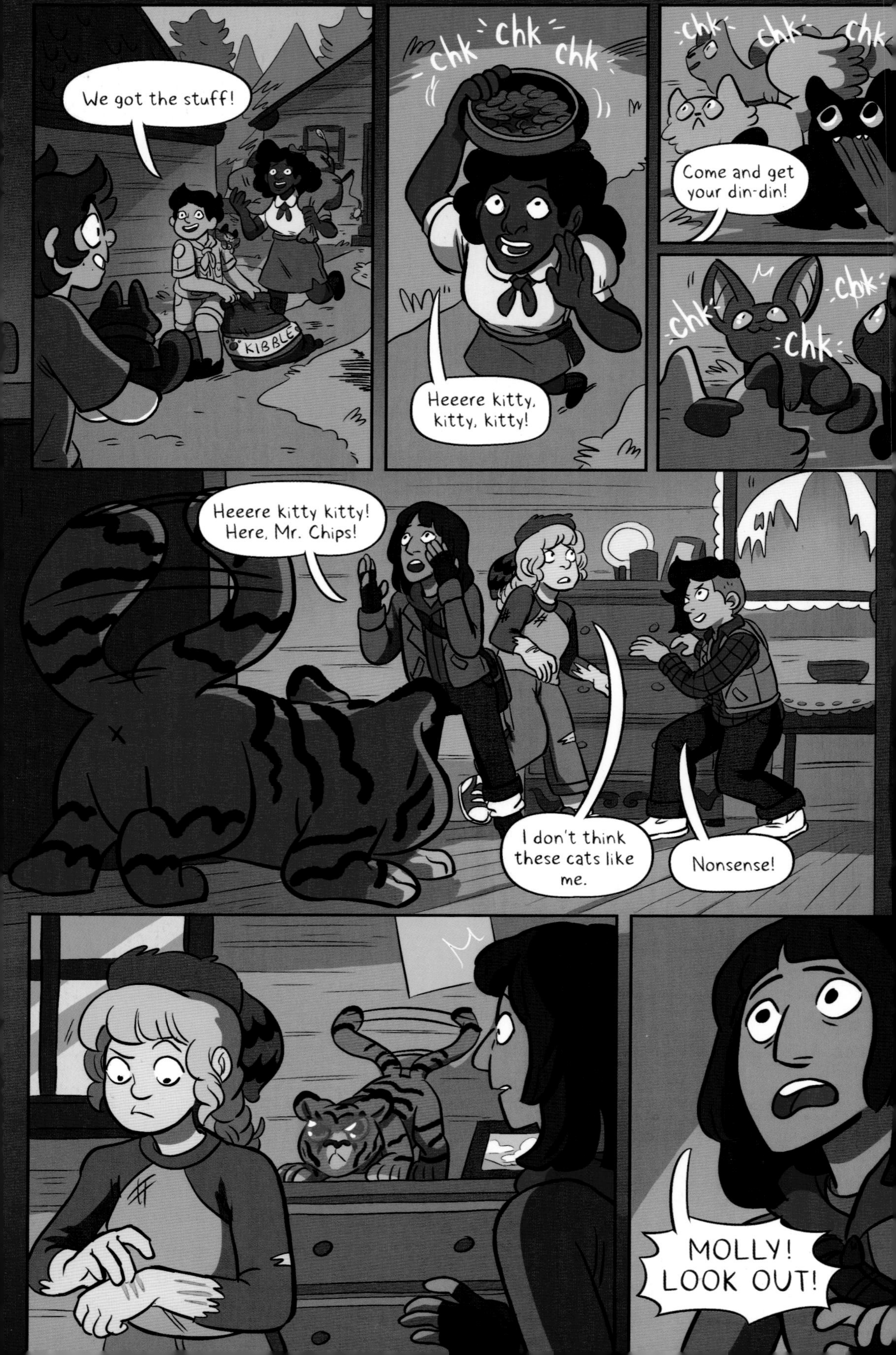
We got the stuff!
KIBBLE
chk chk chk
Heeere kitty, kitty, kitty!
chk chk chk
Come and get your din-din!
chk chk chk
Heeere kitty kitty! Here, Mr. Chips!
I don't think these cats like me.
Nonsense!
MOLLY! LOOK OUT!

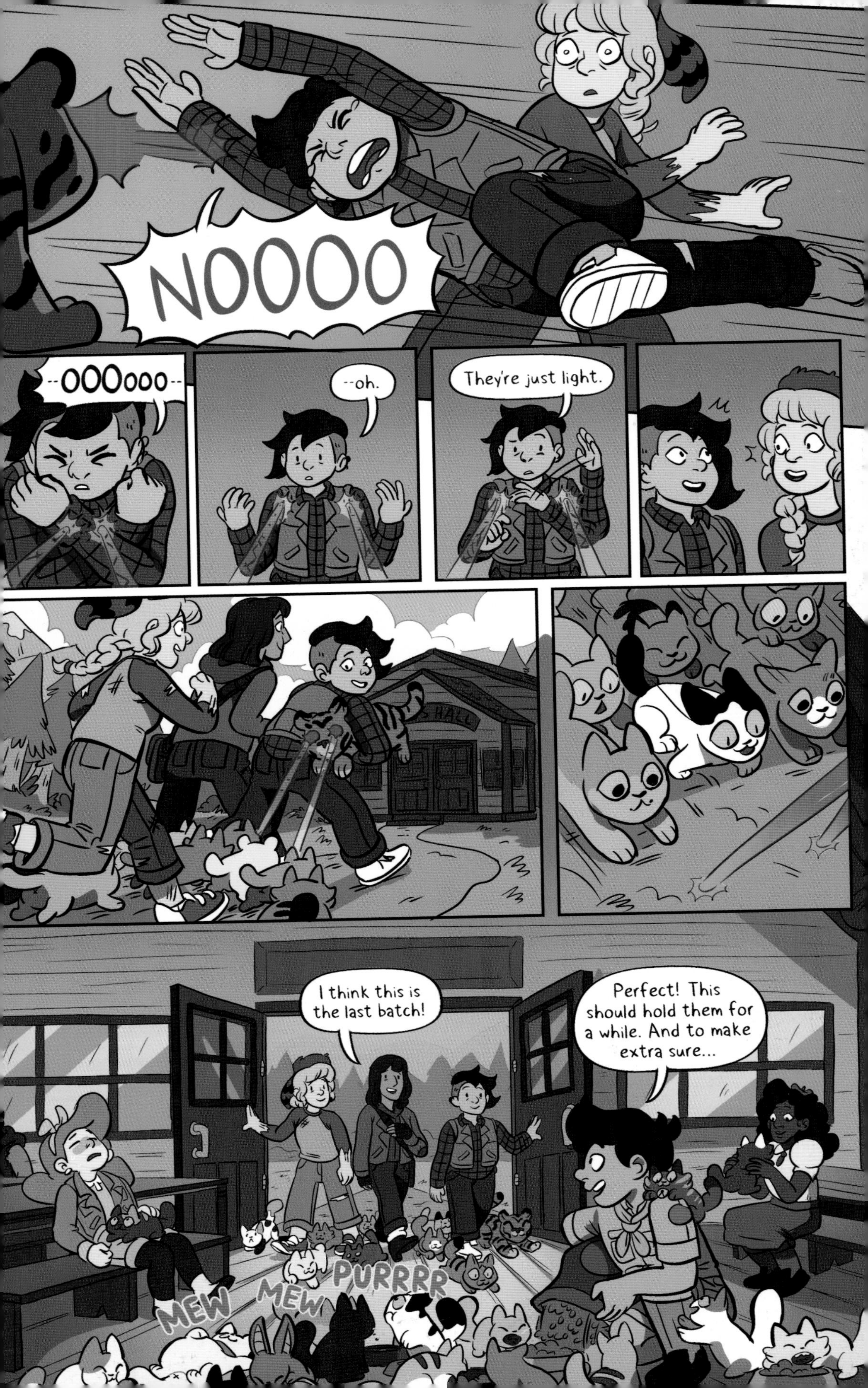
NOOOO
--OOOooo--
--oh.
They're just light.
S HALL
I think this is the last batch!
Perfect! This should hold them for a while. And to make extra sure...
MEW
MEW
PURRRR

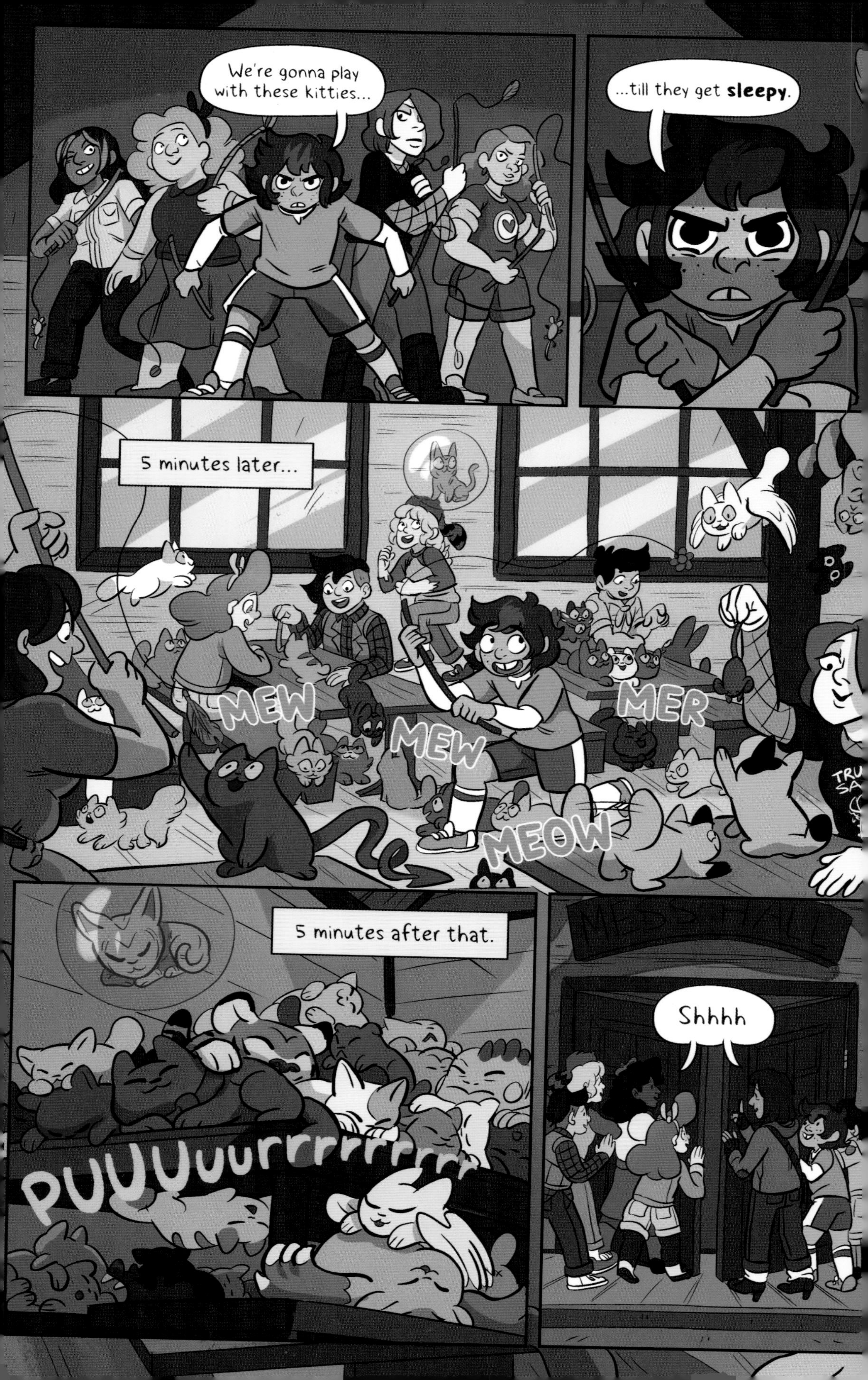
We're gonna play with these kitties...
...till they get **sleepy**.
5 minutes later...
MEW
MEW
MER
MEOW
5 minutes after that.
PUUUuurrrrrrrr
Shhhh

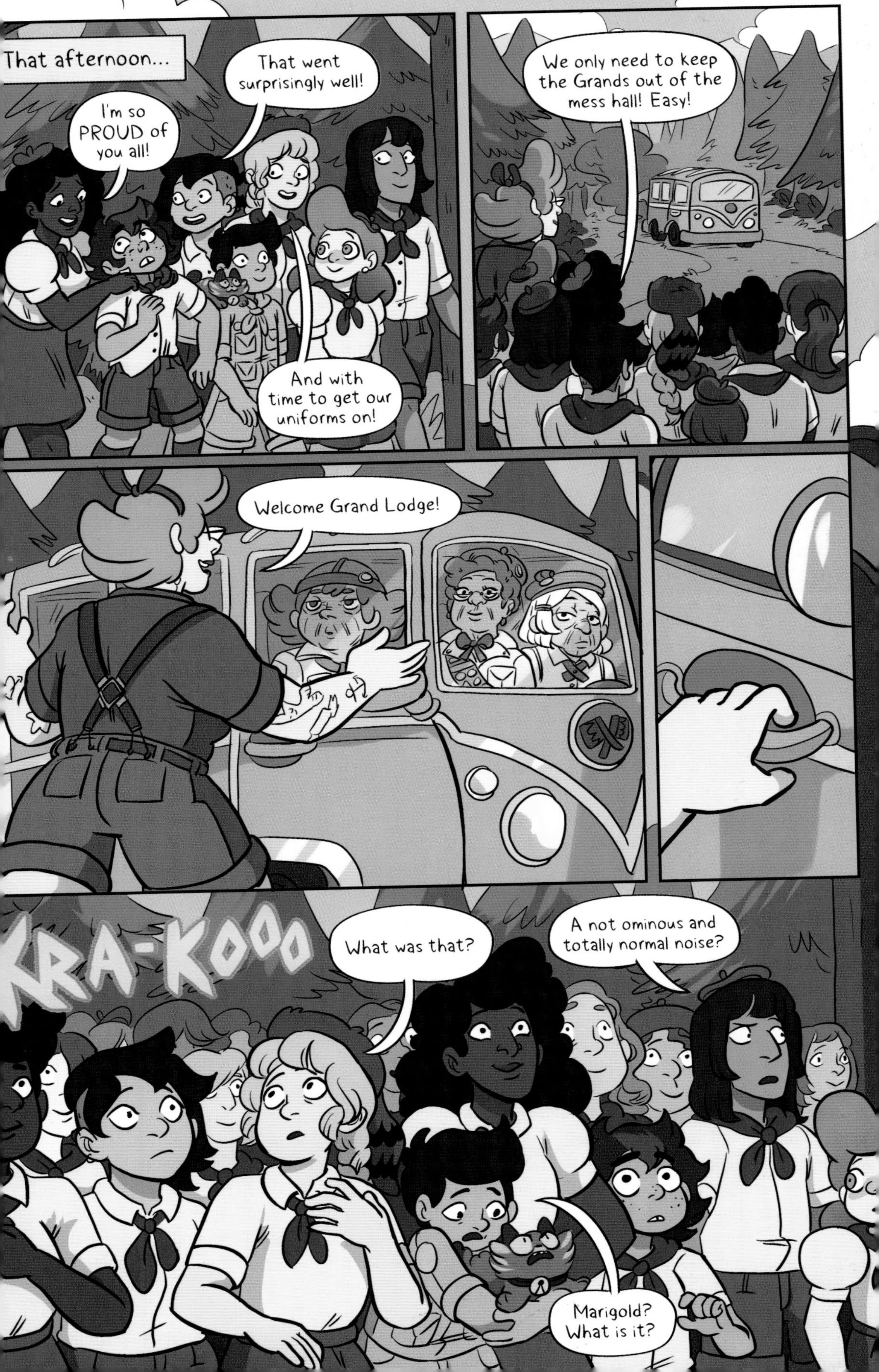
That afternoon...
I'm so PROUD of you all!
That went surprisingly well!
And with time to get our uniforms on!
We only need to keep the Grands out of the mess hall! Easy!
Welcome Grand Lodge!
KRA-KOOO
What was that?
A not ominous and totally normal noise?
Marigold? What is it?

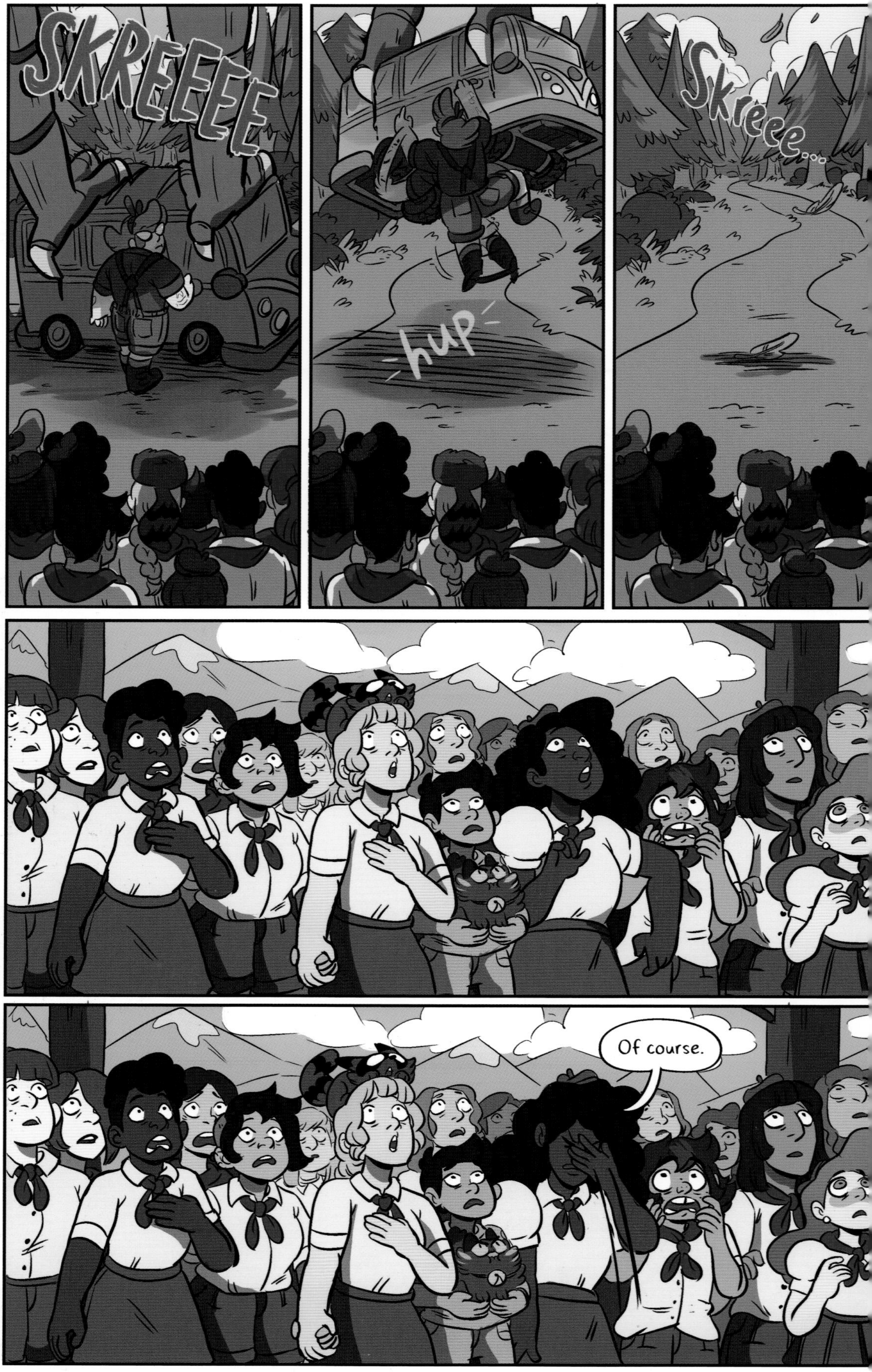
SKREEEE
hup
Skreee...
Of course.

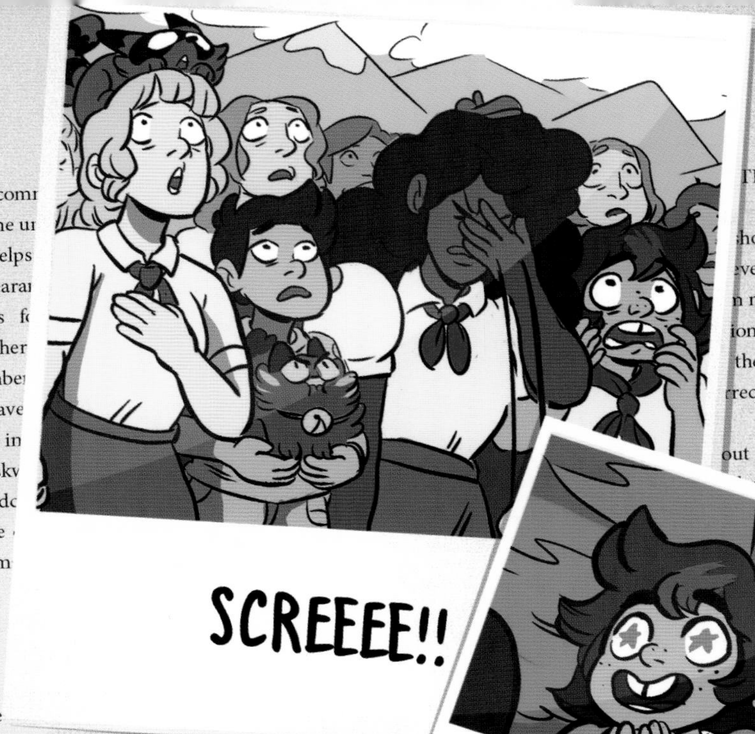
SCREEEE!!

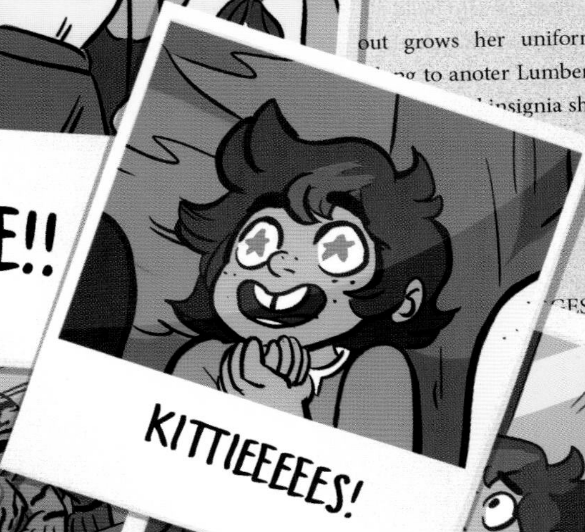
KITTIEEEEES!

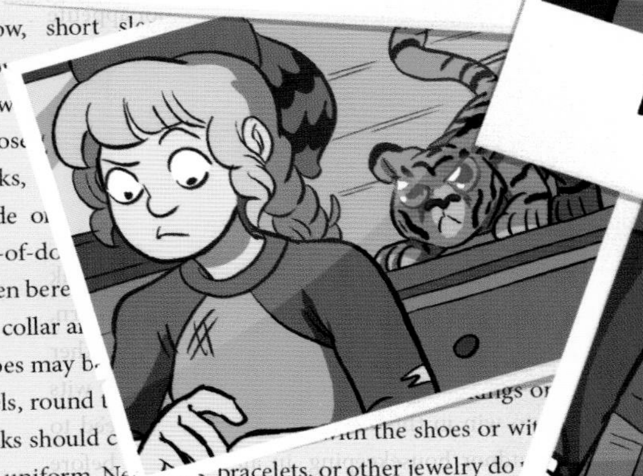

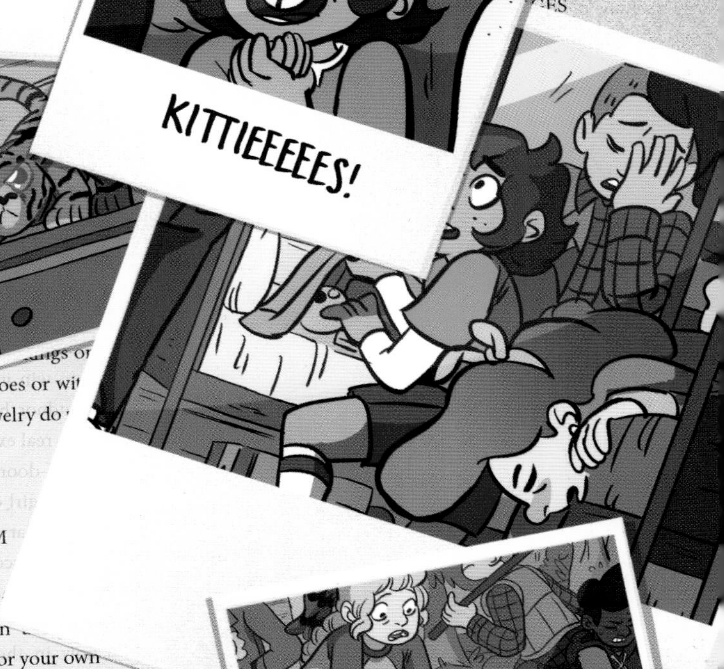

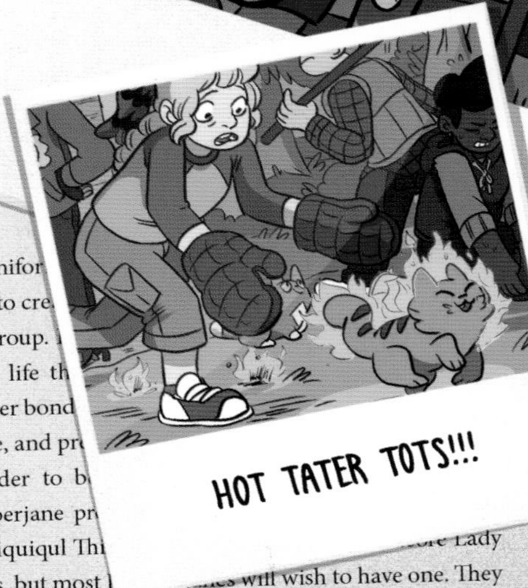
HOT TATER TOTS!!!

will comm

The ur
It helps
appeara
dress f
Further
Lumbe
to have
part in
Thiskv
Hardc
have
them

The
yellow, short sl
emb
the w
choose
slacks,
made o
out-of-do
green bere
the collar a
Shoes may b
heels, round t ... kings or
socks should c ... with the shoes or wi
the uniform. Ne... es, bracelets, or other jewelry do
belong with a Lumberjane uniform.

THE UNIFORM

...hould be worn at camp
...events when Lumberjanes
...n may also be worn at other
...ions. It should be worn as a
... the uniform dress with
...rrect shoes, and stocking or

...out grows her uniform or
...ng to anoter Lumberjane.
... insignia she has
... her
... her

...GES

HOW TO WEAR THE UNIFORM

To look well in a uniform demans first of ... uniform be kept in good condition—clean ... pressed. See that the skirt is the right length for your own height and build, that the belt is adjusted to your waist, that your shoes and stockings are in keeping with the uniform, that you watch your posture and carry yourself with dignity and grace. If the beret is removed indoors, be sure that your hair is neat and kept in place with an insonspicuous clip or ribbon. When you wear a Lumberjane uniform you are identified as a member of this organization and you should be doubly careful to conduct yourself in a way that will show everyone that courtesy and thoughtfullness are part of being a Lumberjane. People are likely to judge a whole nation by the selfishness of a few individuals, to criticize a whole family because of the misconduct of one member, and to feel unkindly toward and organization because of the

The unifor...
helps to cre...
in a group. ...
active life th...
another bond...
future, and pr...
in order to b...
Lumberjane pr...
Penniquiqul Thi... ...ore Lady
Types, but most ... ...es will wish to have one. They can either buy the uniform, or make it themselves from materials available at the trading post.

LUMBERJANES FIELD MANUAL

CHAPTER
TWENTY-SIX

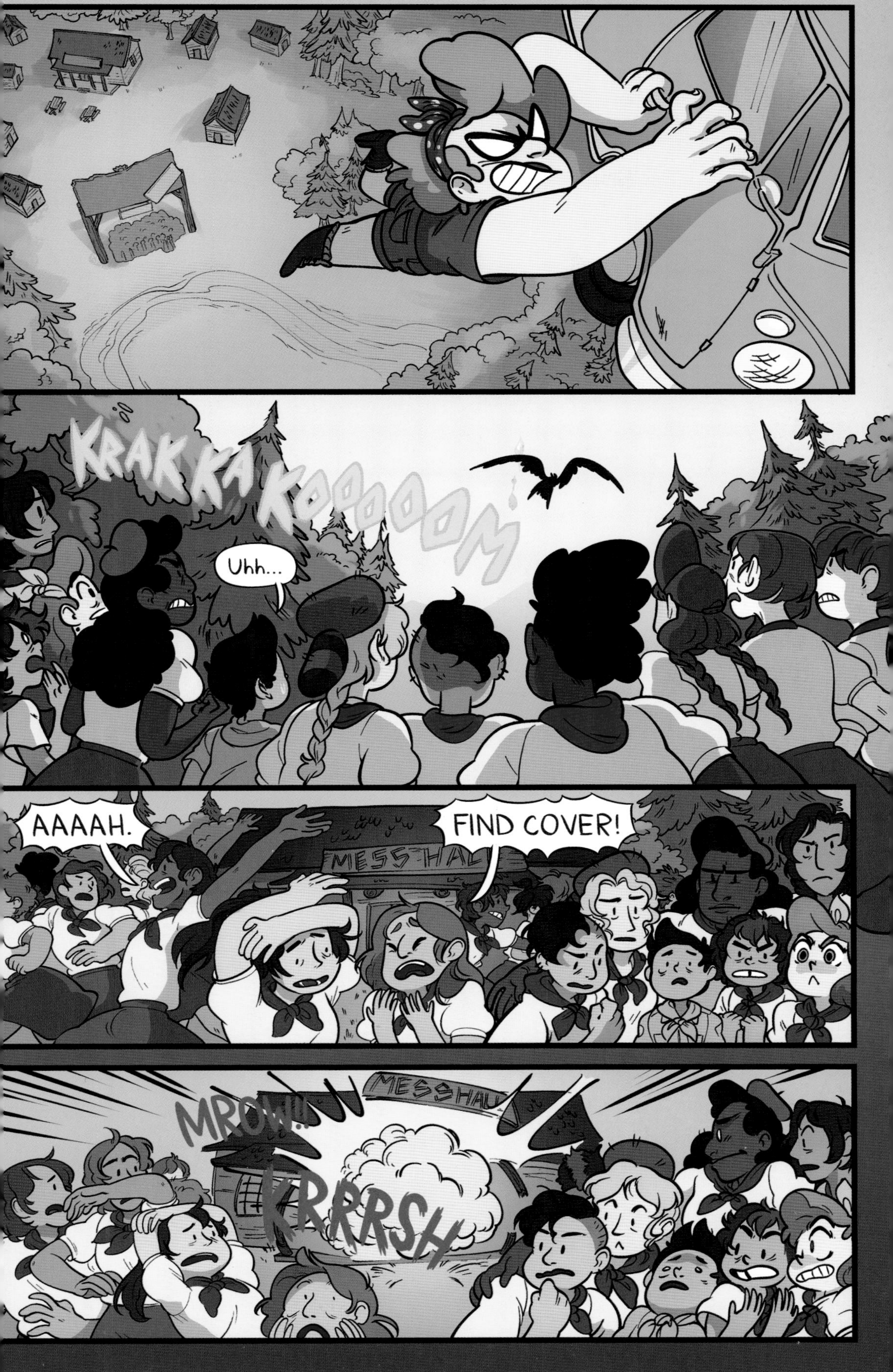
KRAK KA KOOOOOOM
Uhh...
AAAAH.
FIND COVER!
MESS HALL
MESS HALL
MROW!!
KRRRSH

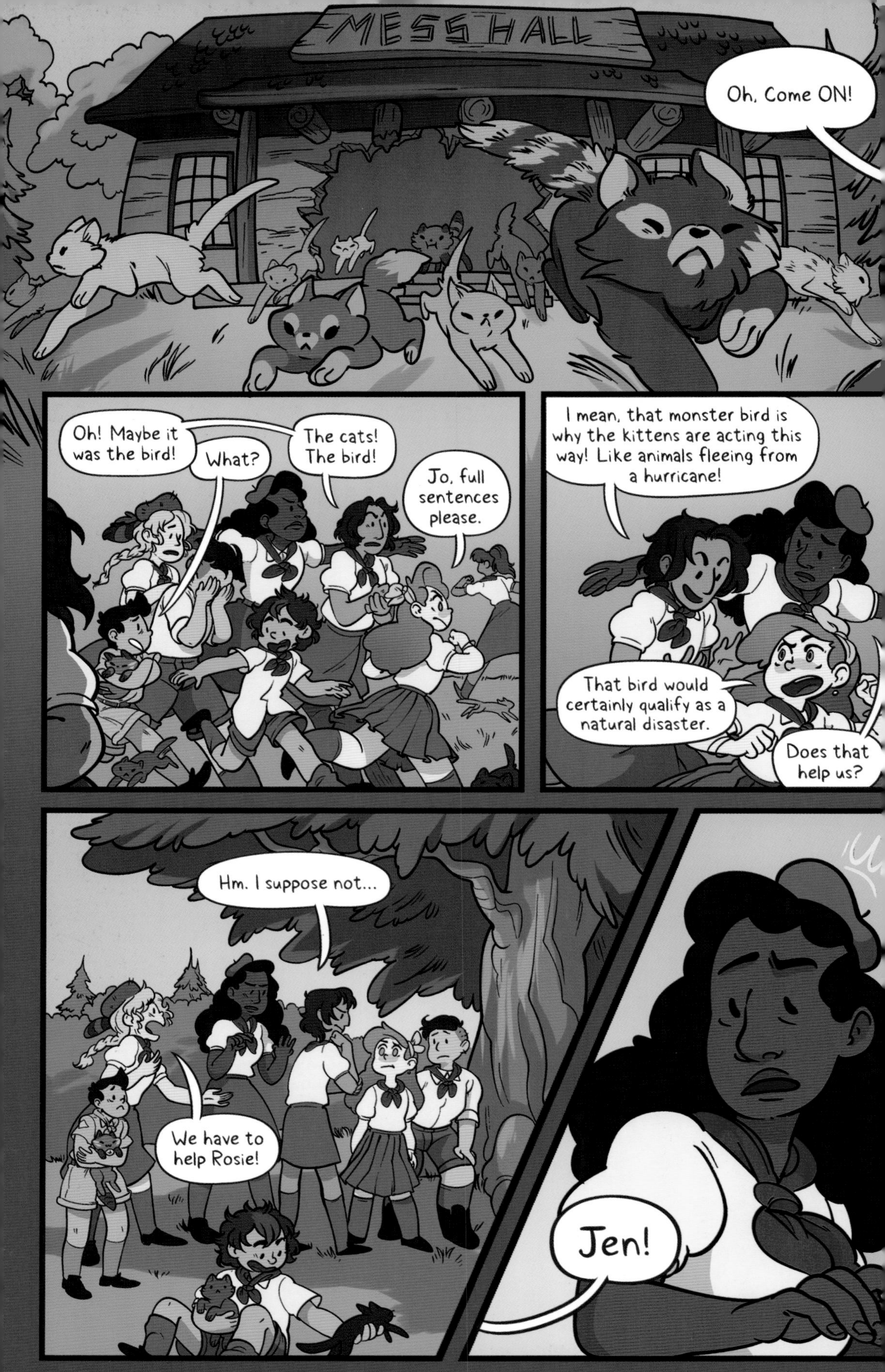
MESS HALL
Oh, Come ON!
Oh! Maybe it was the bird!
What?
The cats! The bird!
Jo, full sentences please.
I mean, that monster bird is why the kittens are acting this way! Like animals fleeing from a hurricane!
That bird would certainly qualify as a natural disaster.
Does that help us?
Hm. I suppose not...
We have to help Rosie!
Jen!

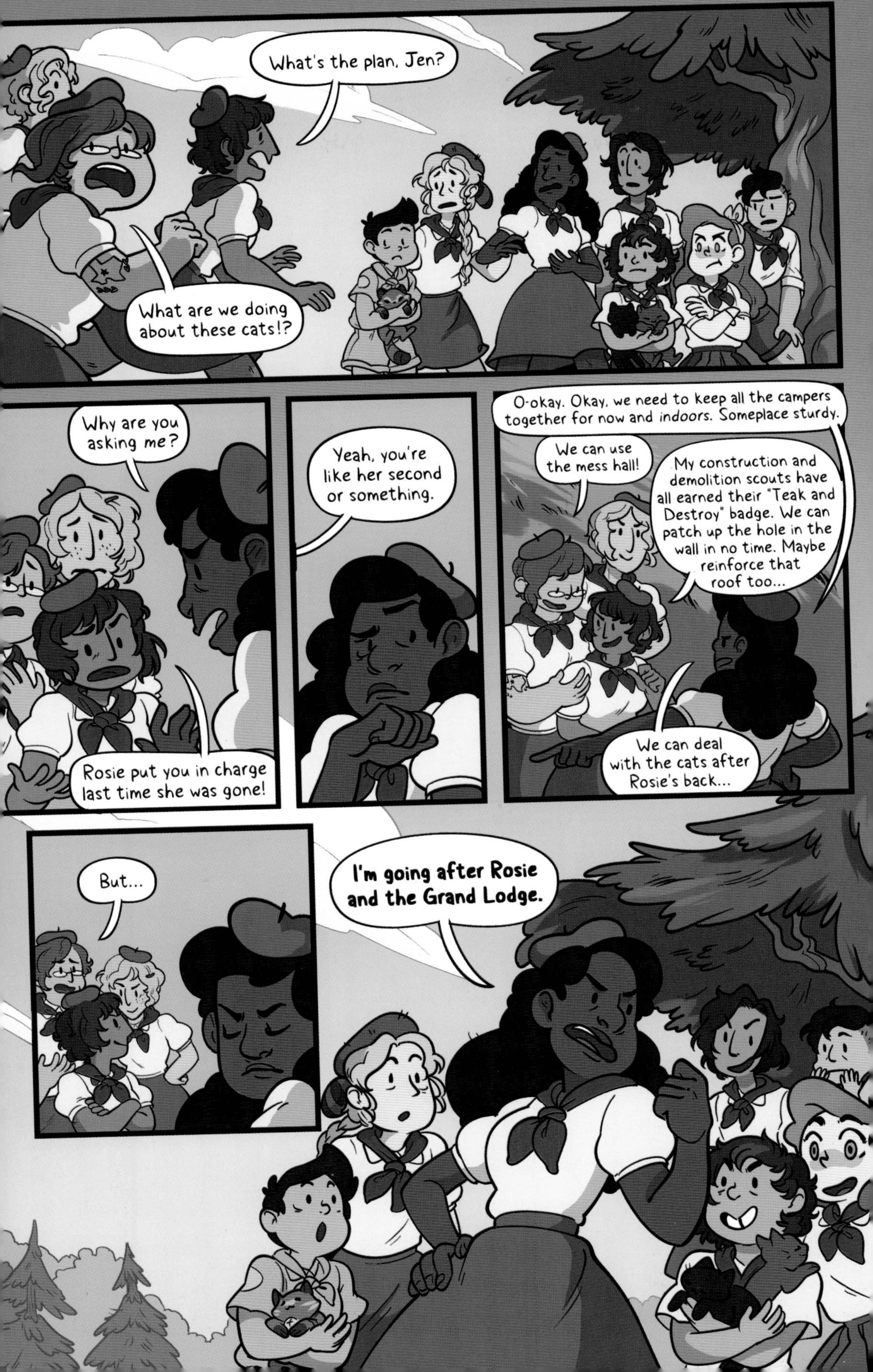
What's the plan, Jen?
What are we doing about these cats!?
Why are you asking me?
Rosie put you in charge last time she was gone!
Yeah, you're like her second or something.
O-okay. Okay, we need to keep all the campers together for now and *indoors*. Someplace sturdy.
We can use the mess hall!
My construction and demolition scouts have all earned their "Teak and Destroy" badge. We can patch up the hole in the wall in no time. Maybe reinforce that roof too...
We can deal with the cats after Rosie's back...
But...
I'm going after Rosie and the Grand Lodge.

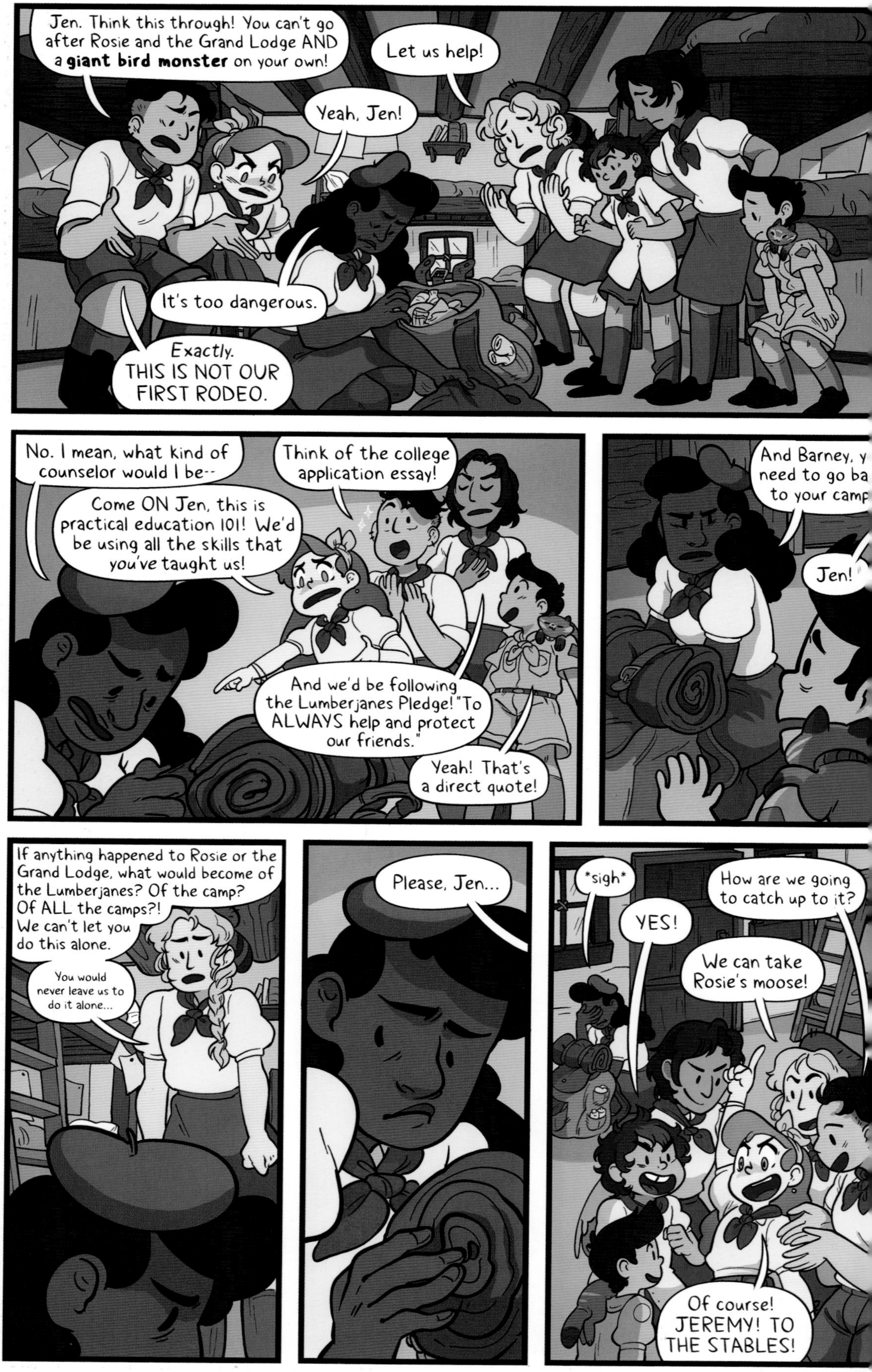

Jen. Think this through! You can't go after Rosie and the Grand Lodge AND a **giant bird monster** on your own!
Let us help!
Yeah, Jen!
It's too dangerous.
Exactly. THIS IS NOT OUR FIRST RODEO.
No. I mean, what kind of counselor would I be--
Think of the college application essay!
Come ON Jen, this is practical education 101! We'd be using all the skills that *you've* taught us!
And we'd be following the Lumberjanes Pledge! "To ALWAYS help and protect our friends."
Yeah! That's a direct quote!
And Barney, y need to go ba to your camp
Jen!
If anything happened to Rosie or the Grand Lodge, what would become of the Lumberjanes? Of the camp? Of ALL the camps?! We can't let you do this alone.
You would never leave us to do it alone...
Please, Jen...
sigh
YES!
How are we going to catch up to it?
We can take Rosie's moose!
Of course! JEREMY! TO THE STABLES!

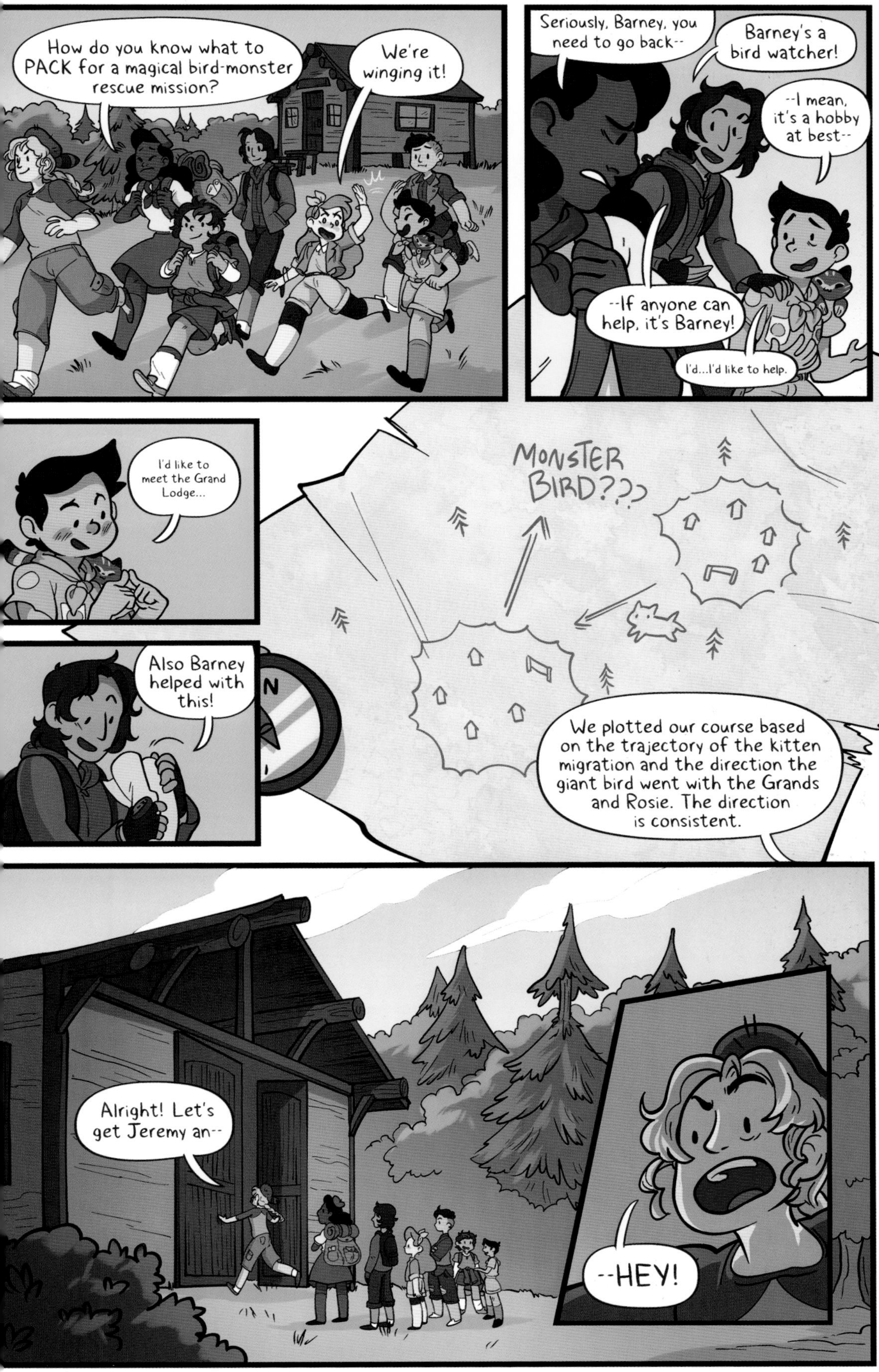
How do you know what to PACK for a magical bird-monster rescue mission?
We're winging it!
Seriously, Barney, you need to go back--
Barney's a bird watcher!
--I mean, it's a hobby at best--
--If anyone can help, it's Barney!
I'd...I'd like to help.
I'd like to meet the Grand Lodge...
MONSTER BIRD???
Also Barney helped with this!
N
We plotted our course based on the trajectory of the kitten migration and the direction the giant bird went with the Grands and Rosie. The direction is consistent.
Alright! Let's get Jeremy an--
--HEY!

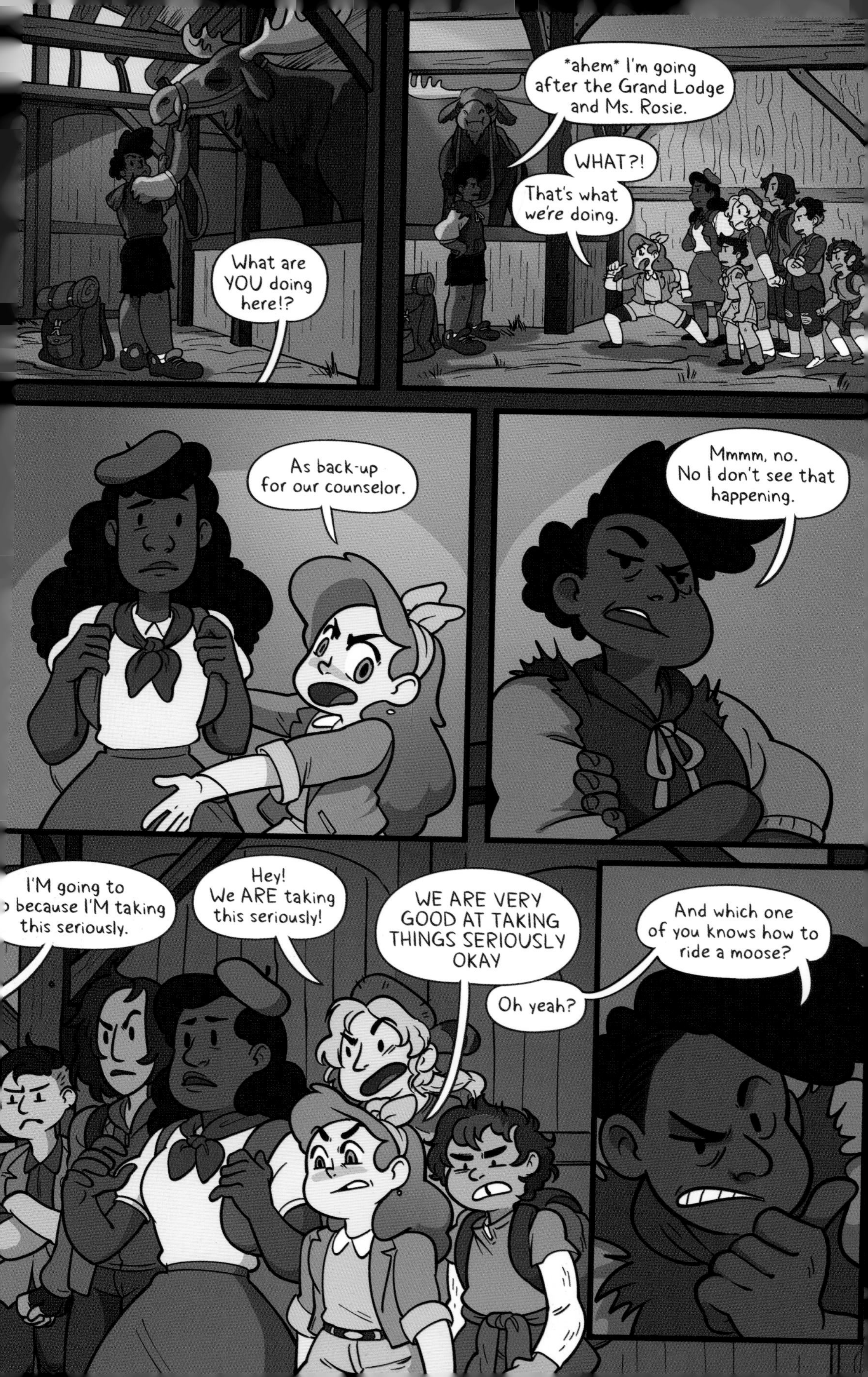
What are YOU doing here!?
ahem I'm going after the Grand Lodge and Ms. Rosie.
WHAT?!
That's what we're doing.
As back-up for our counselor.
Mmmm, no. No I don't see that happening.
I'M going to because I'M taking this seriously.
Hey! We ARE taking this seriously!
WE ARE VERY GOOD AT TAKING THINGS SERIOUSLY OKAY
Oh yeah?
And which one of you knows how to ride a moose?

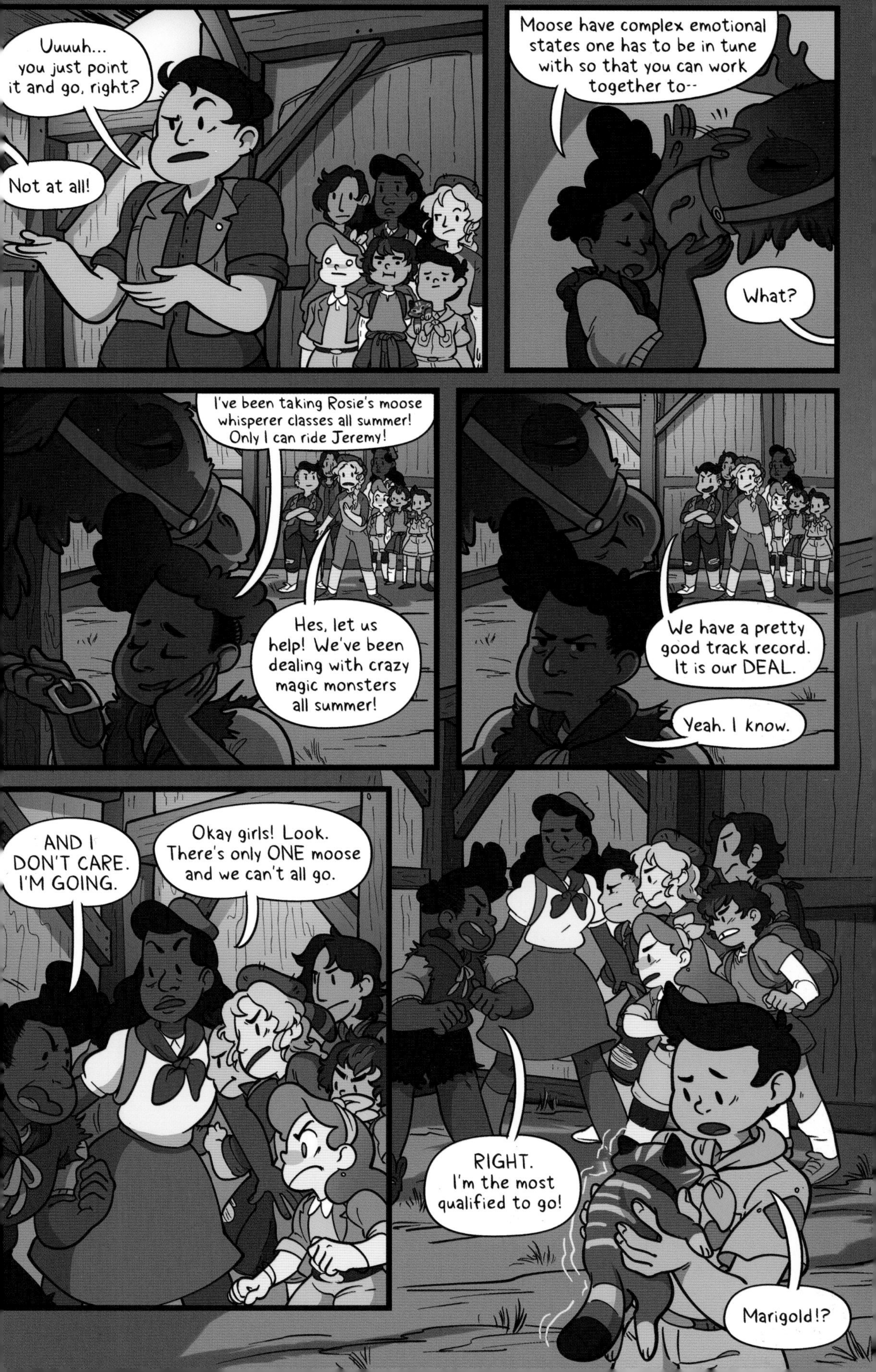
Uuuuh...
you just point it and go, right?
Not at all!
Moose have complex emotional states one has to be in tune with so that you can work together to--
What?
I've been taking Rosie's moose whisperer classes all summer! Only I can ride Jeremy!
Hes, let us help! We've been dealing with crazy magic monsters all summer!
We have a pretty good track record. It is our DEAL.
Yeah. I know.
AND I DON'T CARE. I'M GOING.
Okay girls! Look. There's only ONE moose and we can't all go.
RIGHT. I'm the most qualified to go!
Marigold!?

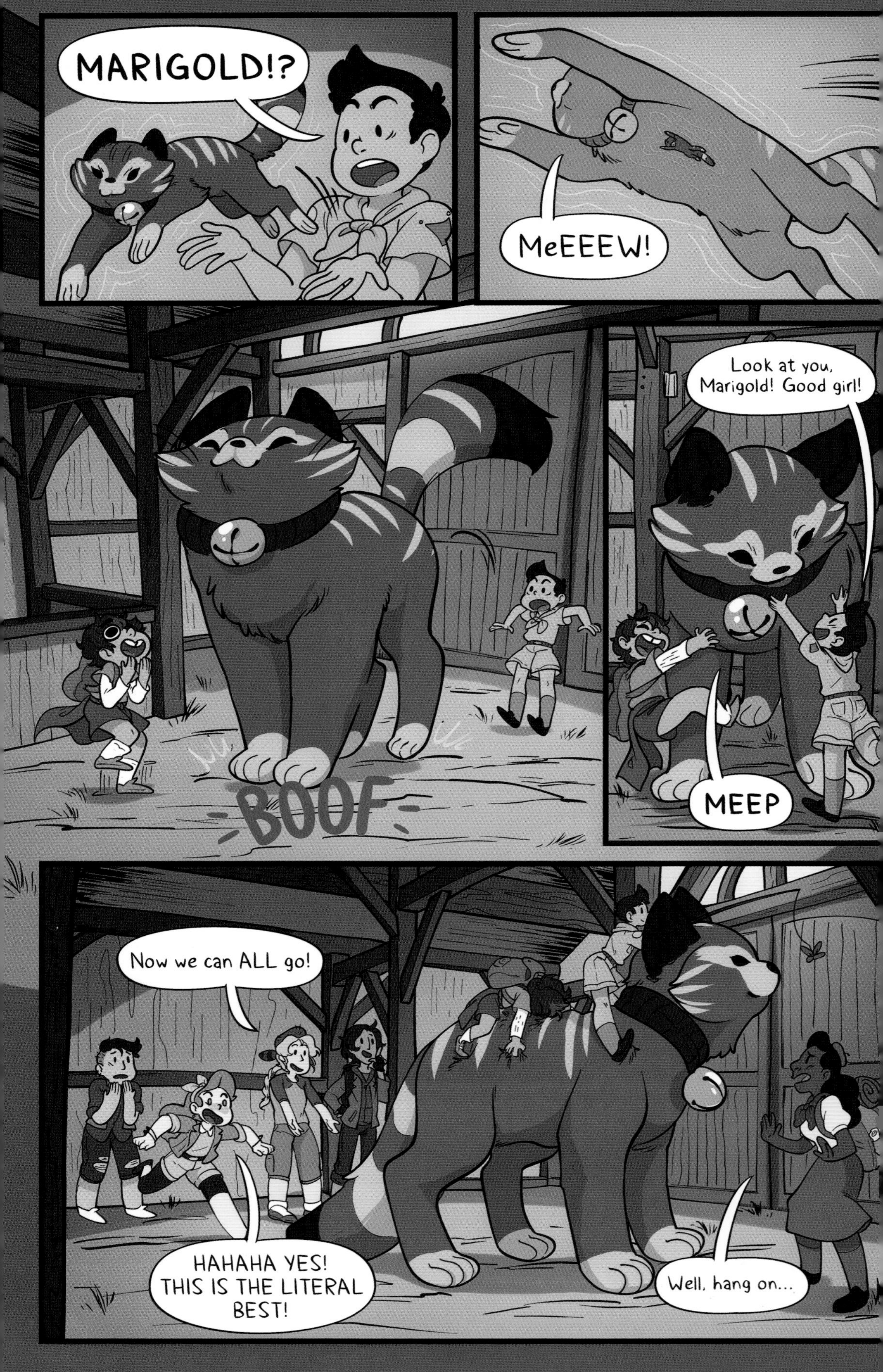
MARIGOLD!?
MeEEEW!
BOOF
Look at you, Marigold! Good girl!
MEEP
Now we can ALL go!
HAHAHA YES! THIS IS THE LITERAL BEST!
Well, hang on...

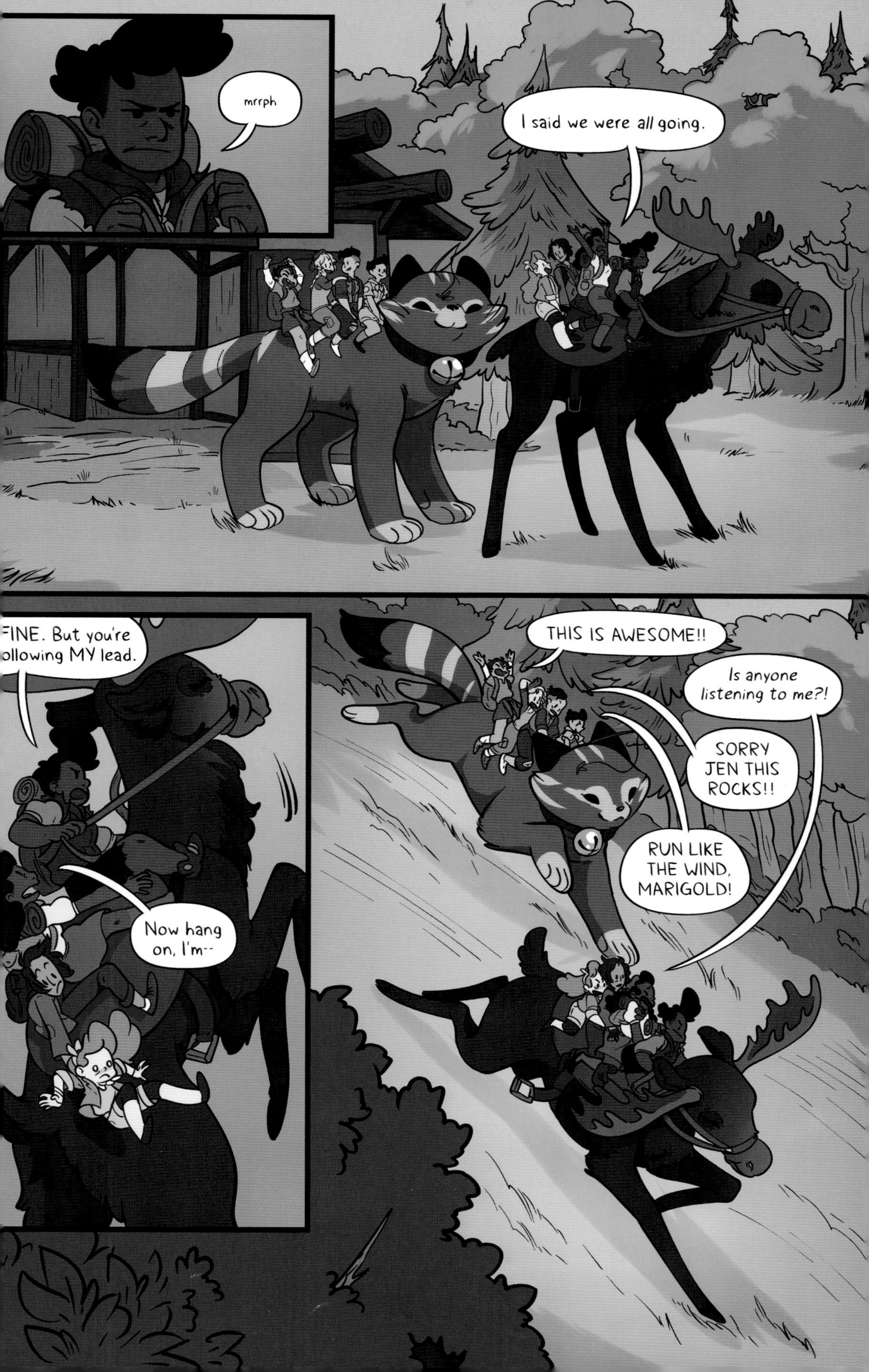
mrrph
I said we were all going.
FINE. But you're following MY lead.
Now hang on, I'm--
THIS IS AWESOME!!
Is anyone listening to me?!
SORRY JEN THIS ROCKS!!
RUN LIKE THE WIND, MARIGOLD!

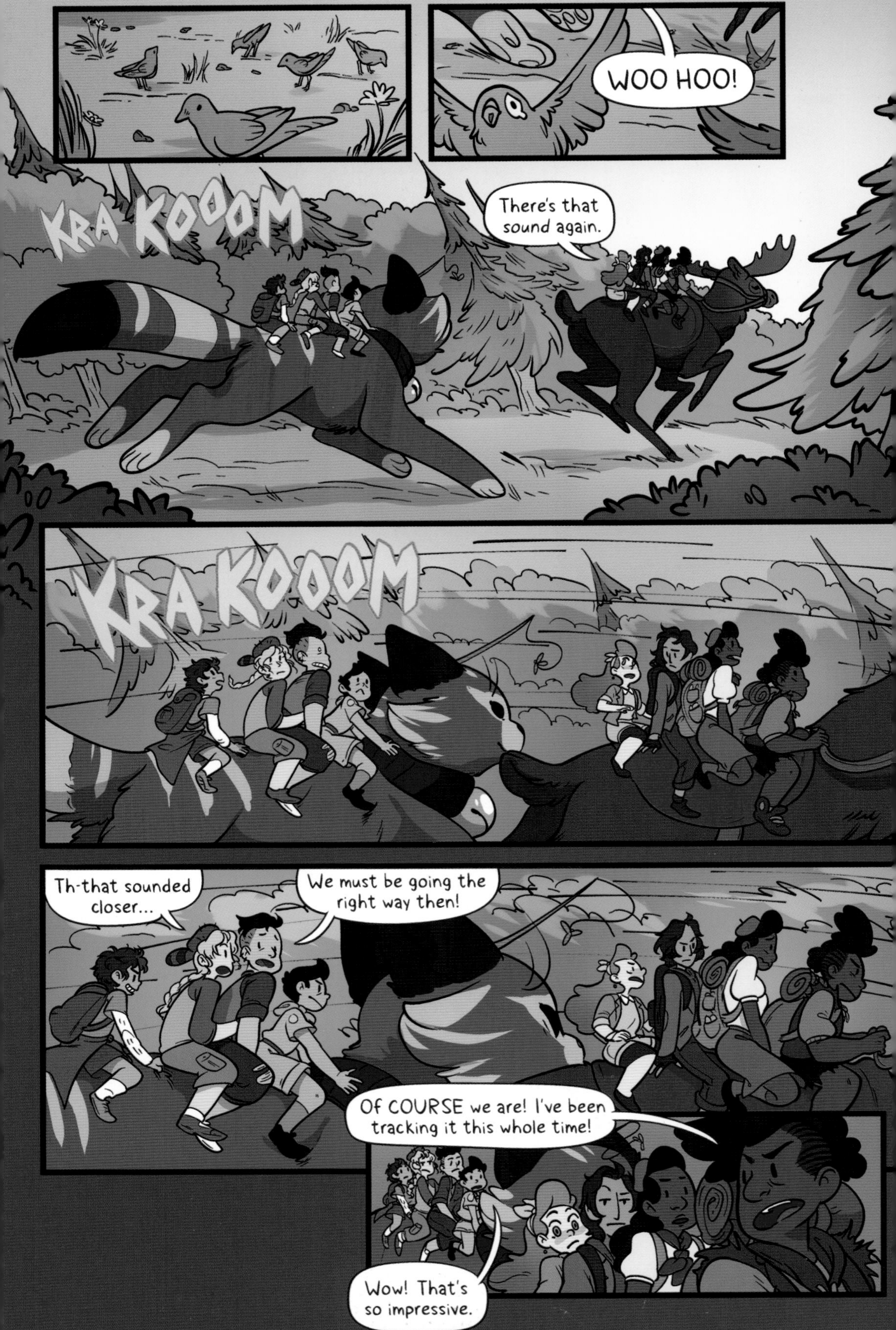
WOO HOO!
KRA KOOOM
There's that sound again.
KRA KOOOM
Th-that sounded closer...
We must be going the right way then!
OF COURSE we are! I've been tracking it this whole time!
Wow! That's so impressive.

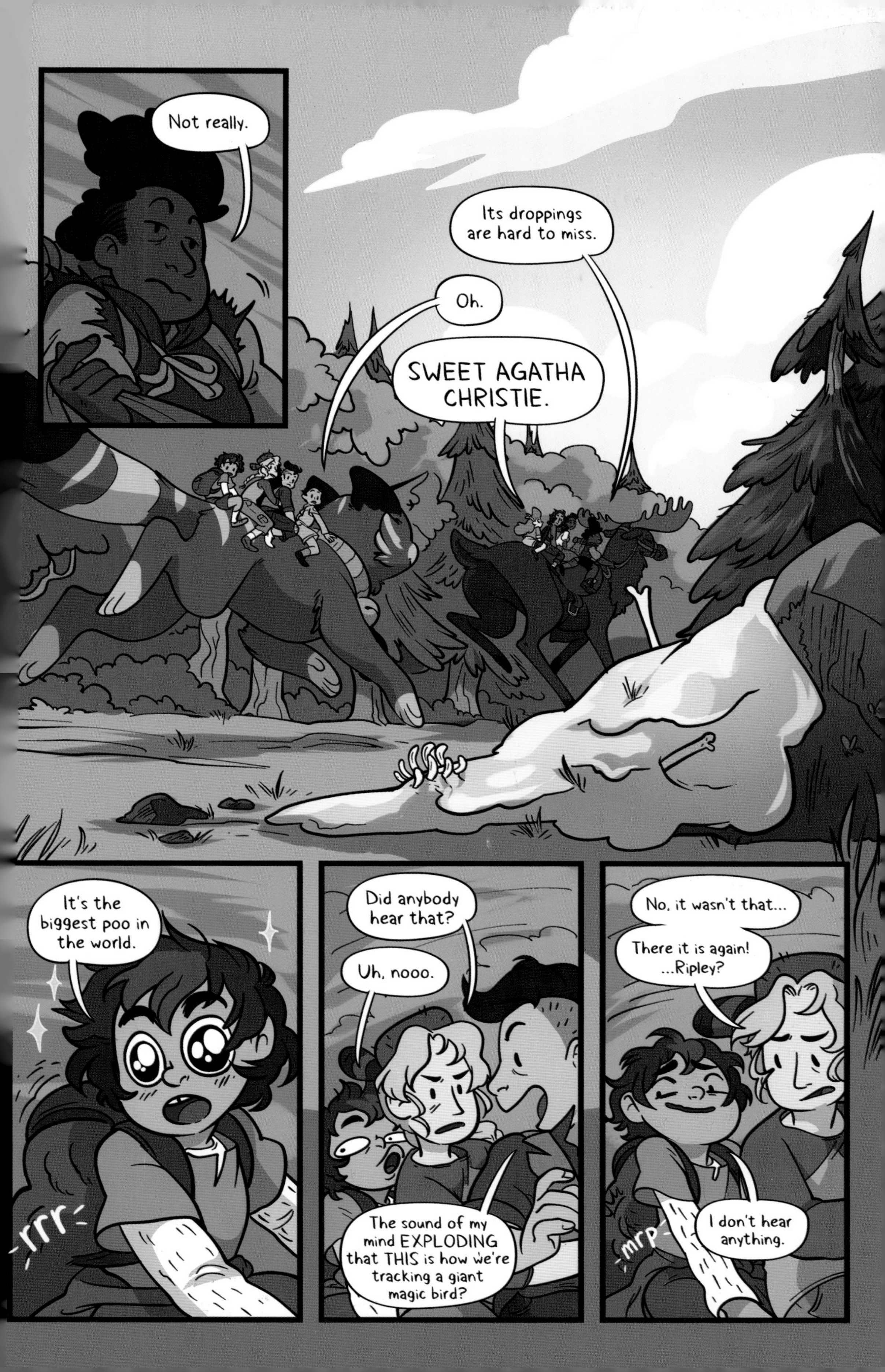
Not really.
Its droppings are hard to miss.
Oh.
SWEET AGATHA CHRISTIE.
It's the biggest poo in the world.
rrr
Did anybody hear that?
Uh, nooo.
The sound of my mind EXPLODING that THIS is how we're tracking a giant magic bird?
No, it wasn't that...
There it is again! ...Ripley?
mrp
I don't hear anything.

--I DON'T HEAR ANYTHING AND ESPECIALLY NOTHING IN THIS BACKPACK!

RIPLEY!

=Myaaaa=

AH. STAY BACK!

WHY, on a dangerous mission to save our camp director, Grand Lodge, and possibly Lumberjanes-dom itself...would you bring kittens along?

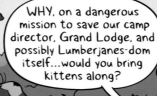

They wanted to come!

=Purr= =Purrr=

sigh

Are you mad at me Jen?

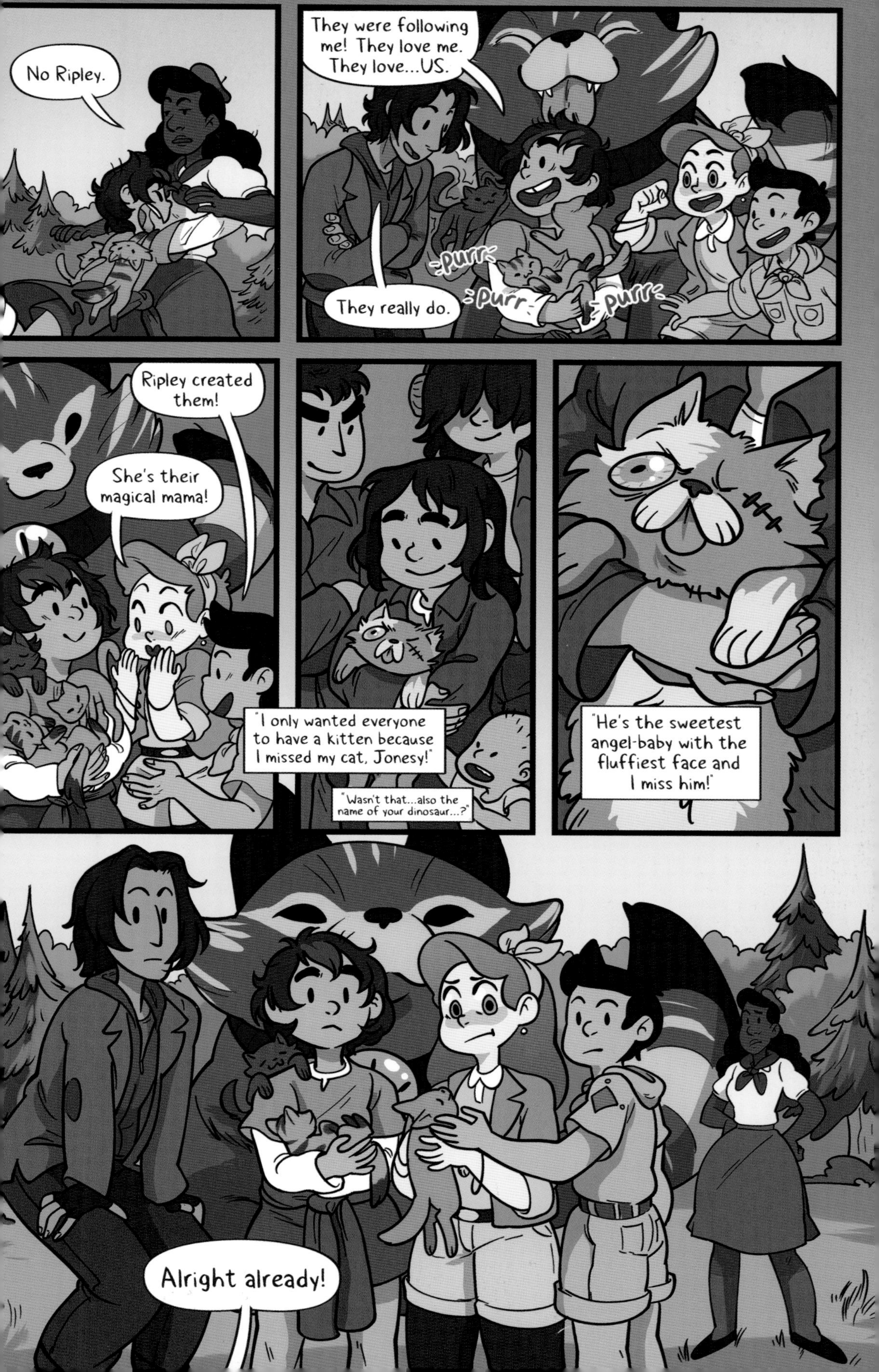
No Ripley.
They were following me! They love me. They love...US.
They really do.
purr
purr
purr
Ripley created them!
She's their magical mama!
"I only wanted everyone to have a kitten because I missed my cat, Jonesy!"
"Wasn't that...also the name of your dinosaur...?"
"He's the sweetest angel-baby with the fluffiest face and I miss him!"
Alright already!

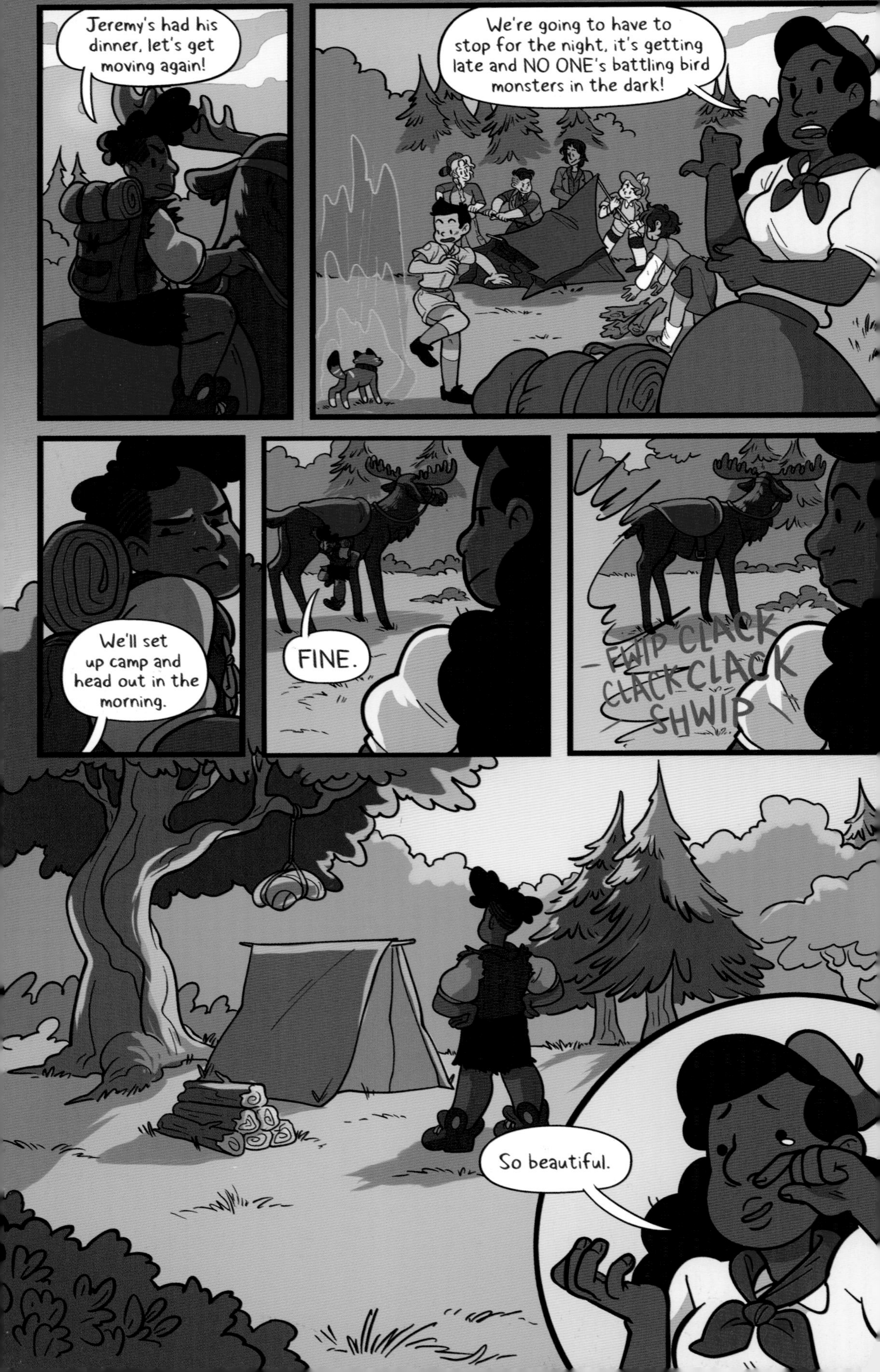
Jeremy's had his dinner, let's get moving again!
We're going to have to stop for the night, it's getting late and NO ONE's battling bird monsters in the dark!
We'll set up camp and head out in the morning.
FINE.
FWIP CLACK
CLACK CLACK
SHWIP
So beautiful.

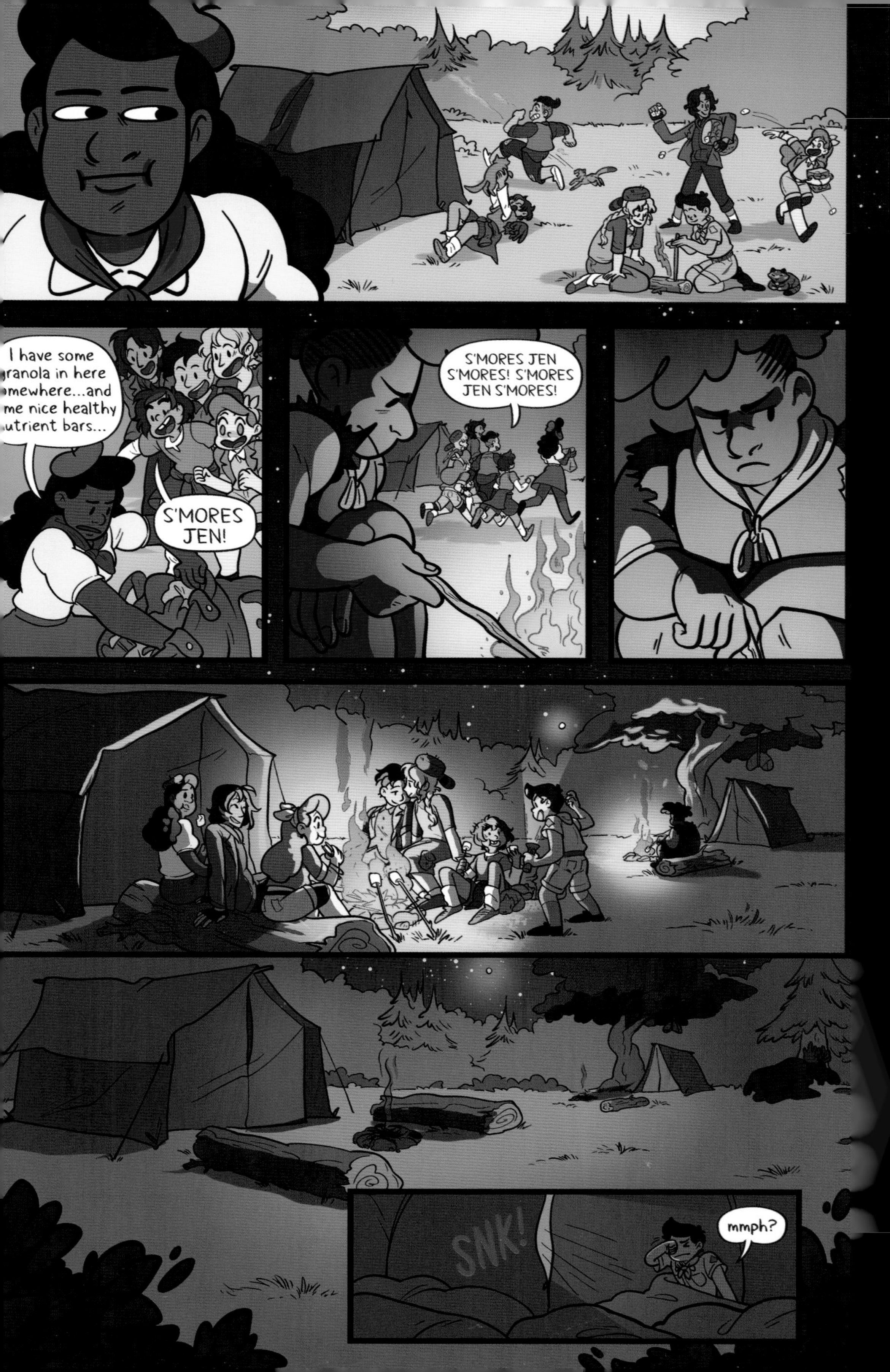
I have some ranola in here mewhere...and me nice healthy utrient bars...
S'MORES JEN!
S'MORES JEN S'MORES! S'MORES JEN S'MORES!
SNK!
mmph?

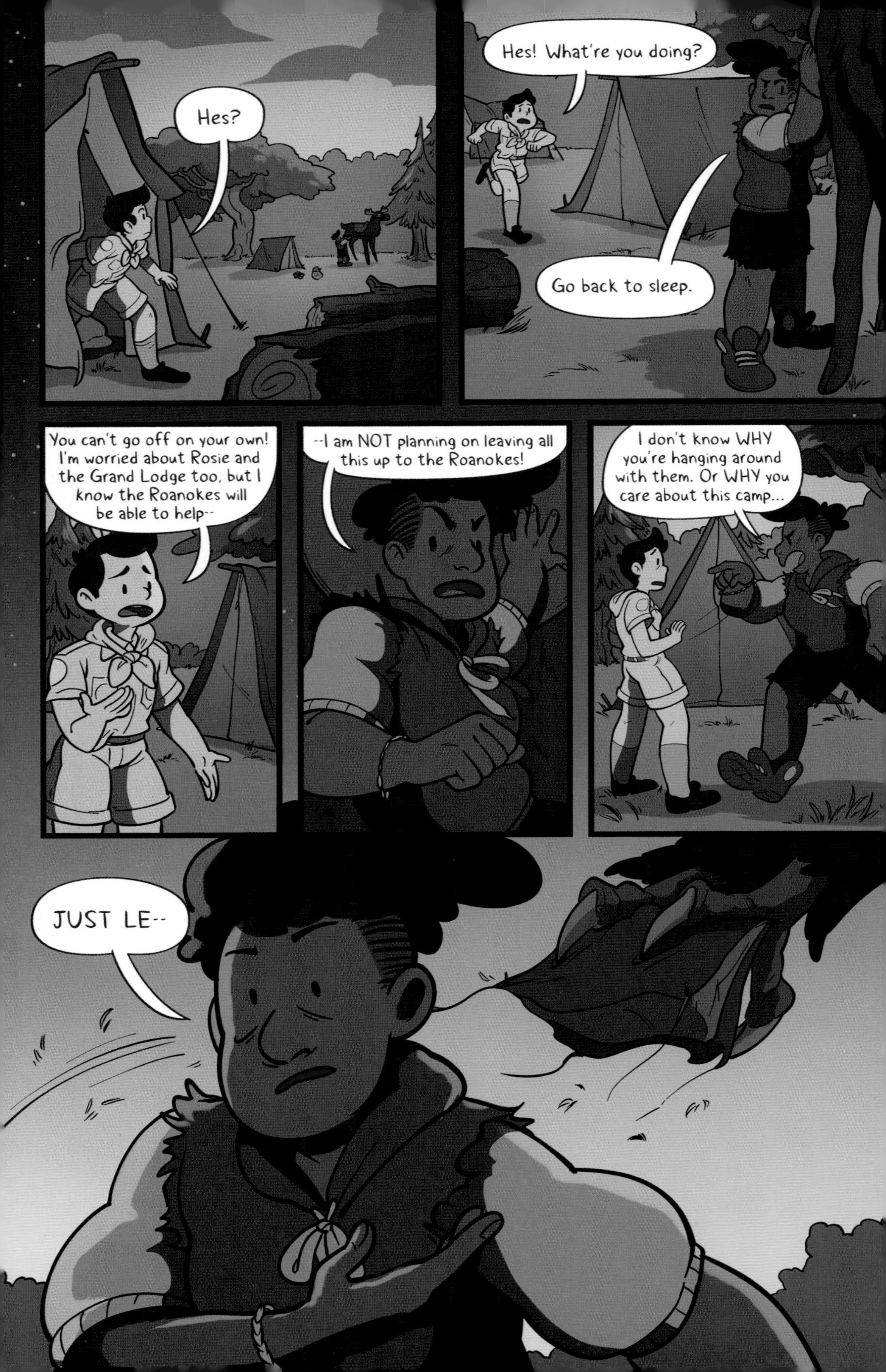
Hes?
Hes! What're you doing?
Go back to sleep.
You can't go off on your own! I'm worried about Rosie and the Grand Lodge too, but I know the Roanokes will be able to help--
--I am NOT planning on leaving all this up to the Roanokes!
I don't know WHY you're hanging around with them. Or WHY you care about this camp...
JUST LE--

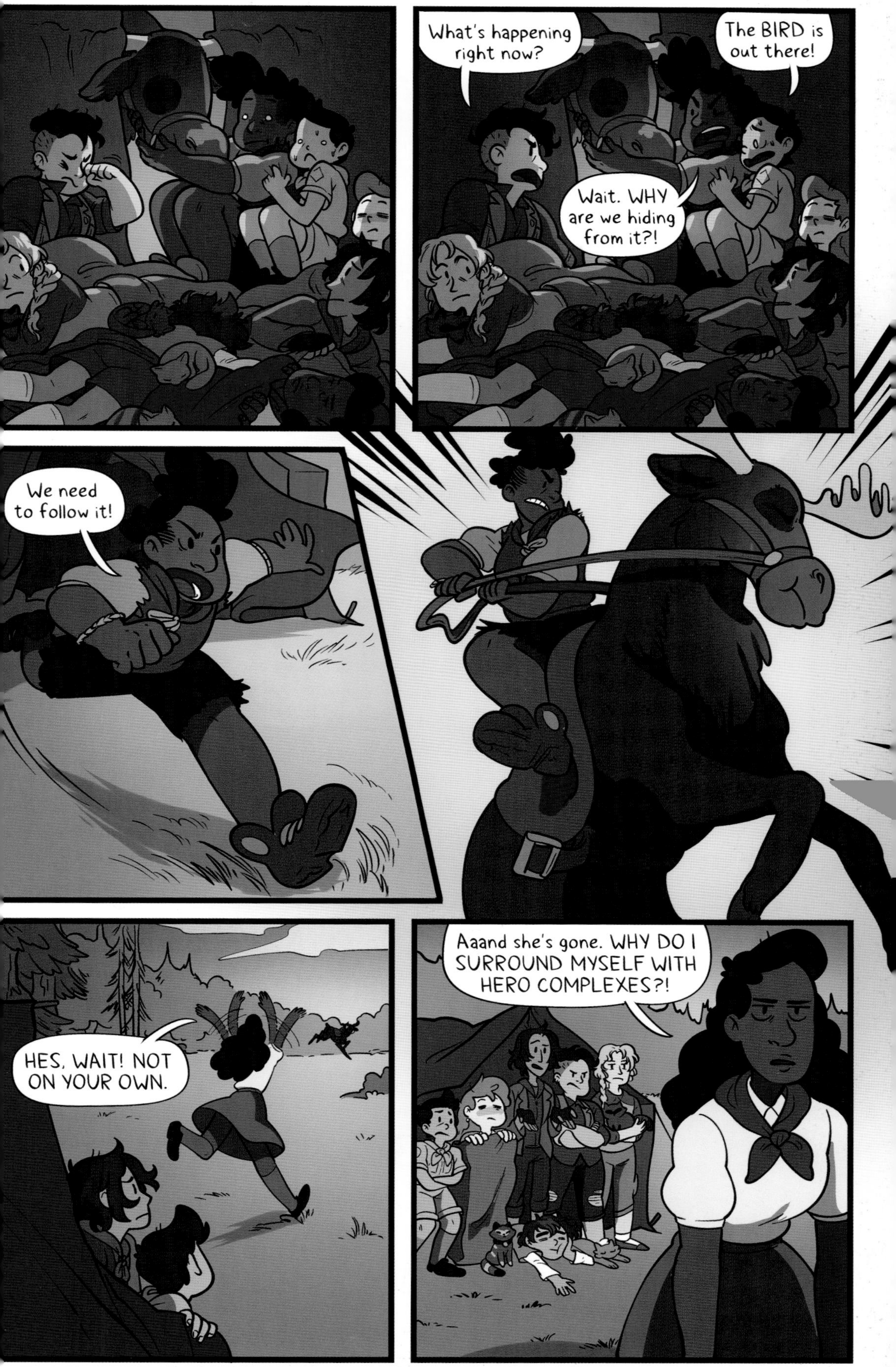
What's happening right now?
The BIRD is out there!
Wait. WHY are we hiding from it?!
We need to follow it!
HES, WAIT! NOT ON YOUR OWN.
Aaand she's gone. WHY DO I SURROUND MYSELF WITH HERO COMPLEXES?!

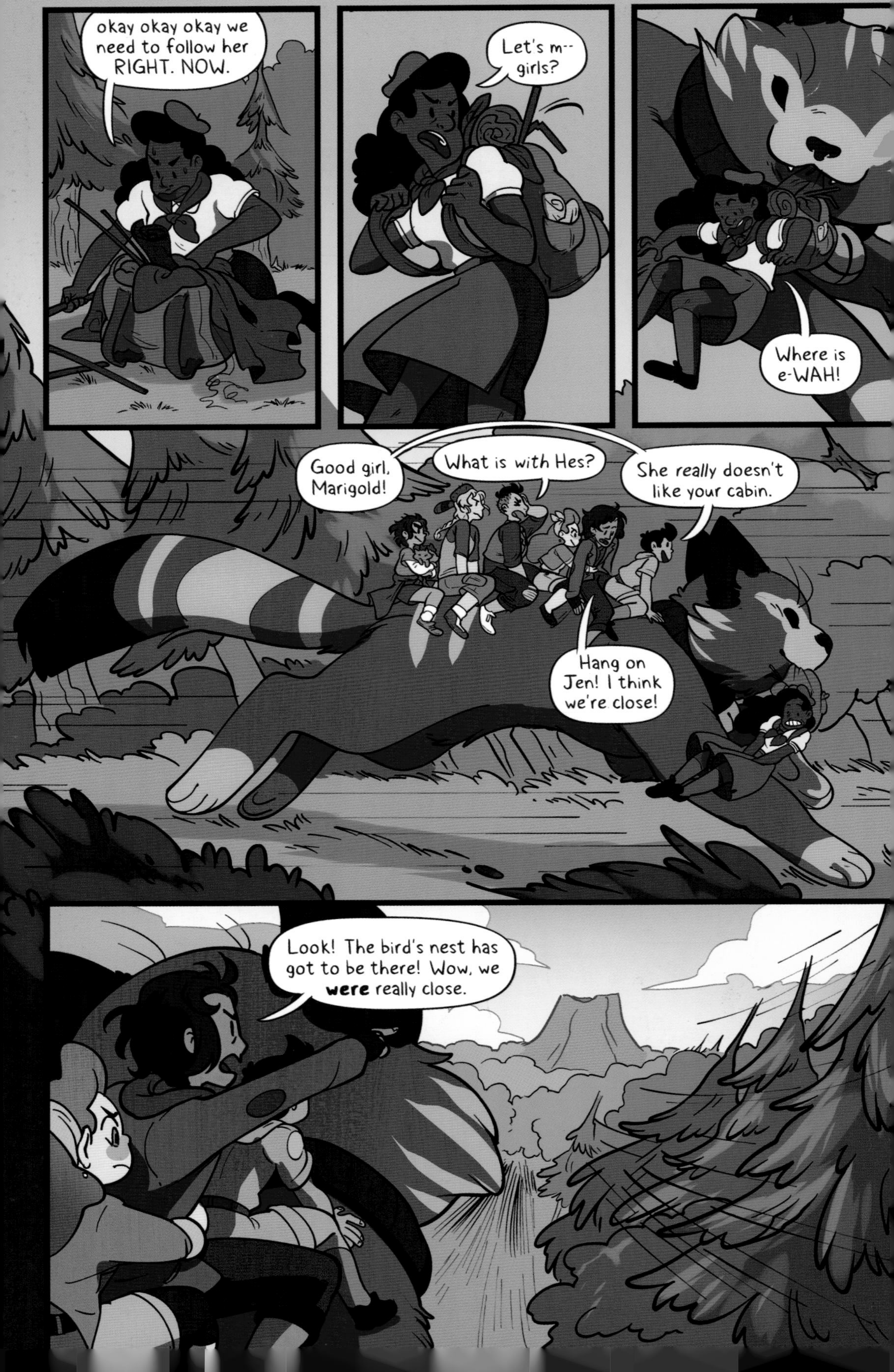
okay okay okay we need to follow her RIGHT. NOW.
Let's m-- girls?
Where is e-WAH!
Good girl, Marigold!
What is with Hes?
She really doesn't like your cabin.
Hang on Jen! I think we're close!
Look! The bird's nest has got to be there! Wow, we **were** really close.

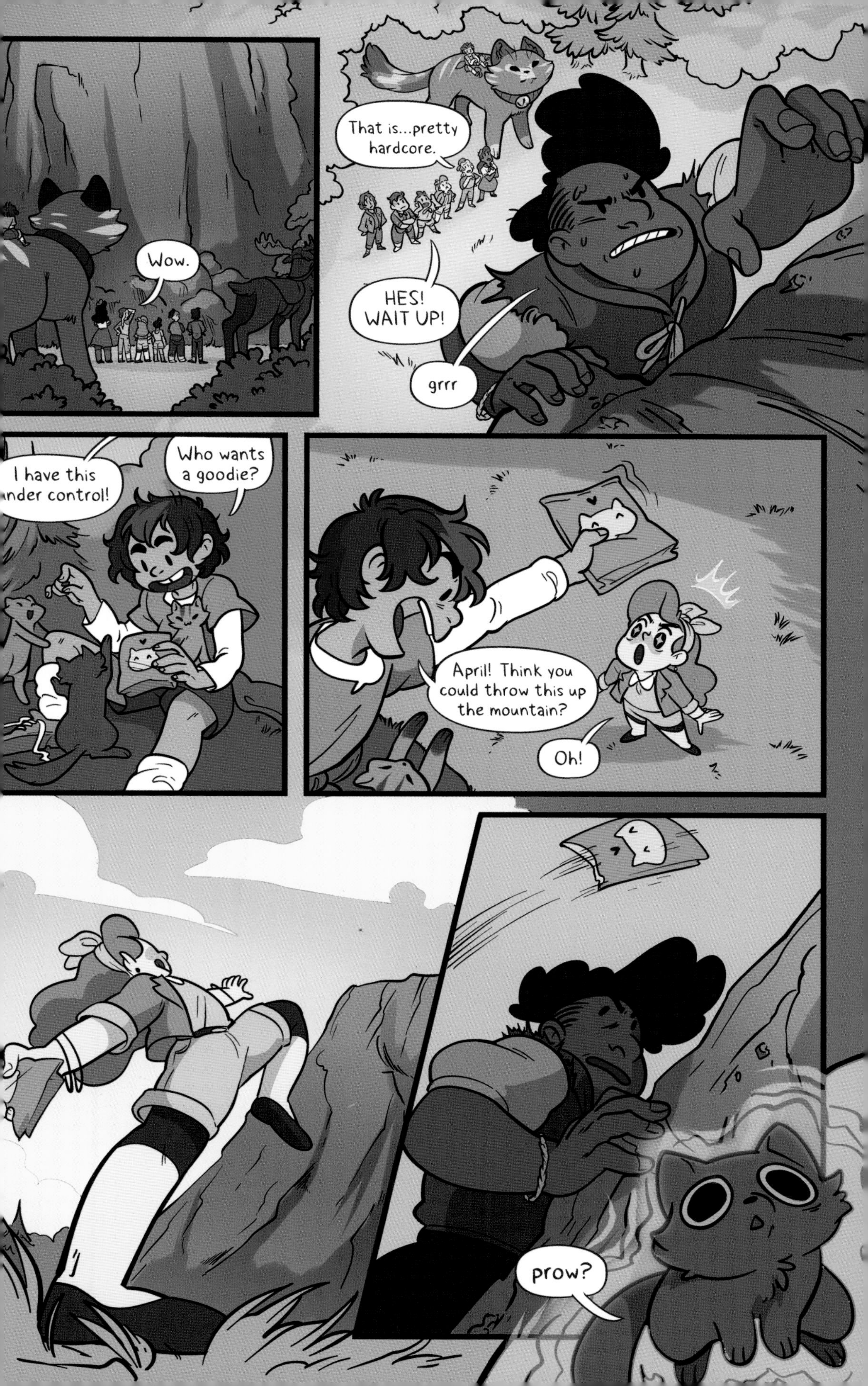
Wow.
That is...pretty hardcore.
HES! WAIT UP!
grrr
I have this nder control!
Who wants a goodie?
April! Think you could throw this up the mountain?
Oh!
prow?

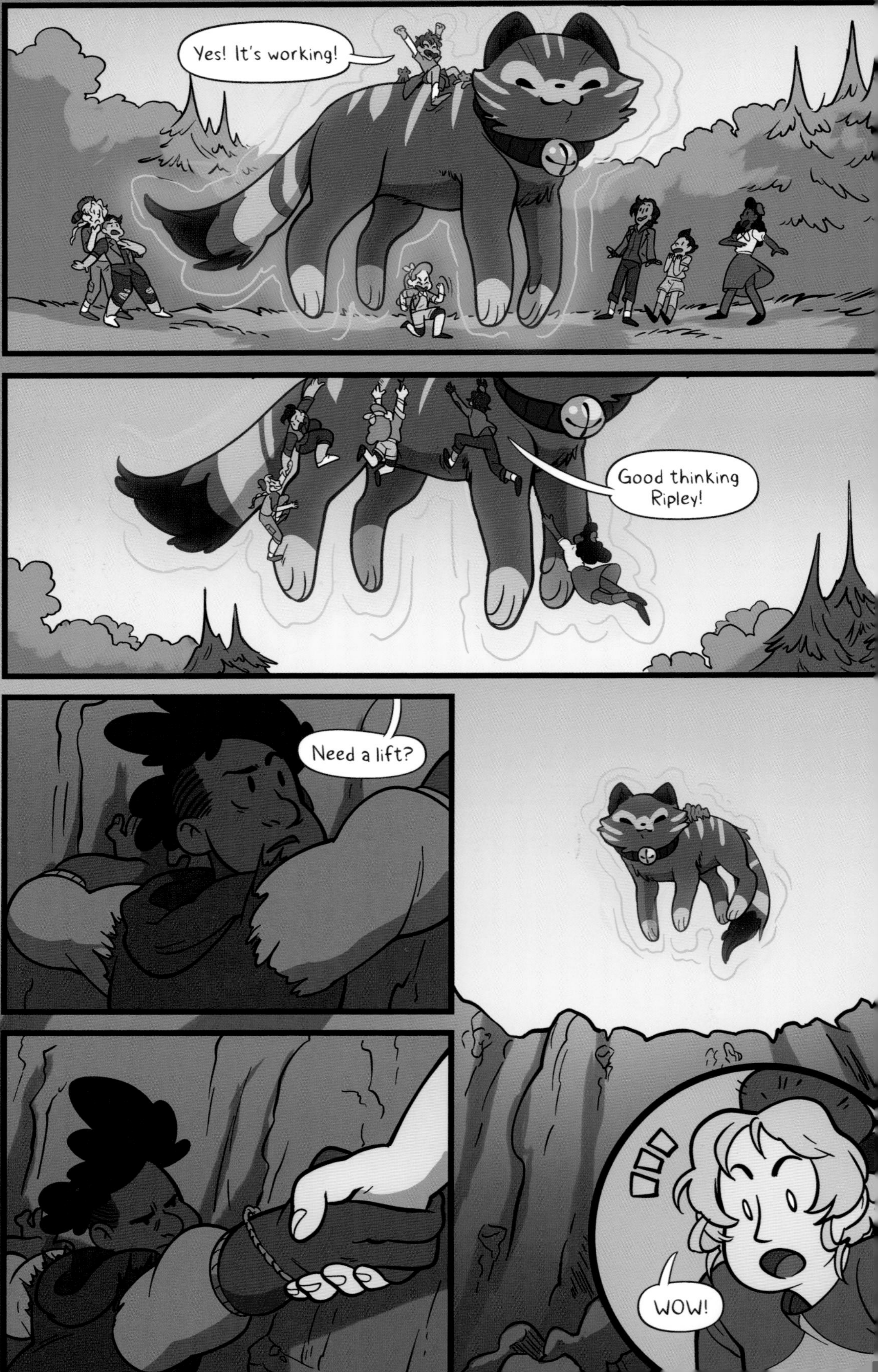
Yes! It's working!
Good thinking Ripley!
Need a lift?
WOW!

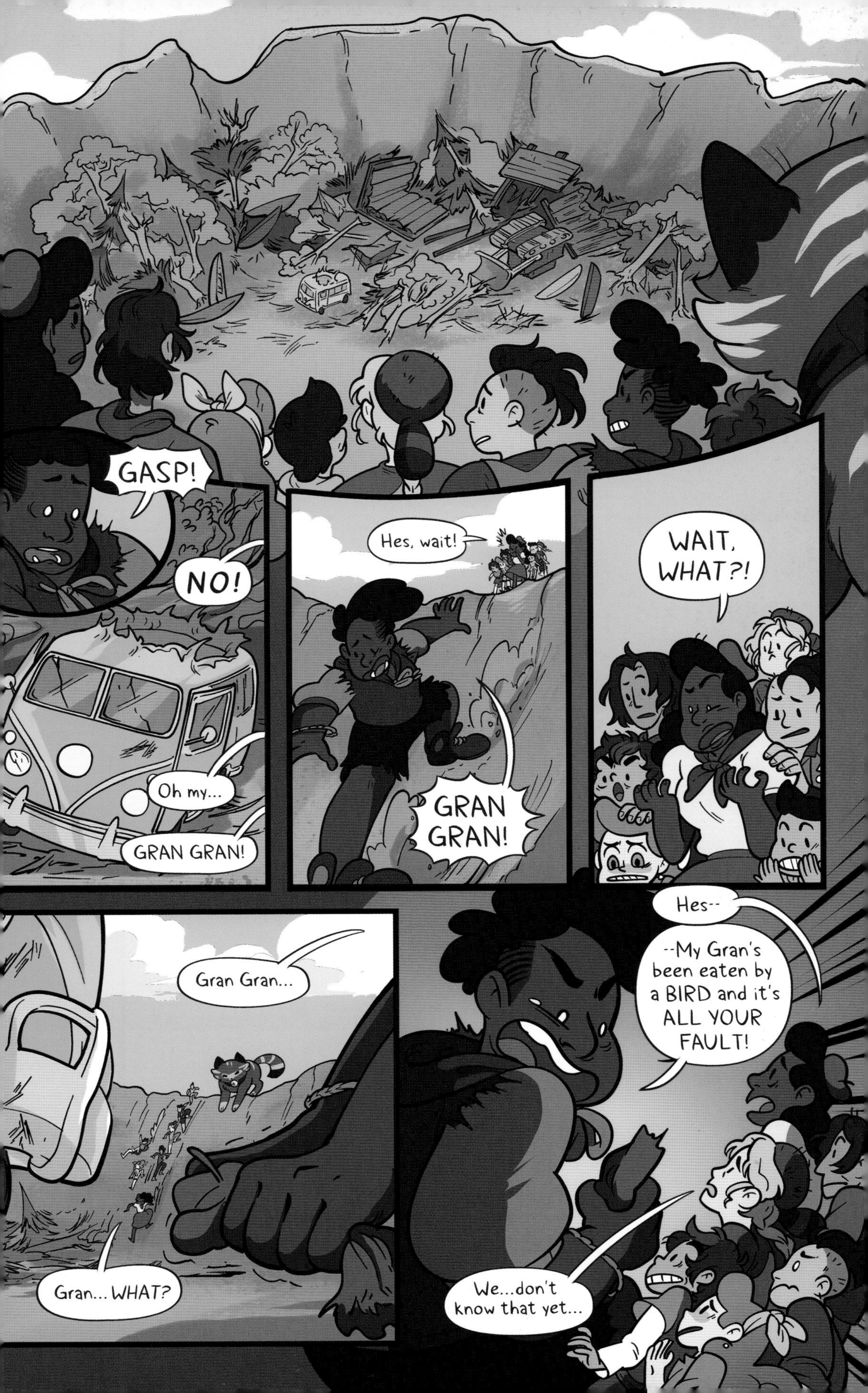
GASP!
NO!
Oh my...
GRAN GRAN!
Hes, wait!
GRAN GRAN!
WAIT, WHAT?!
Gran Gran...
Gran... WHAT?
Hes--
--My Gran's been eaten by a BIRD and it's ALL YOUR FAULT!
We...don't know that yet...

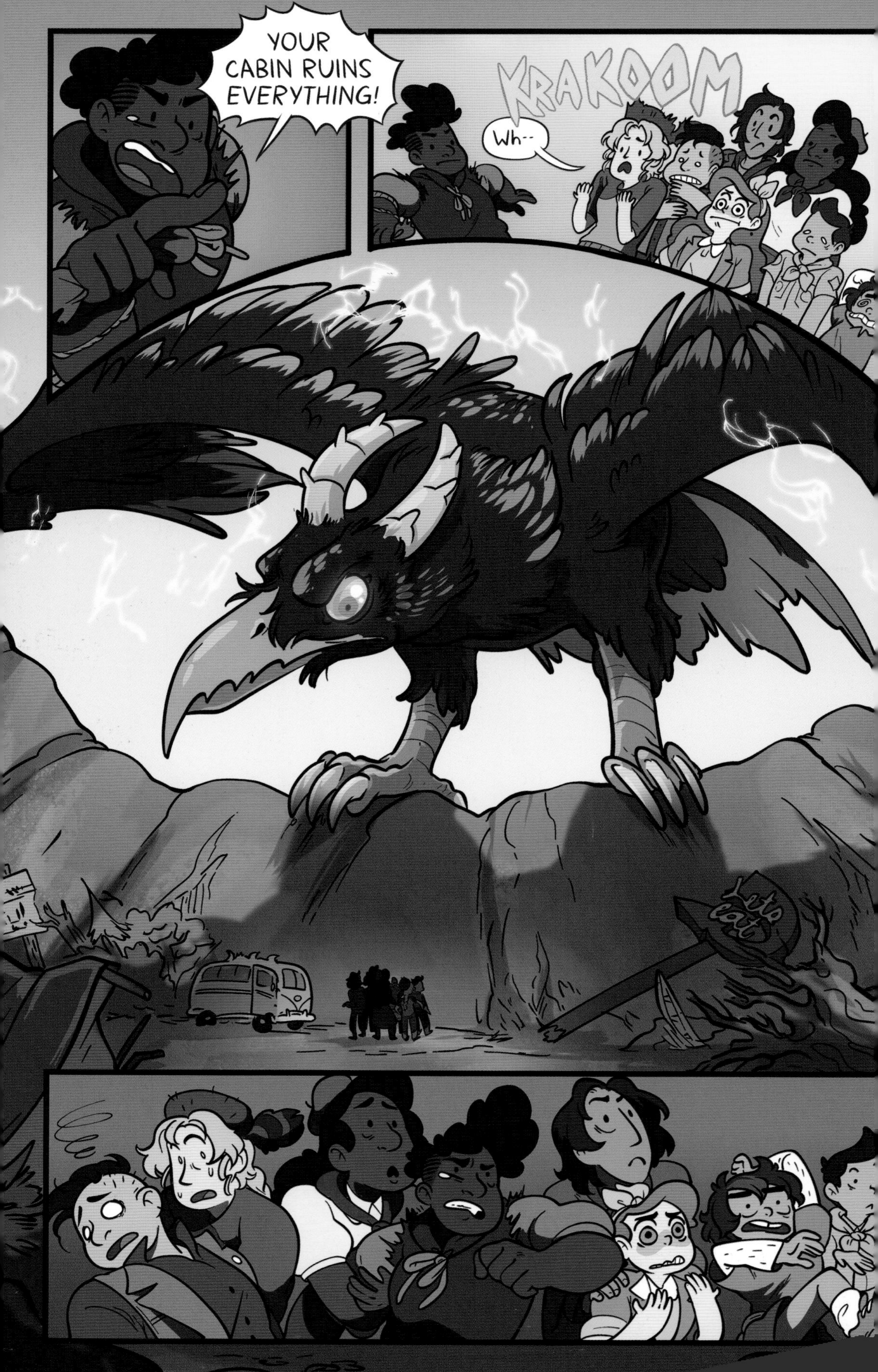
YOUR CABIN RUINS EVERYTHING!
KRAKOOM
Wh--
Lets eat

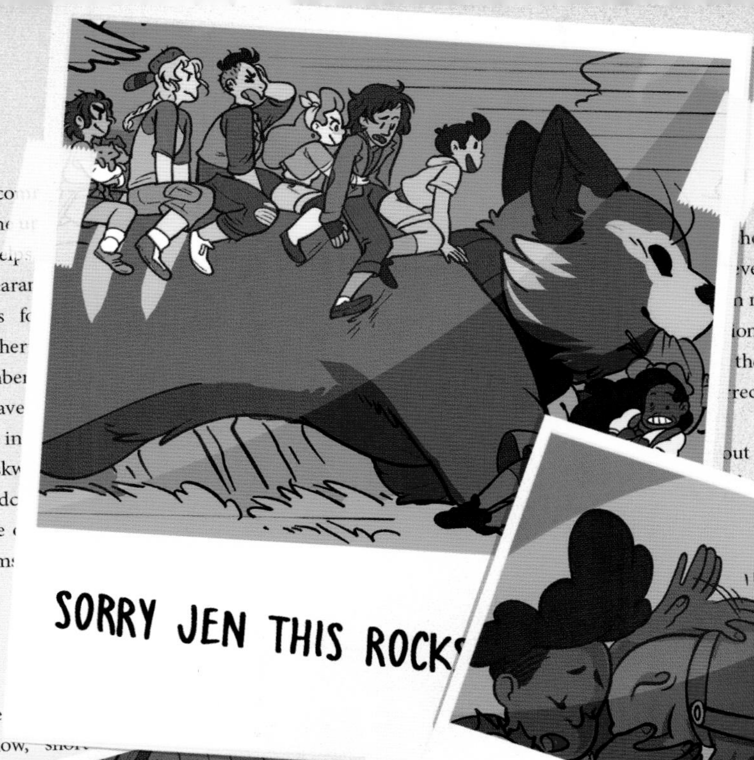
SORRY JEN THIS ROCKS

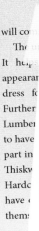

will com

The u

It helps

appearan

dress fo

Further

Lumber

to have

part in

Thiskw

Hardc

have

thems

IE UNIFORM

hould be worn at camp
events when Lumberjanes
n may also be worn at other
ions. It should be worn as a
the uniform dress with
rrect shoes, and stocking or

out grows her uniform or
ter Lumberjane.
a she has
her
her

GES

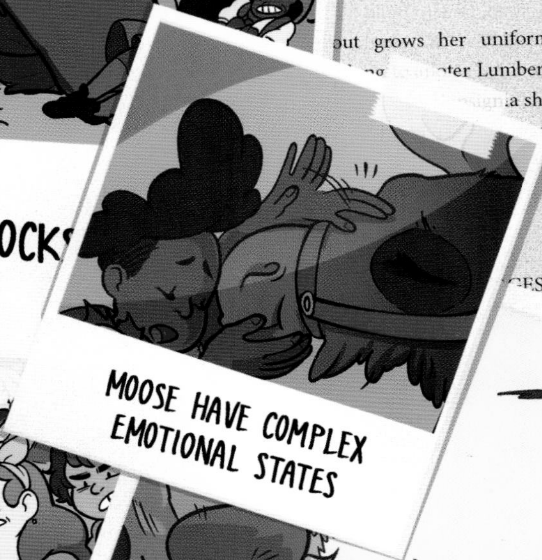
MOOSE HAVE COMPLEX
EMOTIONAL STATES

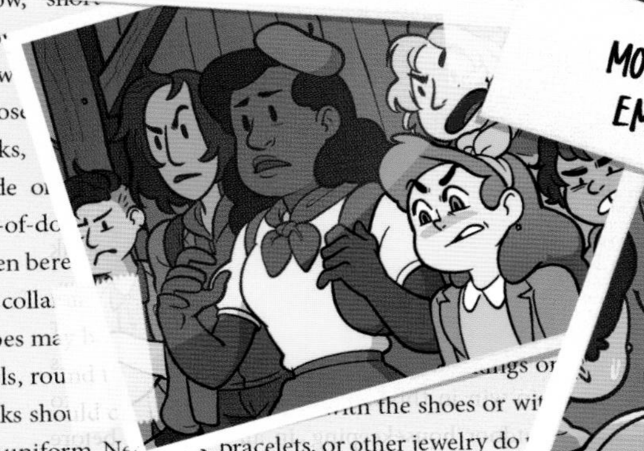

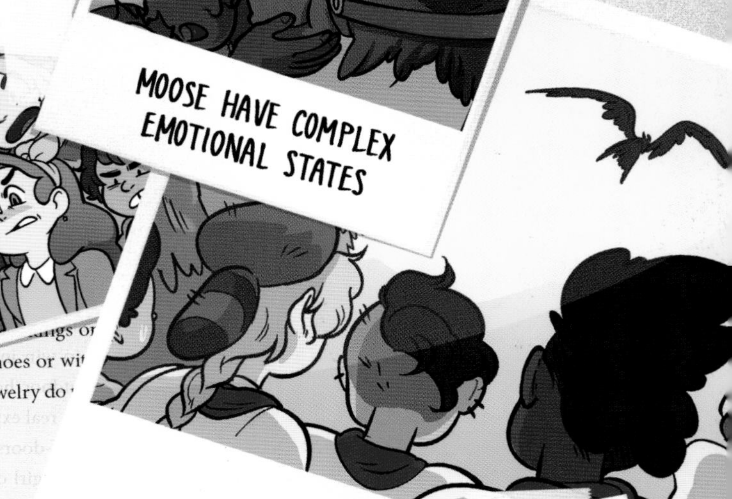

The
yellow,
emb
the w
choos
slacks,
made o
out-of-do
green bere
the colla
Shoes ma
heels, rou
socks shou ... with the shoes or wi
the uniform. Ne... es, bracelets, or other jewelry do
belong with a Lumberjane uniform.

HOW TO WEAR THE UNIFORM

To look well in a uniform demans first of ... uniform be kept in good condition—clean ... pressed. See that the skirt is the right length for your own height and build, that the belt is adjusted to your waist, that your shoes and stockings are in keeping with the uniform, that you watch your posture and carry yourself with dignity and grace. If the beret is removed indoors, be sure that your hair is neat and kept in place with an insonspicuous clip or ribbon. When you wear a Lumberjane uniform you are identified as a member of this organization and you should be doubly careful to conduct yourself in a way that will show everyone that courtesy and thoughtfullness are part of being a Lumberjane. People are likely to judge a whole nation by the selfishness of a few individuals, to criticize a whole family because of the misconduct of one member, and to feel unkindly toward and organization because of the

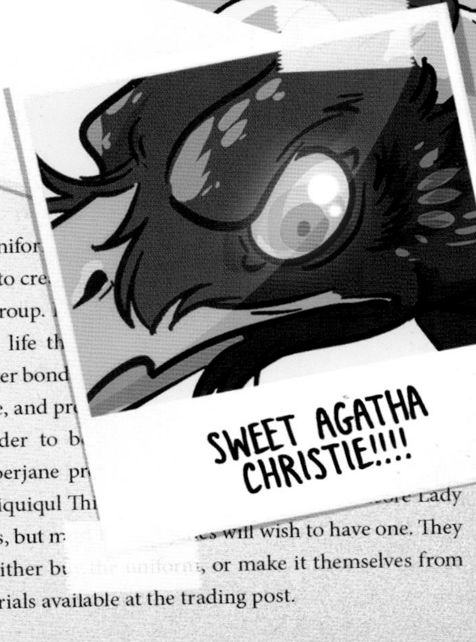
SWEET AGATHA
CHRISTIE!!!!

The unifor
helps to cre
in a group.
active life th
another bond
future, and pr
in order to b
Lumberjane pr
Penniquiqul Thi
Types, but m... es will wish to have one. They
can either bu... the uniform, or make it themselves from
materials available at the trading post.

LUMBERJANES FIELD MANUAL

CHAPTER
TWENTY-SEVEN

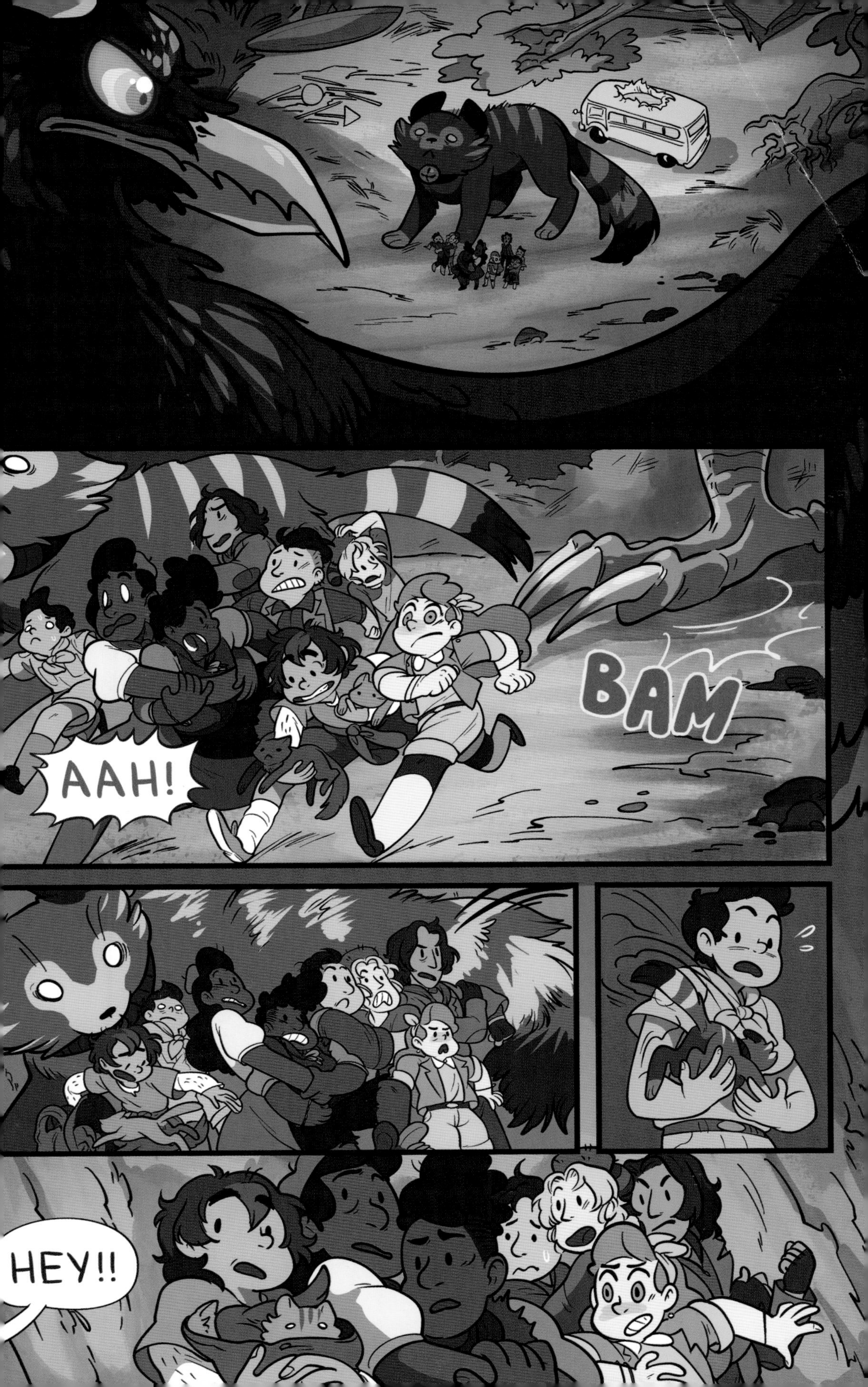
BAM
AAH!
HEY!!

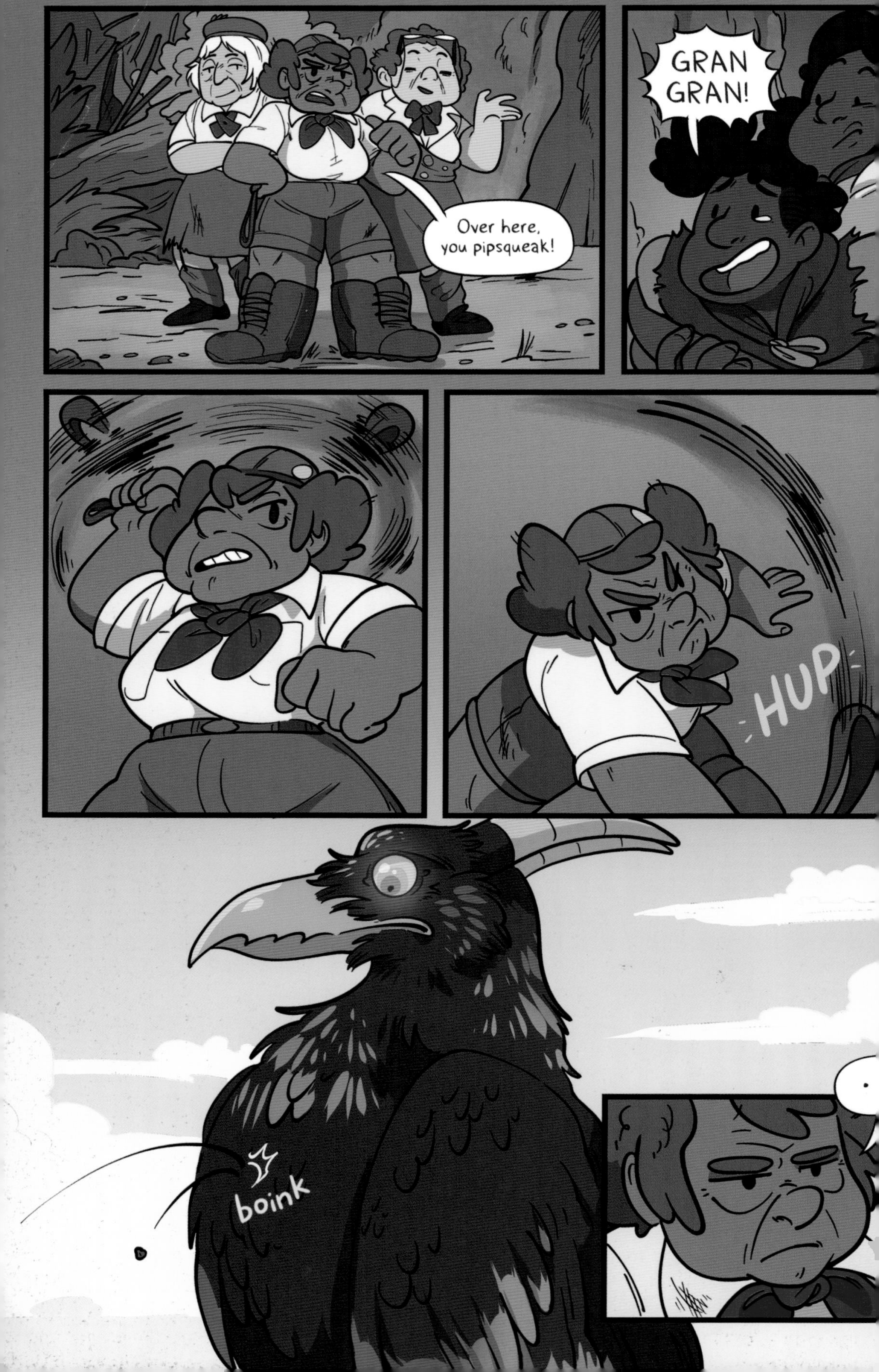
Over here, you pipsqueak!
GRAN GRAN!
HUP
boink

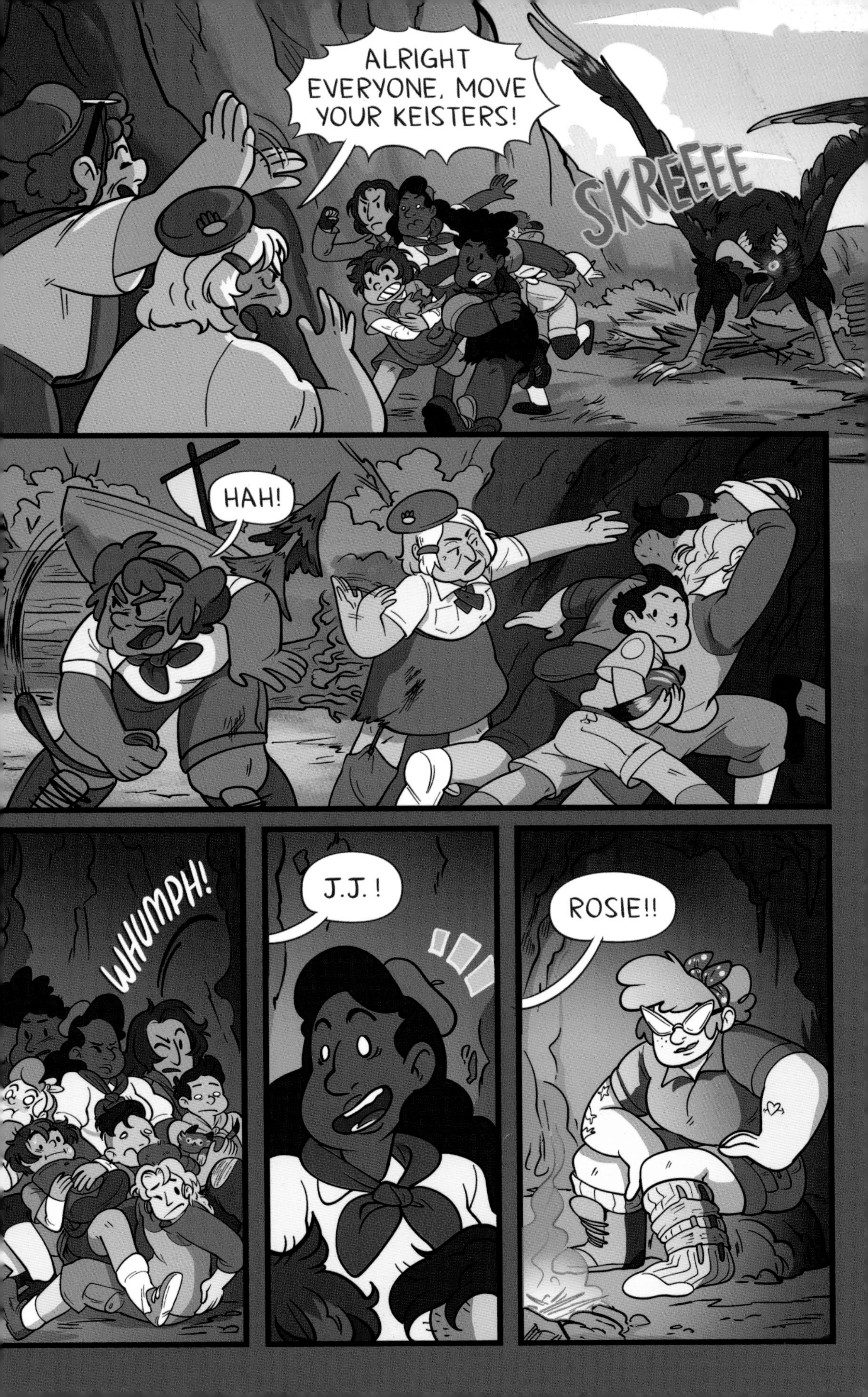
ALRIGHT EVERYONE, MOVE YOUR KEISTERS!
SKREEEE
HAH!
WHUMPH!
J.J. !
ROSIE!!

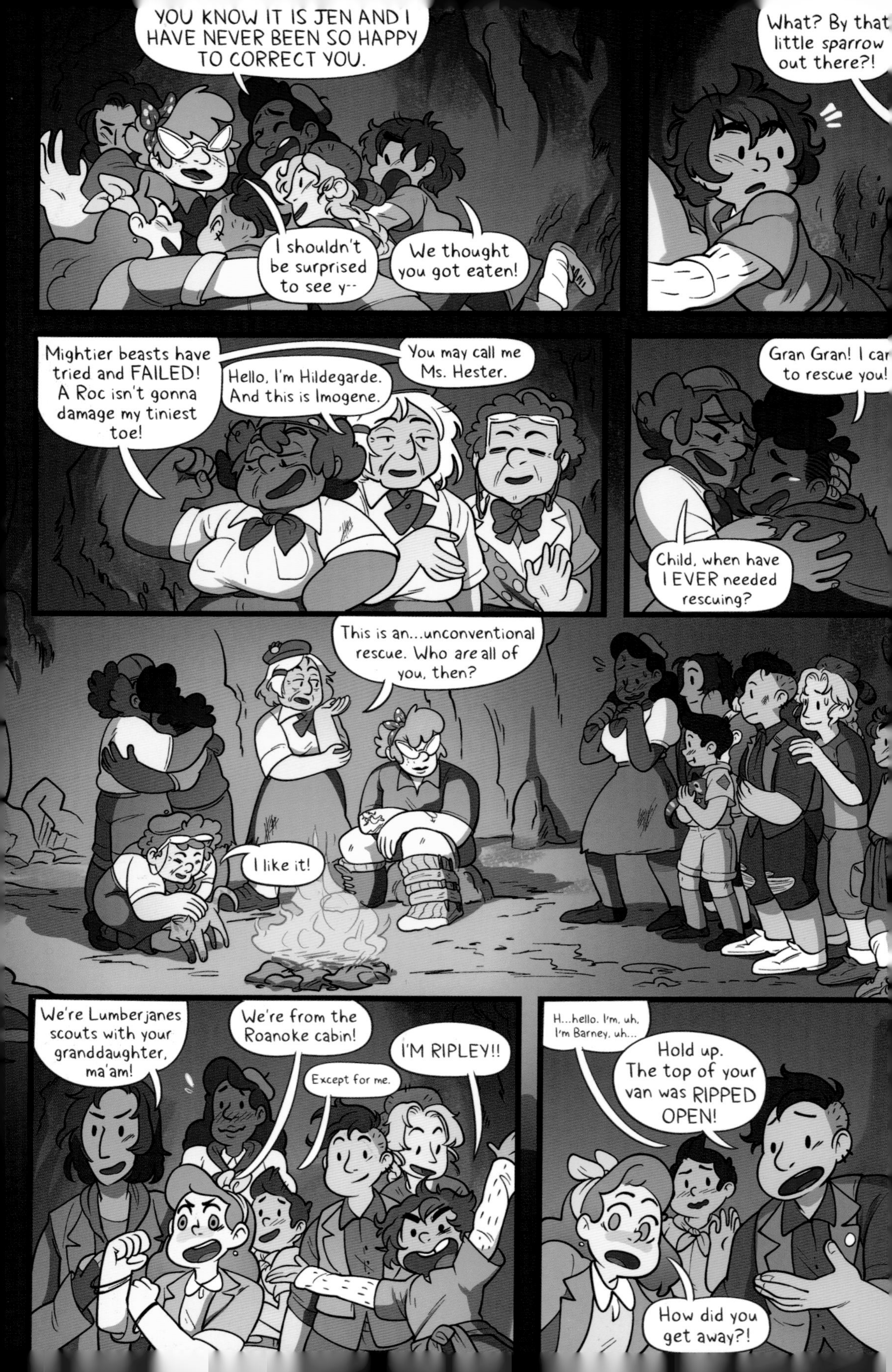
YOU KNOW IT IS JEN AND I HAVE NEVER BEEN SO HAPPY TO CORRECT YOU.
I shouldn't be surprised to see y--
We thought you got eaten!
What? By that little sparrow out there?!
Mightier beasts have tried and FAILED! A Roc isn't gonna damage my tiniest toe!
Hello, I'm Hildegarde. And this is Imogene.
You may call me Ms. Hester.
Gran Gran! I ca to rescue you!
Child, when have I EVER needed rescuing?
This is an...unconventional rescue. Who are all of you, then?
I like it!
We're Lumberjanes scouts with your granddaughter, ma'am!
We're from the Roanoke cabin!
Except for me.
I'M RIPLEY!!
H...hello. I'm, uh, I'm Barney, uh...
Hold up. The top of your van was RIPPED OPEN!
How did you get away?!

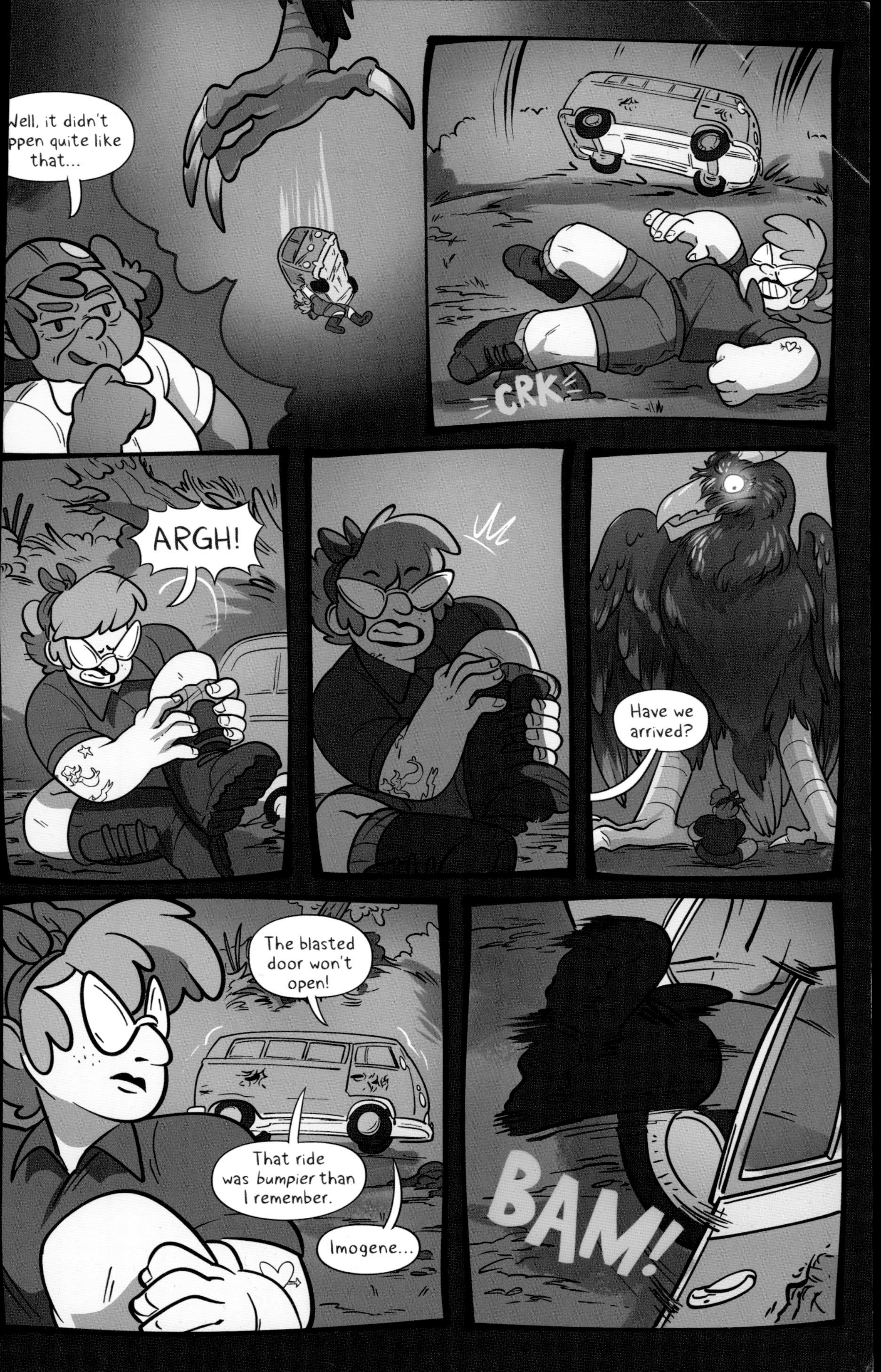
Well, it didn't
ppen quite like
that...
CRK
ARGH!
Have we
arrived?
The blasted
door won't
open!
That ride
was *bumpier* than
I remember.
Imogene...
BAM!

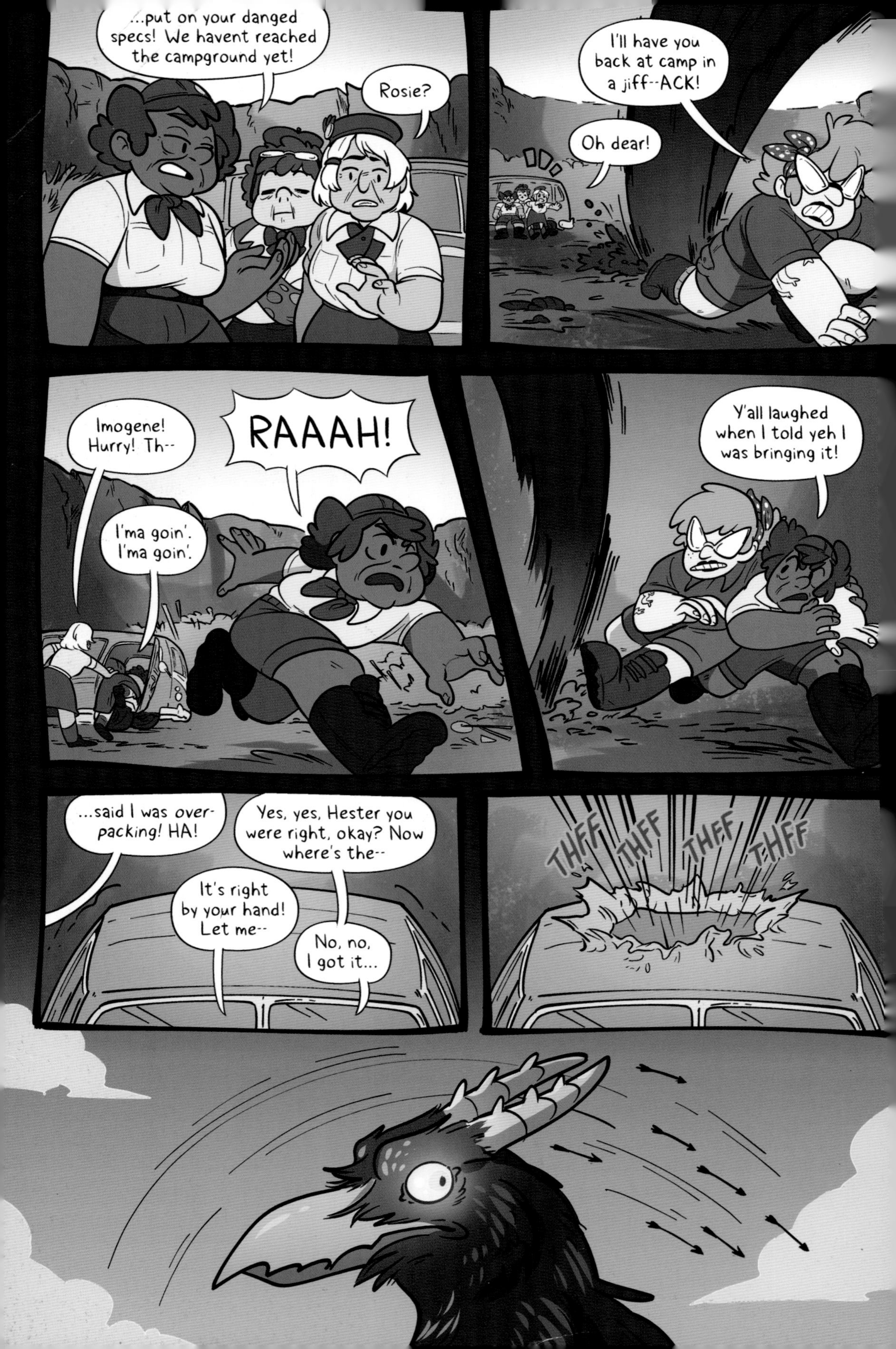
...put on your danged specs! We havent reached the campground yet!
Rosie?
I'll have you back at camp in a jiff--ACK!
Oh dear!
Imogene! Hurry! Th--
RAAAH!
I'ma goin'. I'ma goin'.
Y'all laughed when I told yeh I was bringing it!
...said I was over-packing! HA!
Yes, yes, Hester you were right, okay? Now where's the--
It's right by your hand! Let me--
No, no, I got it...
THFF THFF THFF THFF

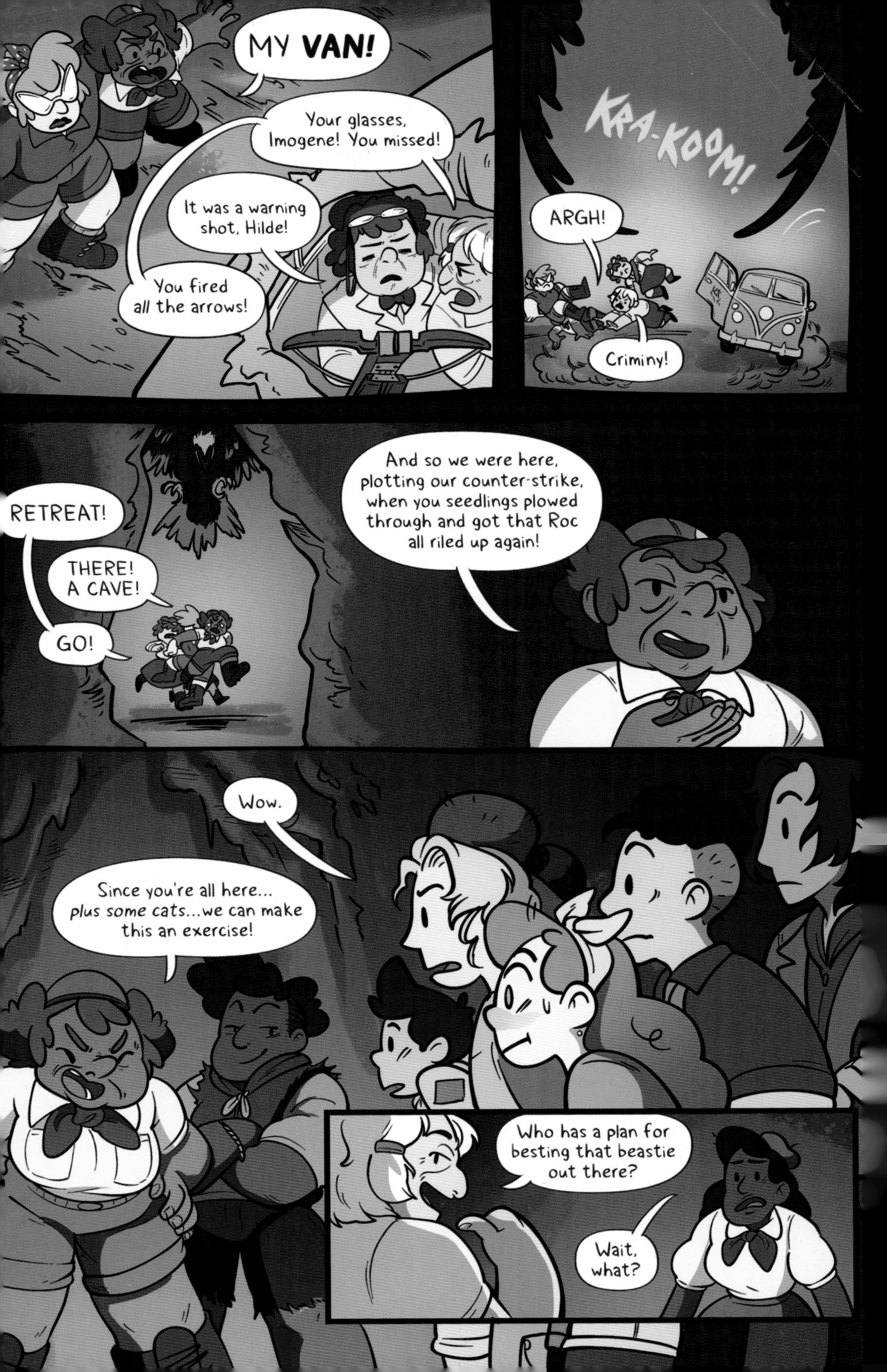
MY VAN!
Your glasses, Imogene! You missed!
It was a warning shot, Hilde!
You fired all the arrows!
KRA-KOOM!
ARGH!
Criminy!
RETREAT!
THERE! A CAVE!
GO!
And so we were here, plotting our counter-strike, when you seedlings plowed through and got that Roc all riled up again!
Wow.
Since you're all here... plus some cats...we can make this an exercise!
Who has a plan for besting that beastie out there?
Wait, what?

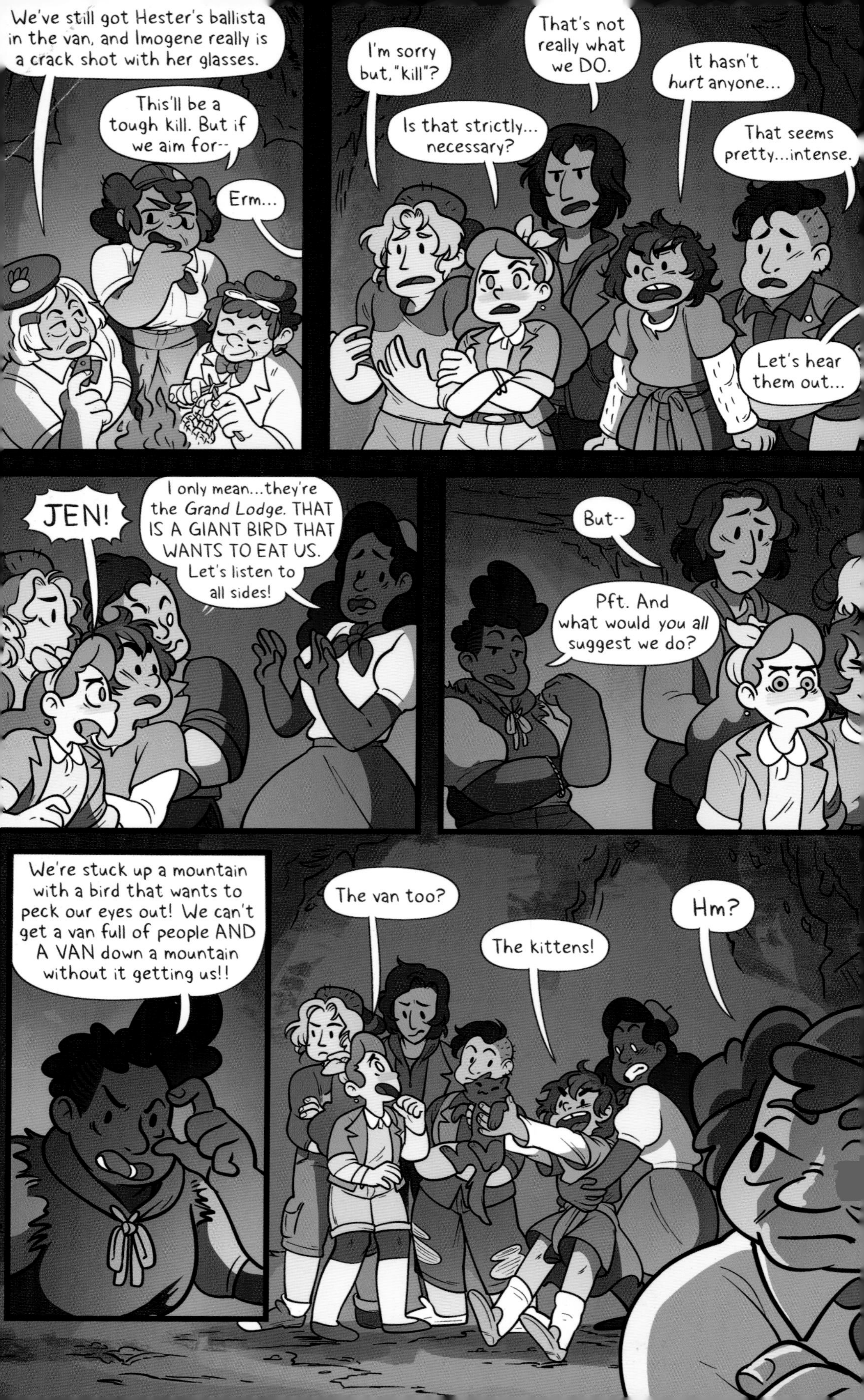
We've still got Hester's ballista in the van, and Imogene really is a crack shot with her glasses.
This'll be a tough kill. But if we aim for--
Erm...
I'm sorry but, "kill"?
Is that strictly... necessary?
That's not really what we DO.
It hasn't hurt anyone...
That seems pretty...intense.
Let's hear them out...
JEN!
I only mean...they're the *Grand Lodge.* THAT IS A GIANT BIRD THAT WANTS TO EAT US. Let's listen to all sides!
But--
Pft. And what would *you* all suggest we do?
We're stuck up a mountain with a bird that wants to peck our eyes out! We can't get a van full of people AND A VAN down a mountain without it getting us!!
The van too?
The kittens!
Hm?

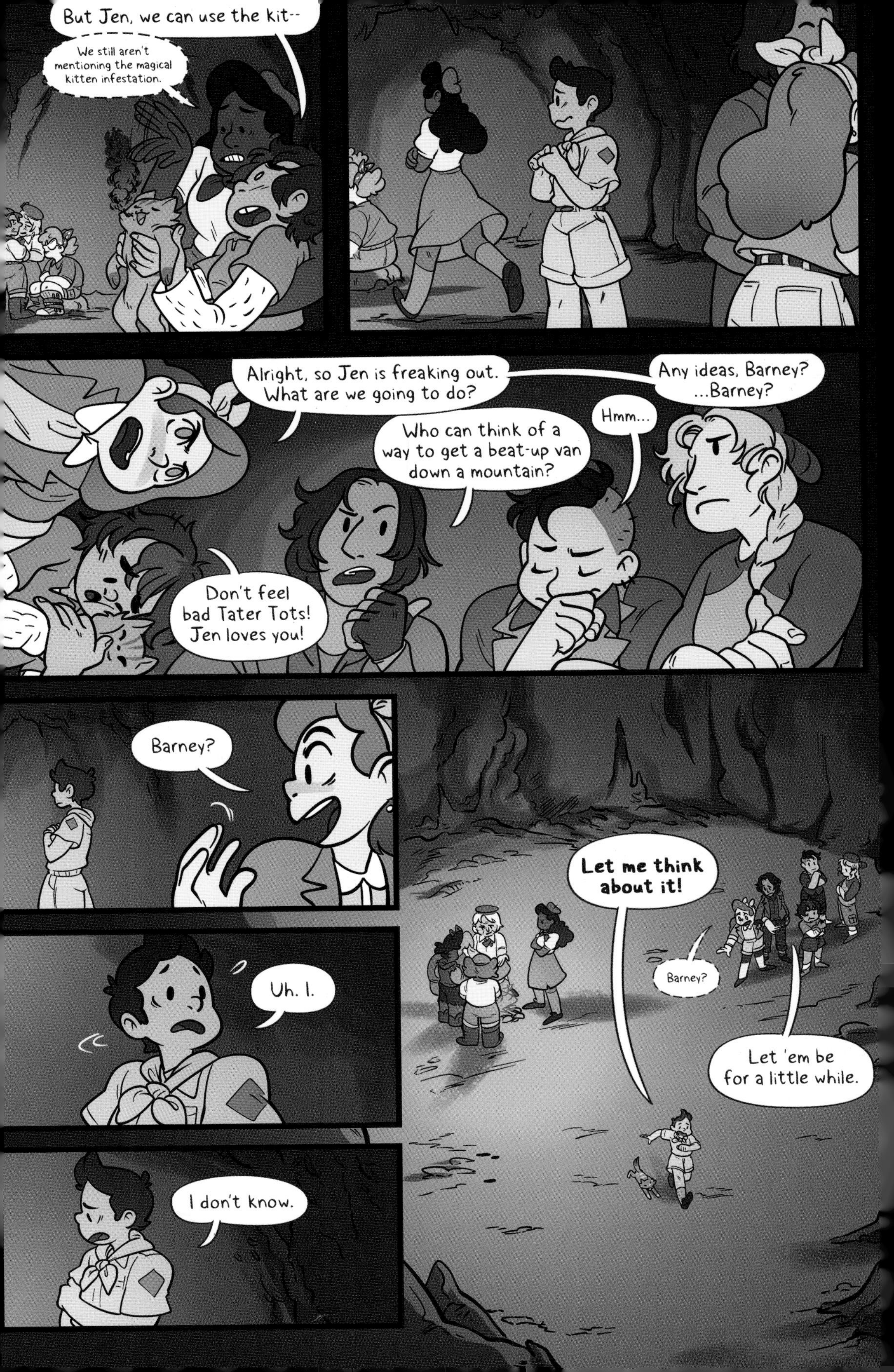
But Jen, we can use the kit--
We still aren't mentioning the magical kitten infestation.
Alright, so Jen is freaking out. What are we going to do?
Any ideas, Barney? ...Barney?
Hmm...
Who can think of a way to get a beat-up van down a mountain?
Don't feel bad Tater Tots! Jen loves you!
Barney?
Uh. I.
I don't know.
Let me think about it!
Barney?
Let 'em be for a little while.

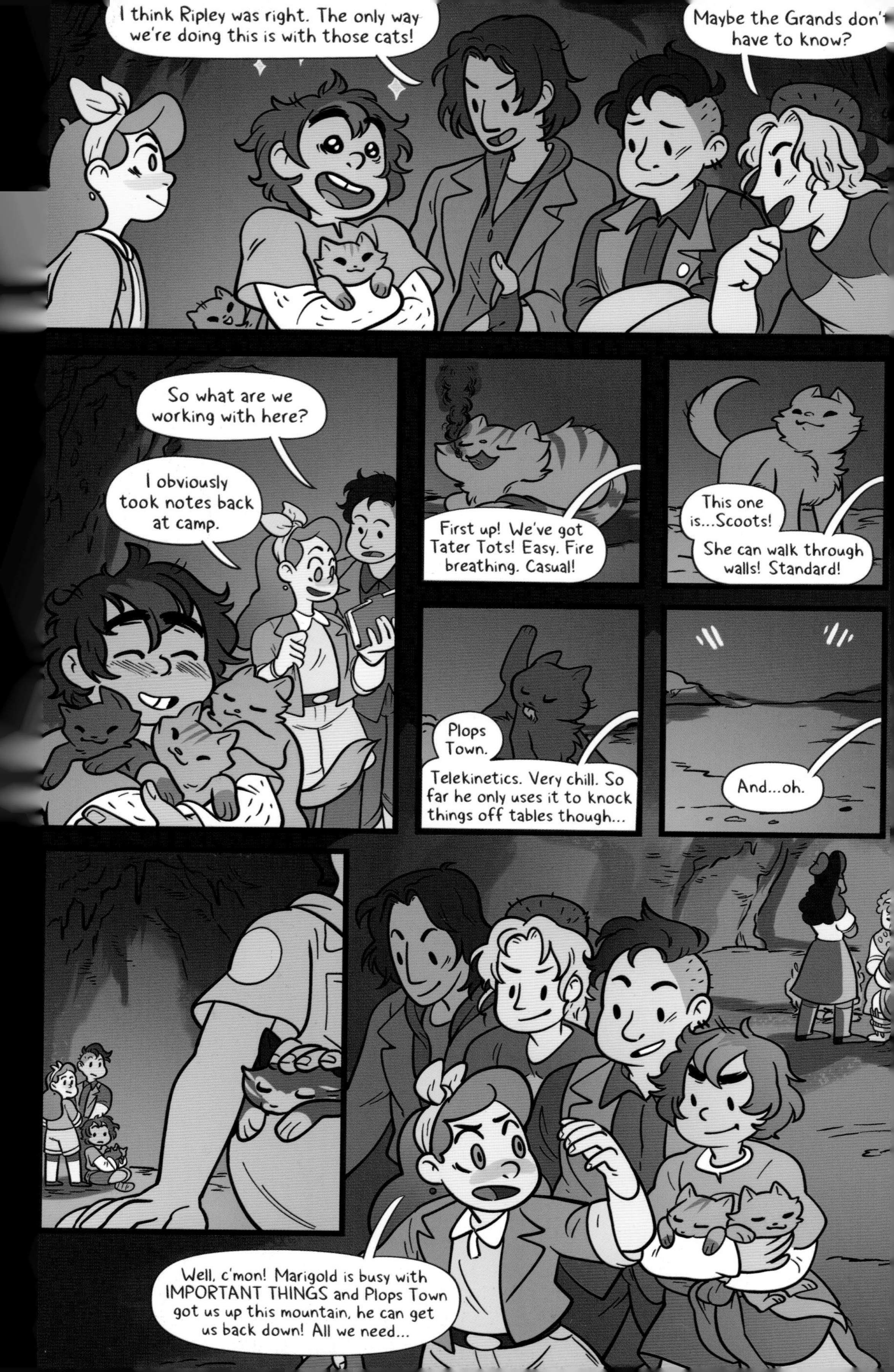
I think Ripley was right. The only way we're doing this is with those cats!
Maybe the Grands don't have to know?
So what are we working with here?
I obviously took notes back at camp.
First up! We've got Tater Tots! Easy. Fire breathing. Casual!
This one is...Scoots!
She can walk through walls! Standard!
Plops Town.
Telekinetics. Very chill. So far he only uses it to knock things off tables though...
And...oh.
Well, c'mon! Marigold is busy with IMPORTANT THINGS and Plops Town got us up this mountain, he can get us back down! All we need...

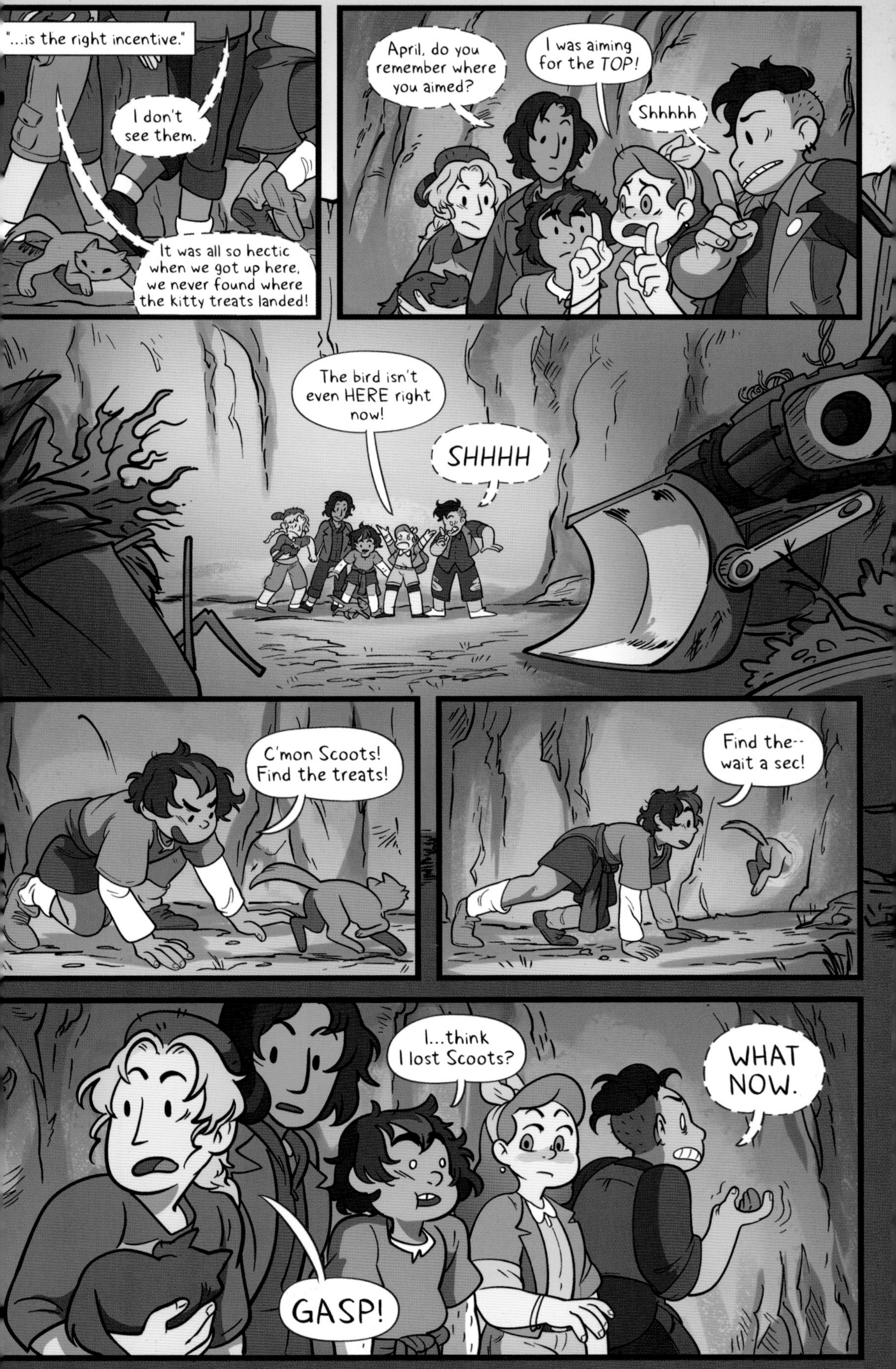
"...is the right incentive."
I don't see them.
It was all so hectic when we got up here, we never found where the kitty treats landed!
April, do you remember where you aimed?
I was aiming for the TOP!
Shhhhh
The bird isn't even HERE right now!
SHHHH
C'mon Scoots! Find the treats!
Find the-- wait a sec!
I...think I lost Scoots?
WHAT NOW.
GASP!

It's okay, Mal. It's a standard issue bird.

I don't believe THAT for a second!

Look what it has!

The kitten treats!

Drop it! Shoo!

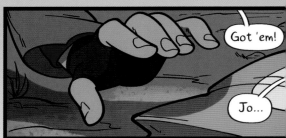

Got 'em!

Jo...

What--

KRAK

-hisssssss-

KOOM

IT'S BACK.

SLAM

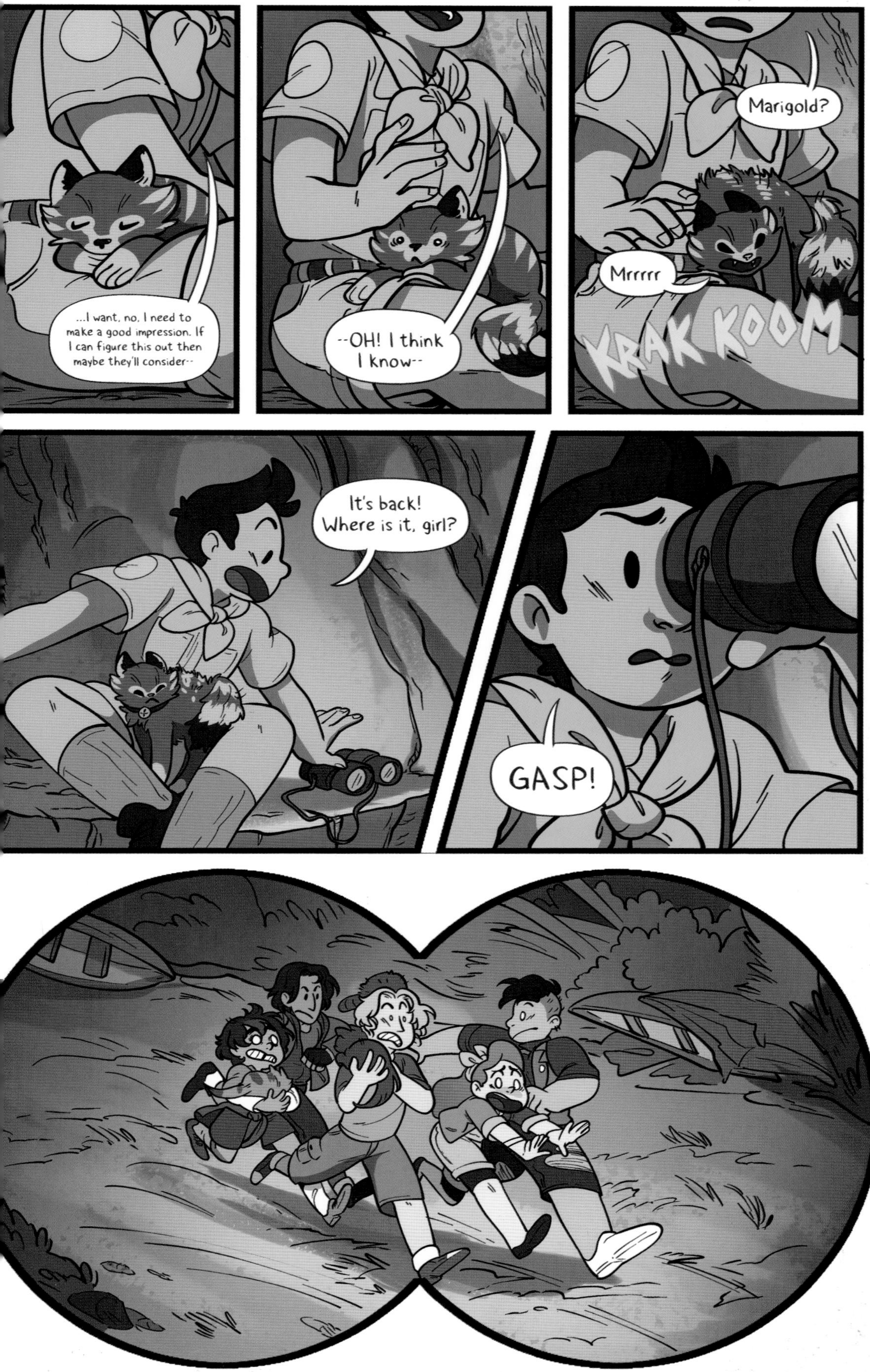
...I want, no, I need to make a good impression. If I can figure this out then maybe they'll consider--
--OH! I think I know--
Marigold?
Mrrrrr
KRAK KOOM
It's back! Where is it, girl?
GASP!

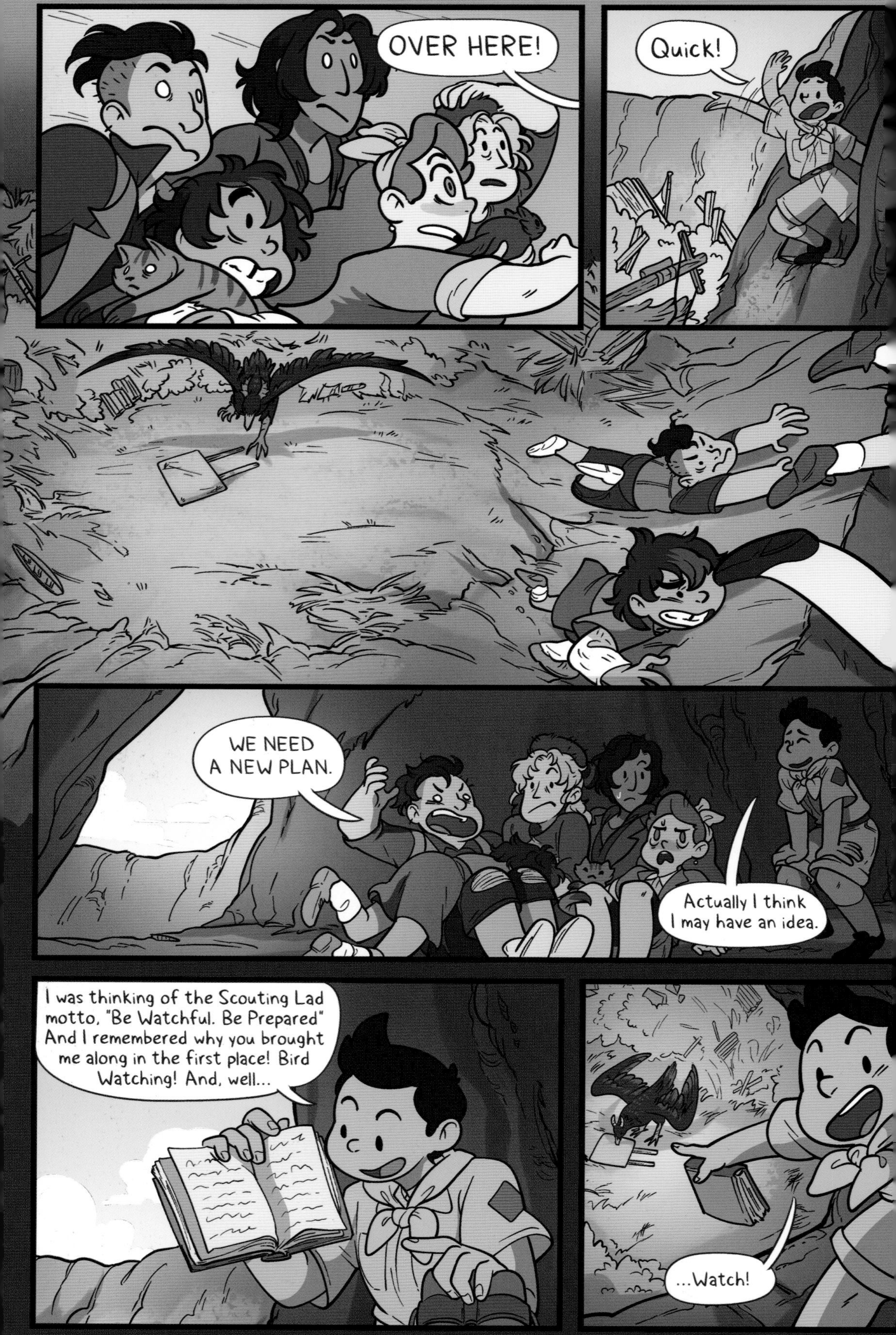
OVER HERE!
Quick!
WE NEED A NEW PLAN.
Actually I think I may have an idea.
I was thinking of the Scouting Lad motto, "Be Watchful. Be Prepared" And I remembered why you brought me along in the first place! Bird Watching! And, well...
...Watch!

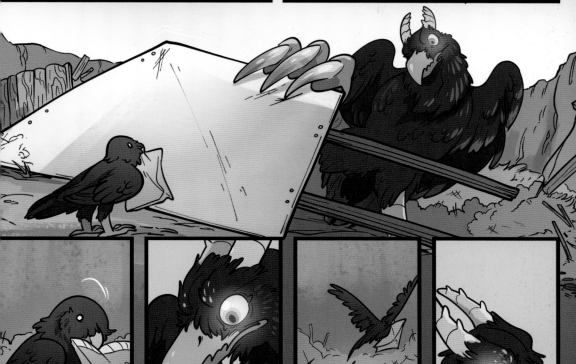

You see, some birds build complex nests to try and impress and attract a mate. I think that's why it's collecting all this random stuff!

SKREEEE

Aaaw. It only wants to impress the tiny bird.

Poor Roc!

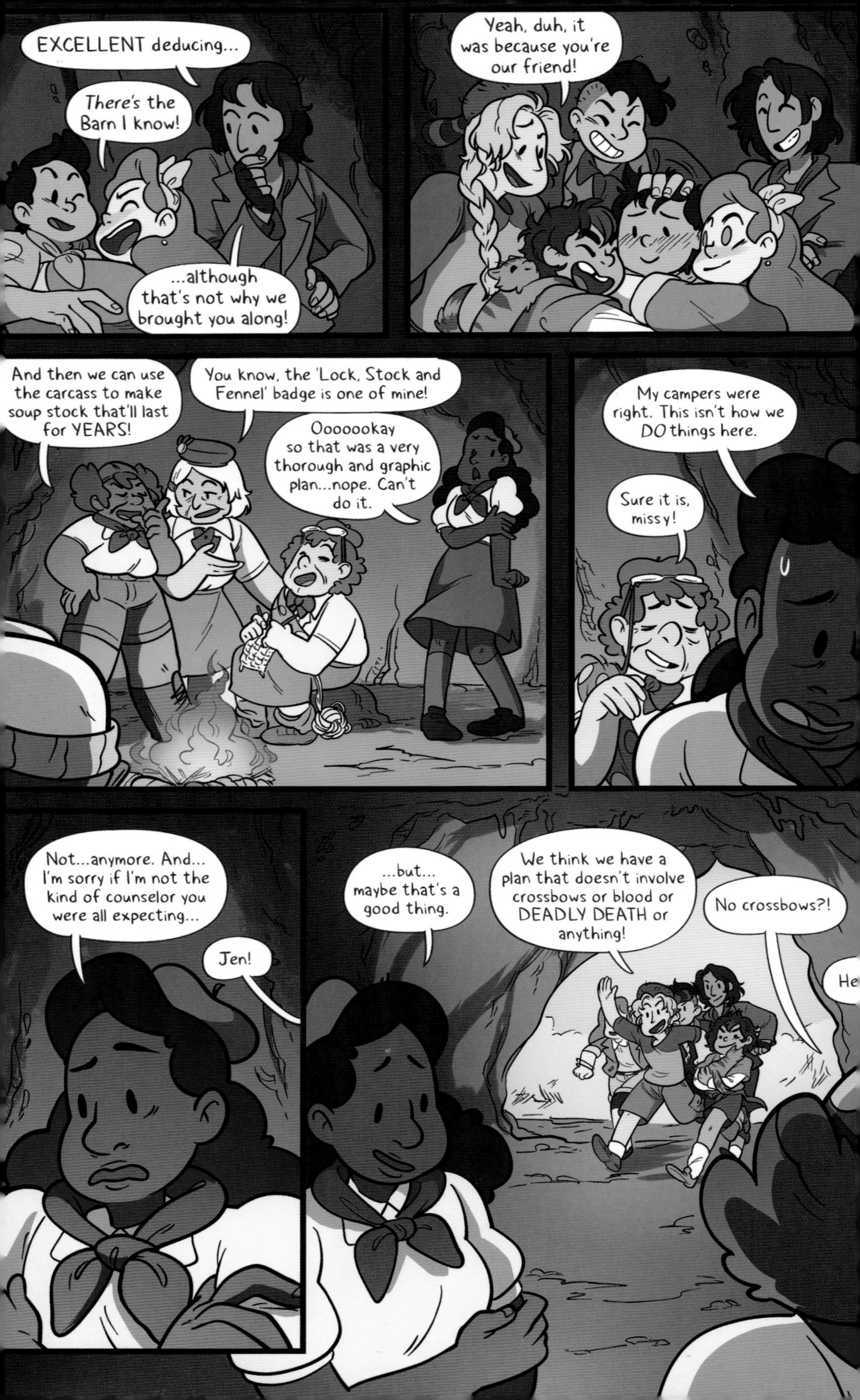
EXCELLENT deducing...
There's the Barn I know!
...although that's not why we brought you along!
Yeah, duh, it was because you're our friend!
And then we can use the carcass to make soup stock that'll last for YEARS!
You know, the 'Lock, Stock and Fennel' badge is one of mine!
Ooooookay so that was a very thorough and graphic plan...nope. Can't do it.
My campers were right. This isn't how we DO things here.
Sure it is, missy!
Not...anymore. And... I'm sorry if I'm not the kind of counselor you were all expecting...
Jen!
...but... maybe that's a good thing.
We think we have a plan that doesn't involve crossbows or blood or DEADLY DEATH or anything!
No crossbows?!

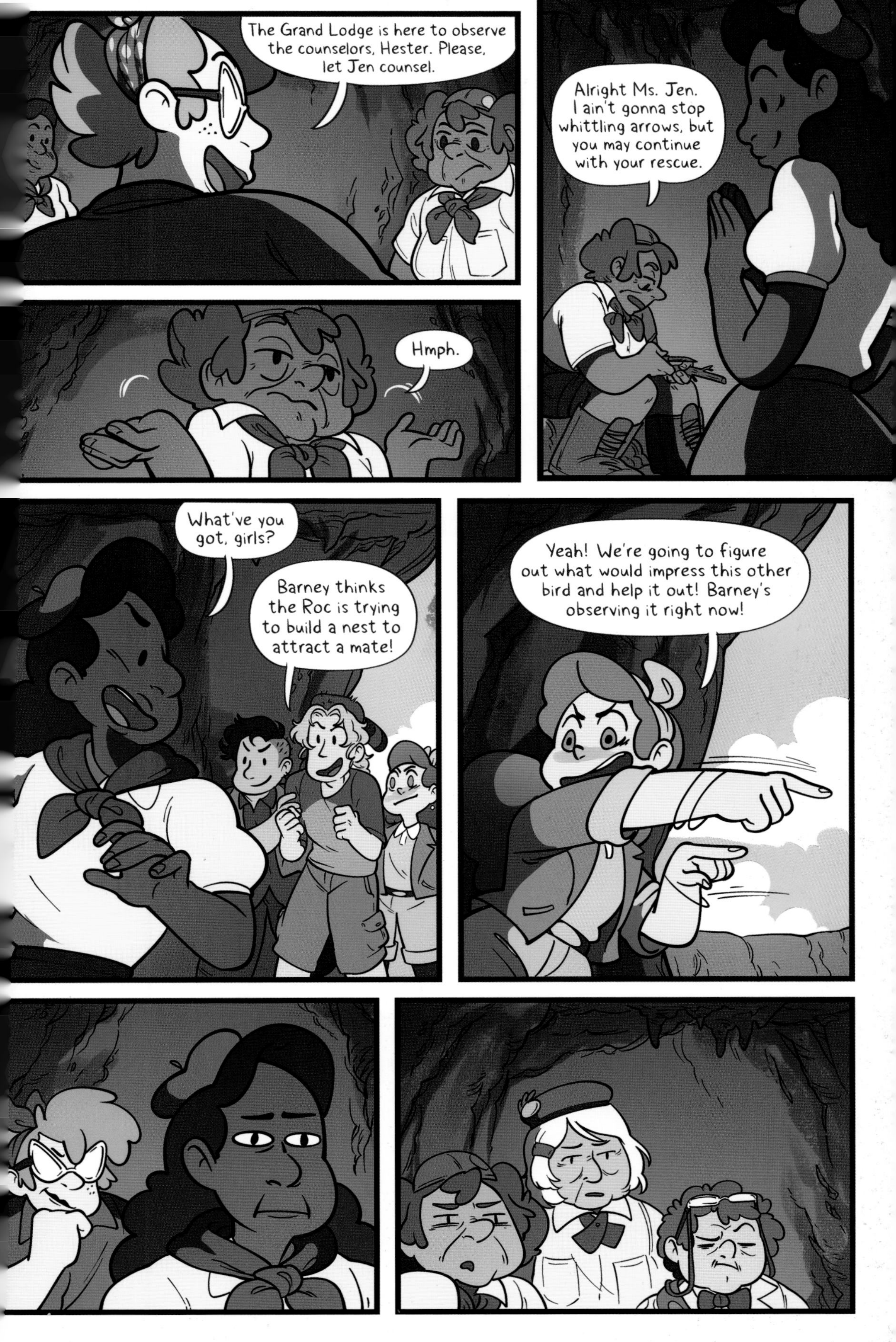
The Grand Lodge is here to observe the counselors, Hester. Please, let Jen counsel.
Hmph.
Alright Ms. Jen. I ain't gonna stop whittling arrows, but you may continue with your rescue.
What've you got, girls?
Barney thinks the Roc is trying to build a nest to attract a mate!
Yeah! We're going to figure out what would impress this other bird and help it out! Barney's observing it right now!

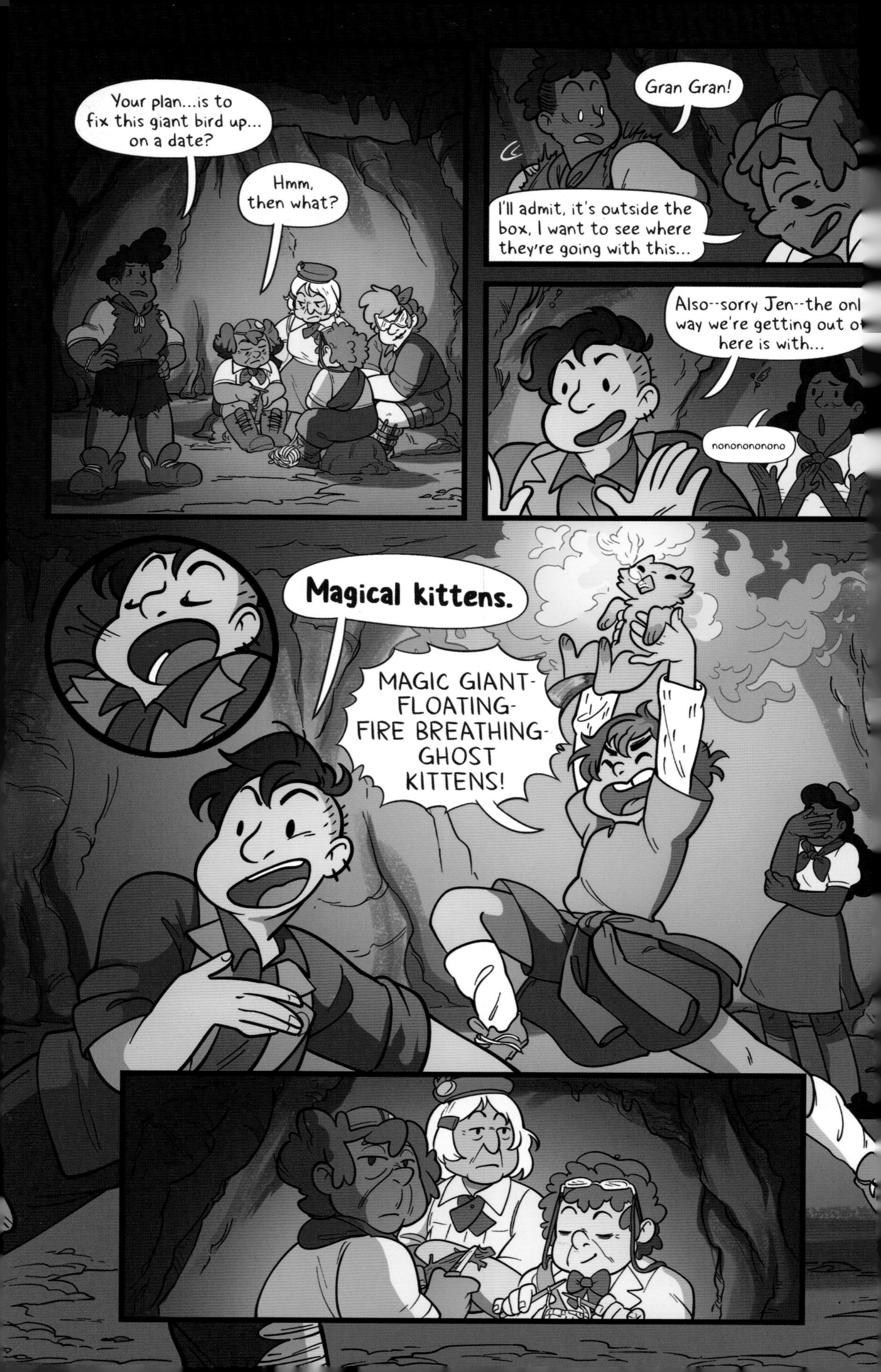

Your plan...is to fix this giant bird up... on a date?
Hmm, then what?
Gran Gran!
I'll admit, it's outside the box, I want to see where they're going with this...
Also--sorry Jen--the onl way we're getting out o here is with...
nonononono
Magical kittens.
MAGIC GIANT-FLOATING-FIRE BREATHING-GHOST KITTENS!

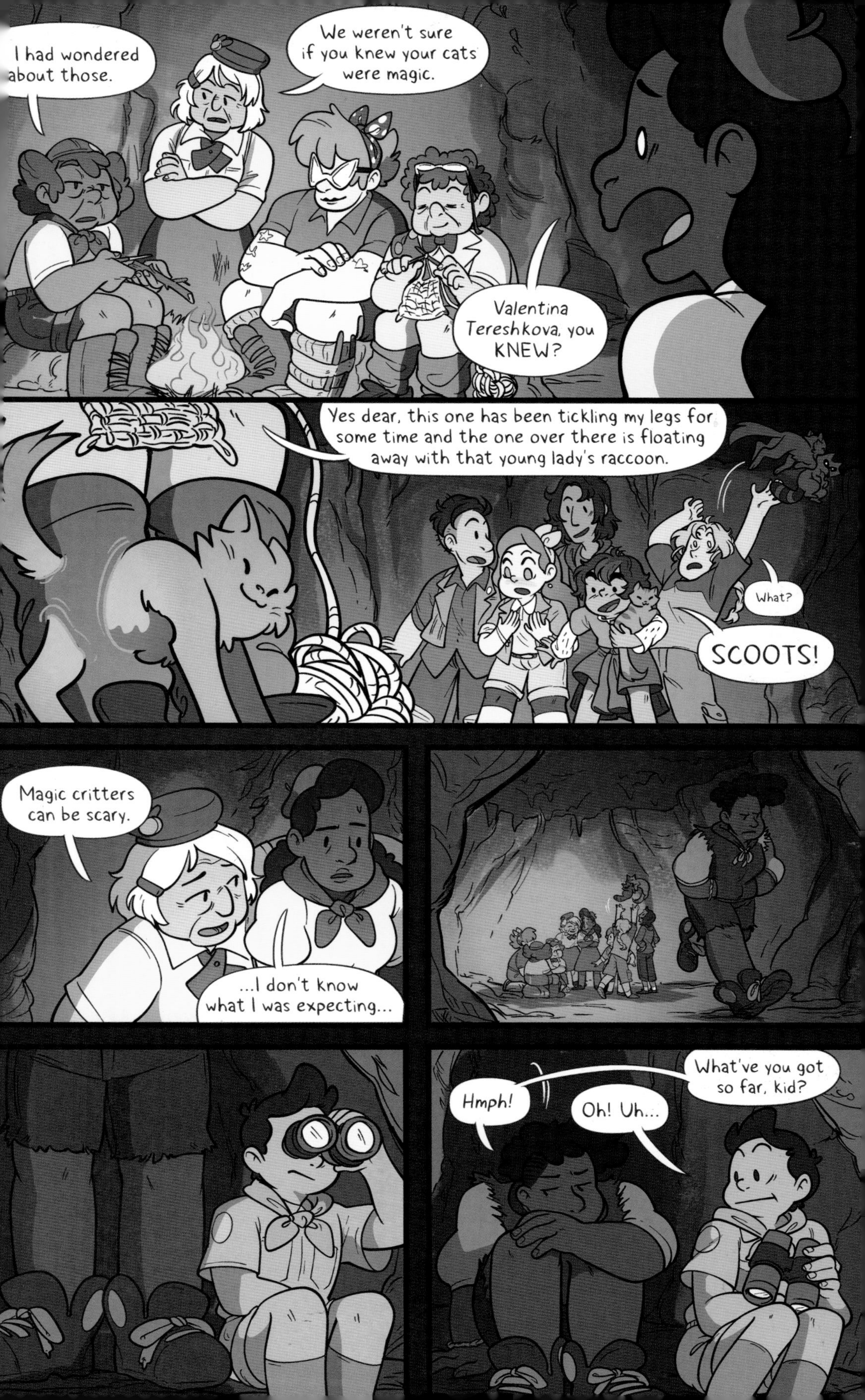
I had wondered about those.
We weren't sure if you knew your cats were magic.
Valentina Tereshkova, you KNEW?
Yes dear, this one has been tickling my legs for some time and the one over there is floating away with that young lady's raccoon.
What?
SCOOTS!
Magic critters can be scary.
...I don't know what I was expecting...
What've you got so far, kid?
Hmph!
Oh! Uh...

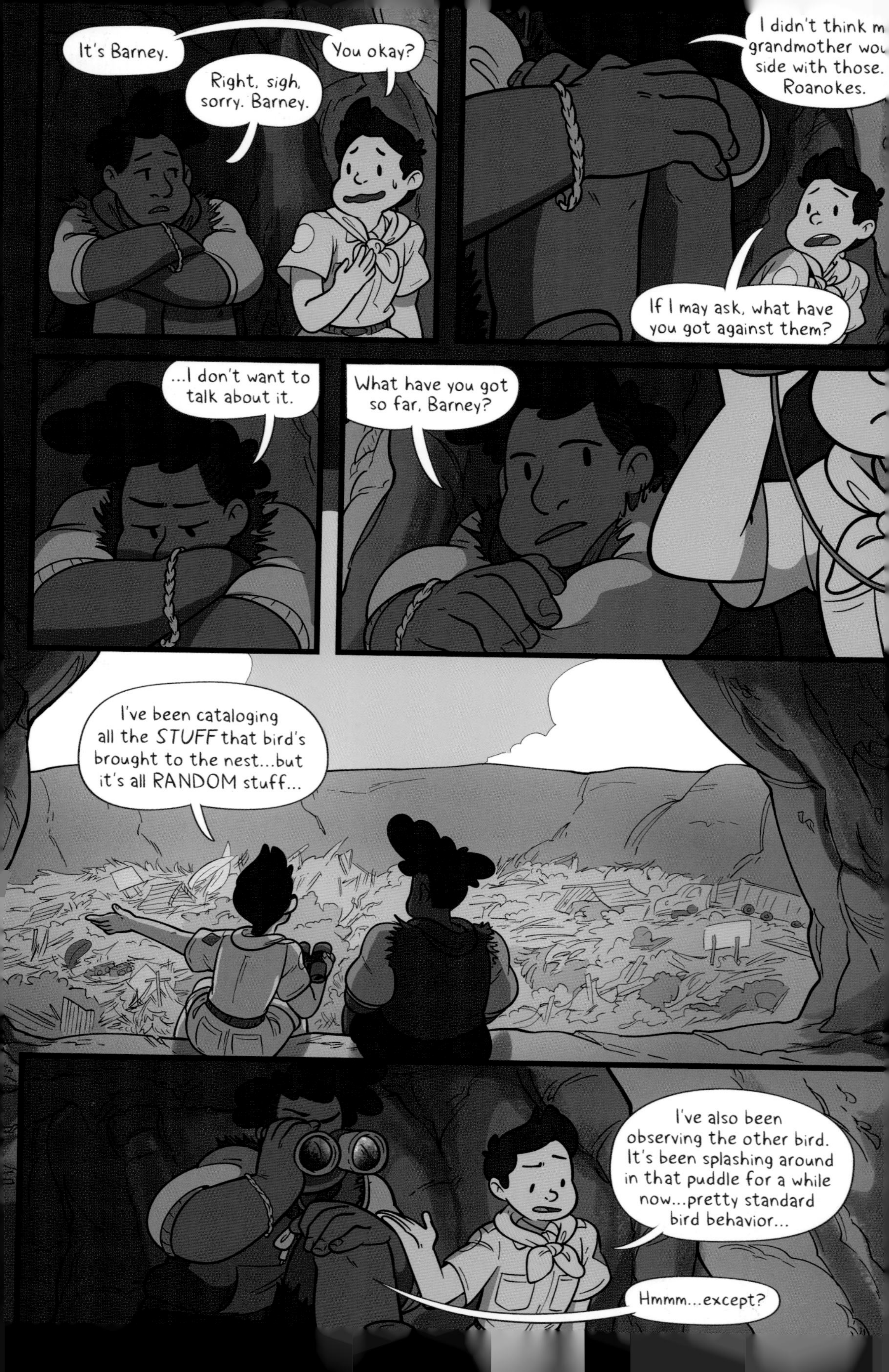
It's Barney.
You okay?
Right, sigh, sorry. Barney.
I didn't think my grandmother wou side with those. Roanokes.
If I may ask, what have you got against them?
...I don't want to talk about it.
What have you got so far, Barney?
I've been cataloging all the STUFF that bird's brought to the nest...but it's all RANDOM stuff...
I've also been observing the other bird. It's been splashing around in that puddle for a while now...pretty standard bird behavior...
Hmmm...except?

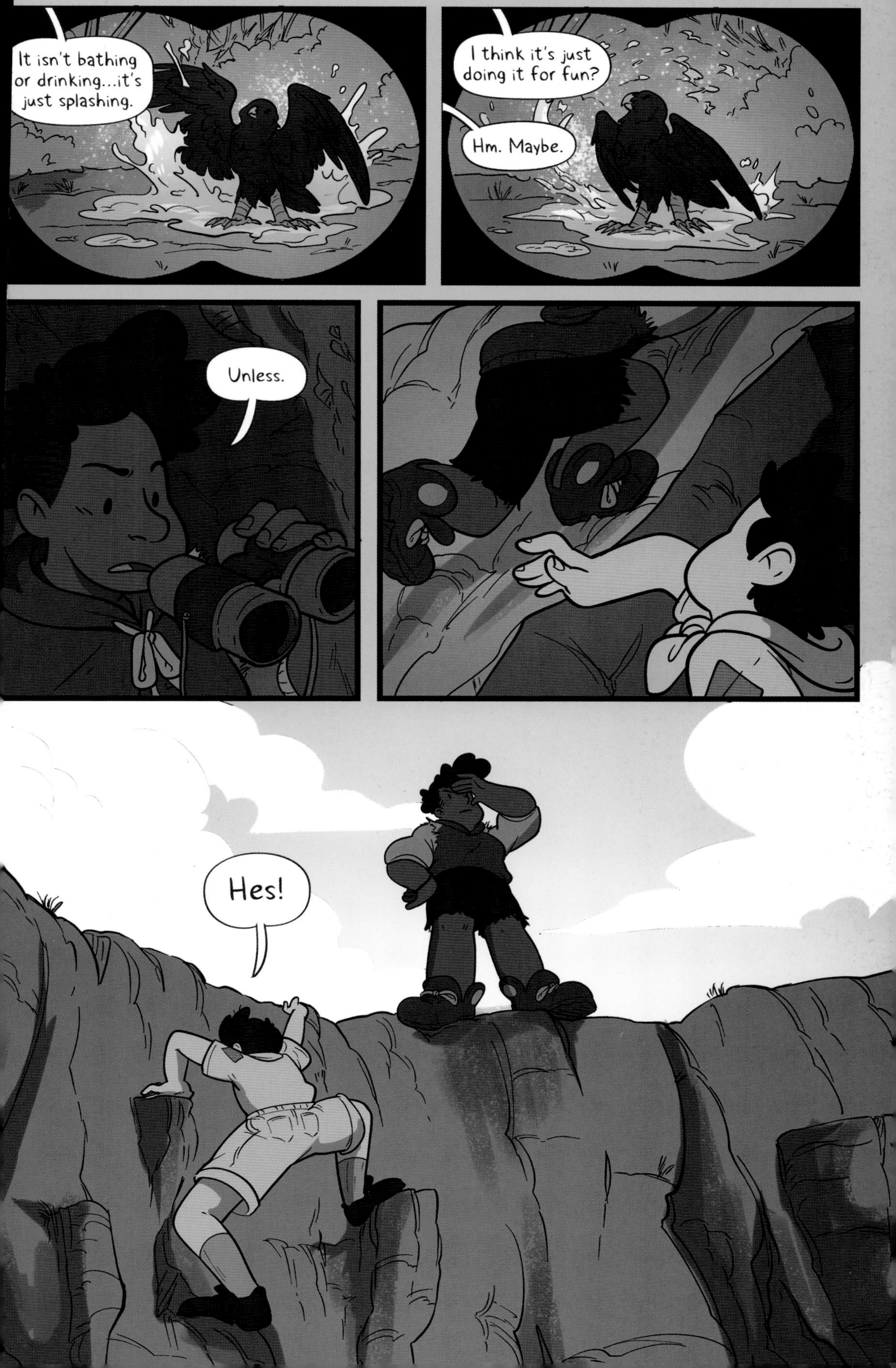
It isn't bathing or drinking...it's just splashing.
I think it's just doing it for fun?
Hm. Maybe.
Unless.
Hes!

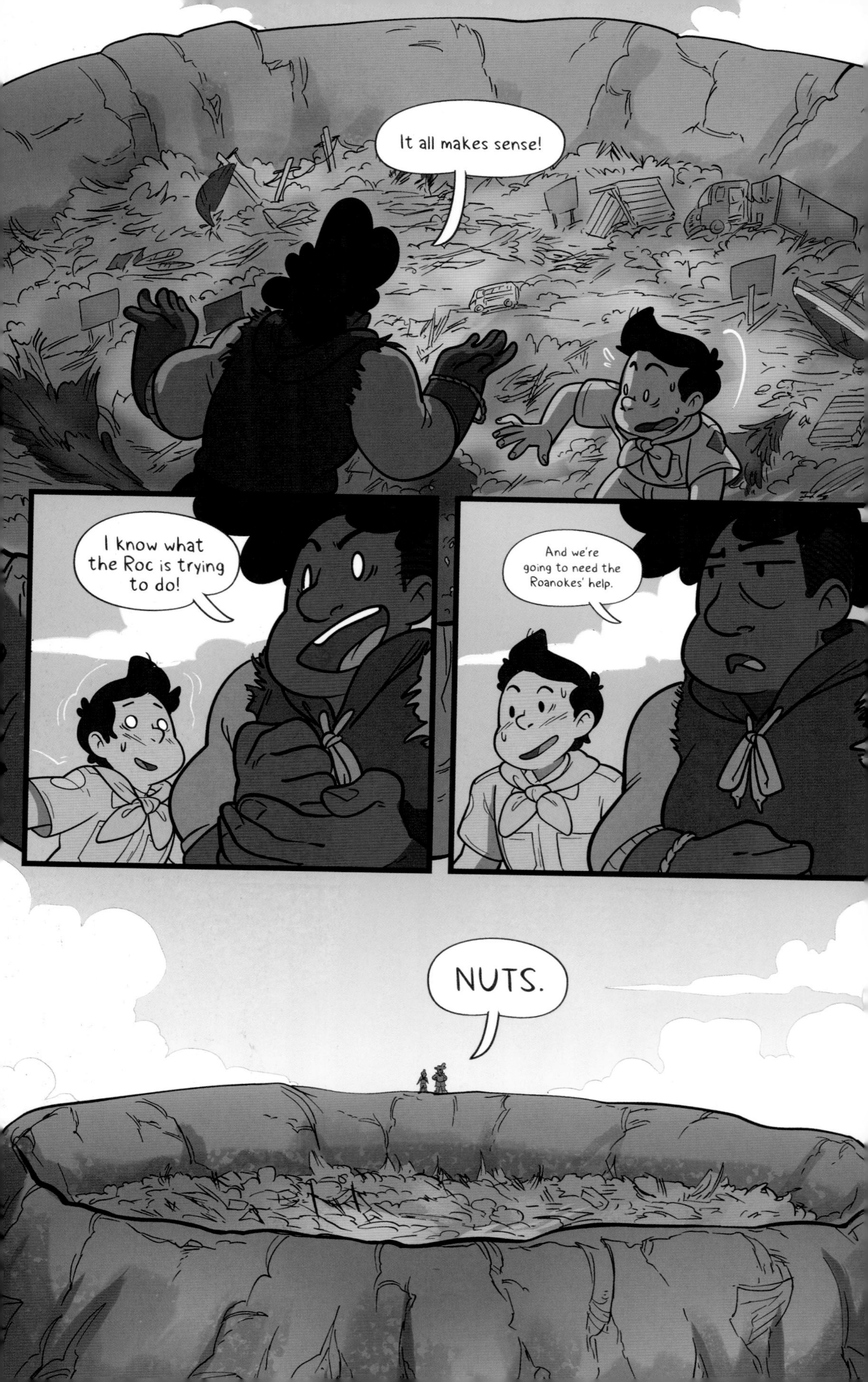
It all makes sense!
I know what the Roc is trying to do!
And we're going to need the Roanokes' help.
NUTS.

will co

The
It hel
appearan
dress f
Further
Lumber
to have
part in
Thiskv
Hardc
have
them

AAAAAAAAAAAAAAAH

The
yellow, short sl
emb
the w
choose
slacks,
made o
out-of-dc
green bere
the colla
Shoes ma
heels, rou
socks shou
the uniform. Ne
belong with a Lumberjane uniform.

MAGIC GIANT FLOATING FIRE BREATHING GHOST KITTENS

HOW TO WEAR THE UNIFORM

To look well in a uniform demans first of
uniform be kept in good condition—clean
pressed. See that the skirt is the right length for your own
height and build, that the belt is adjusted to your waist,
that your shoes and stockings are in keeping with the
uniform, that you watch your posture and carry yourself
with dignity and grace. If the beret is removed indoors,
be sure that your hair is neat and kept in place with an
insonspicuous clip or ribbon. When you wear a
Lumberjane uniform you are identified as a member of
this organization and you should be doubly careful to
conduct yourself in a way that will show everyone that
courtesy and thoughtfullness are part of being a
Lumberjane. People are likely to judge a whole nation by
the selfishness of a few individuals, to criticize a whole
family because of the misconduct of one member, and to
feel unkindly toward and organization because of the

IE UNIFORM

hould be worn at camp
events when Lumberjanes
n may also be worn at other
ons. It should be worn as a
the uniform dress with
rect shoes, and stocking or

out grows her uniform or
ter Lumberjane.
a she has
her
f her

GES

The unifor
helps to cre
in a group.
active life th
another bond
future, and pr
in order to b
Lumberjane pr
Penniquiqul Thi
Types, but m
can either bu
materials available at the trading post.

ROSIEEEEEE!!!

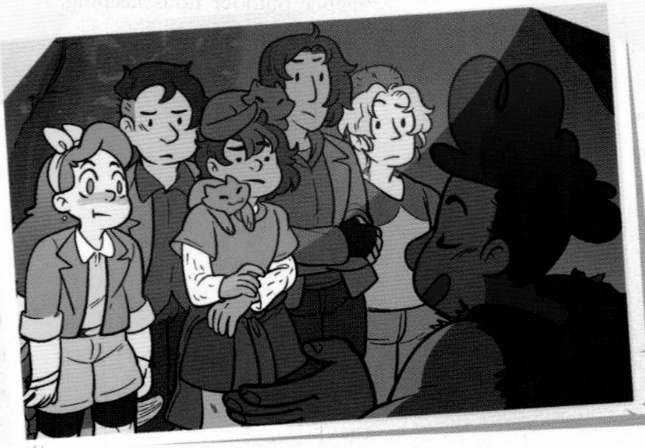

LUMBERJANES FIELD MANUAL

CHAPTER TWENTY-EIGHT

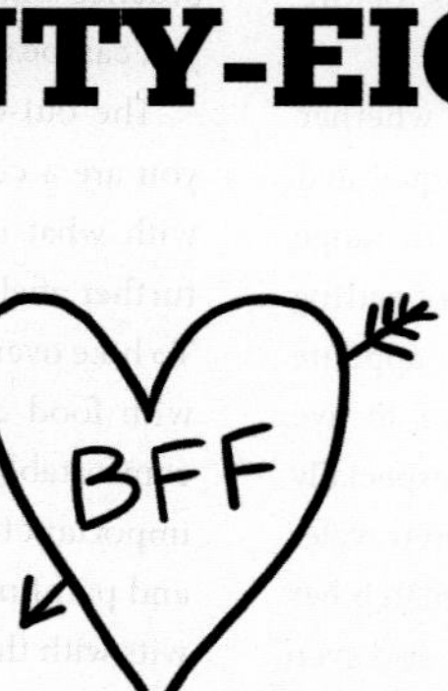
BFF

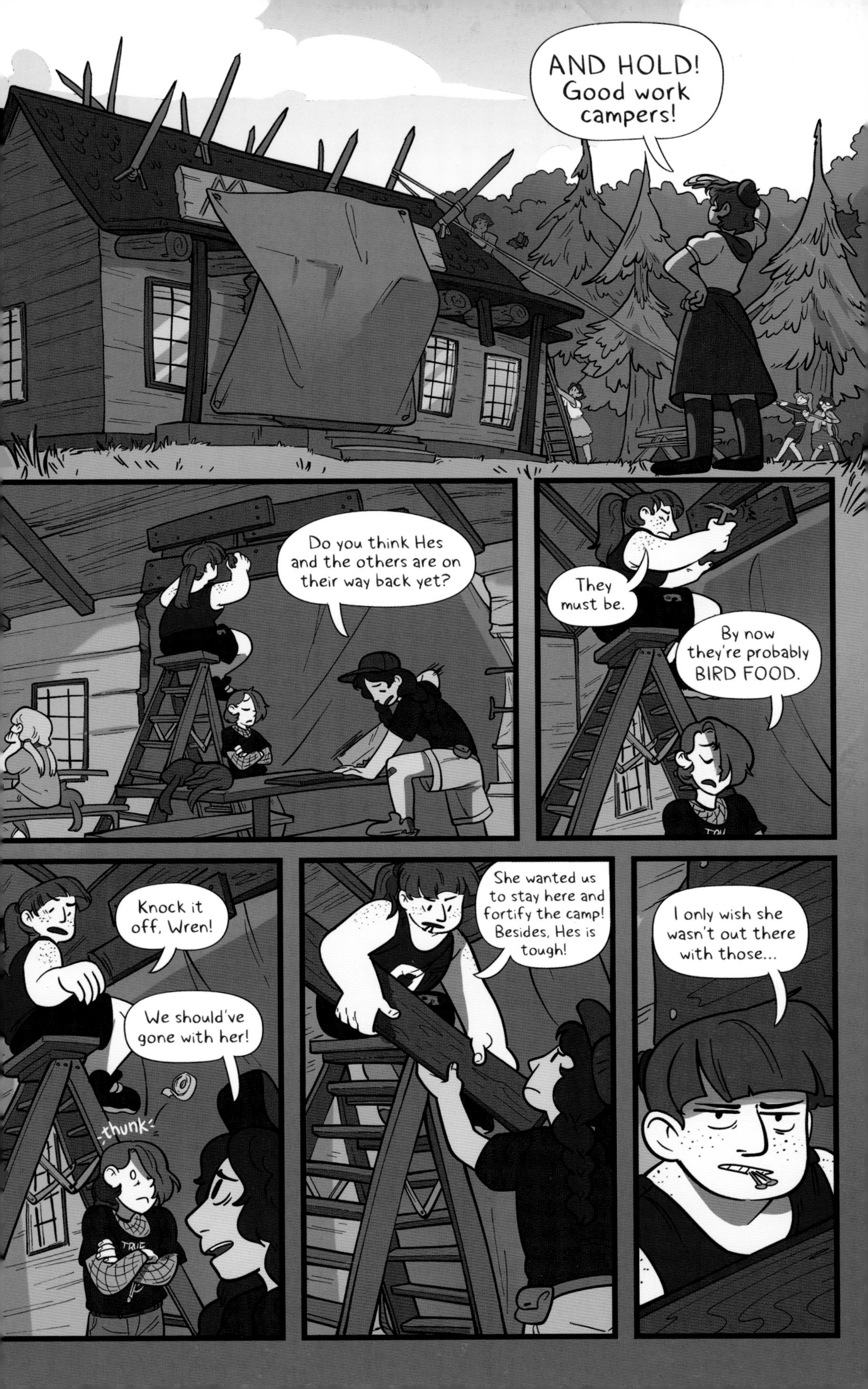
AND HOLD! Good work campers!
Do you think Hes and the others are on their way back yet?
They must be.
By now they're probably BIRD FOOD.
Knock it off, Wren!
We should've gone with her!
thunk
She wanted us to stay here and fortify the camp! Besides, Hes is tough!
I only wish she wasn't out there with those...

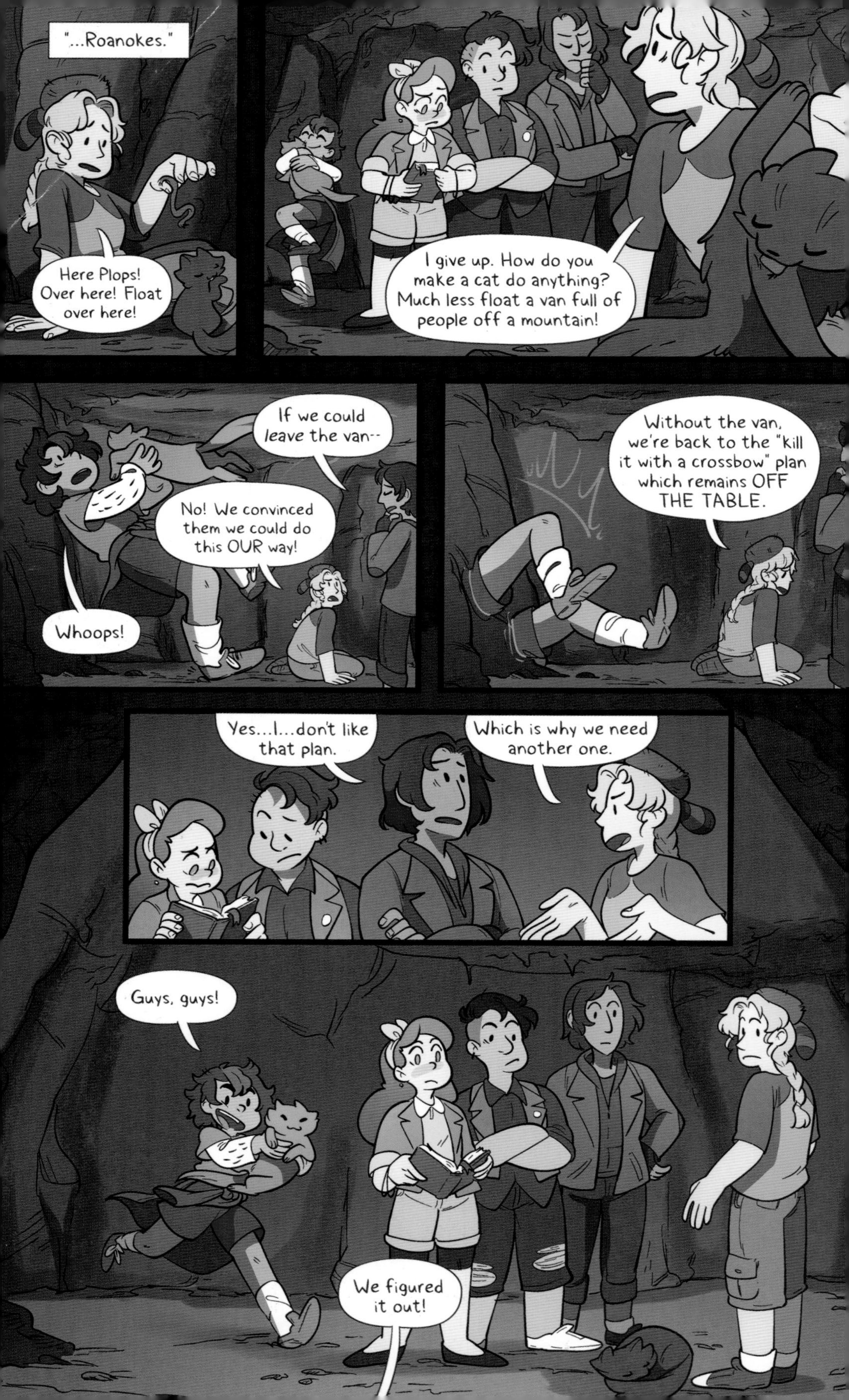
"...Roanokes."
Here Plops! Over here! Float over here!
I give up. How do you make a cat do anything? Much less float a van full of people off a mountain!
If we could leave the van--
No! We convinced them we could do this OUR way!
Whoops!
Without the van, we're back to the "kill it with a crossbow" plan which remains OFF THE TABLE.
Yes...I...don't like that plan.
Which is why we need another one.
Guys, guys!
We figured it out!

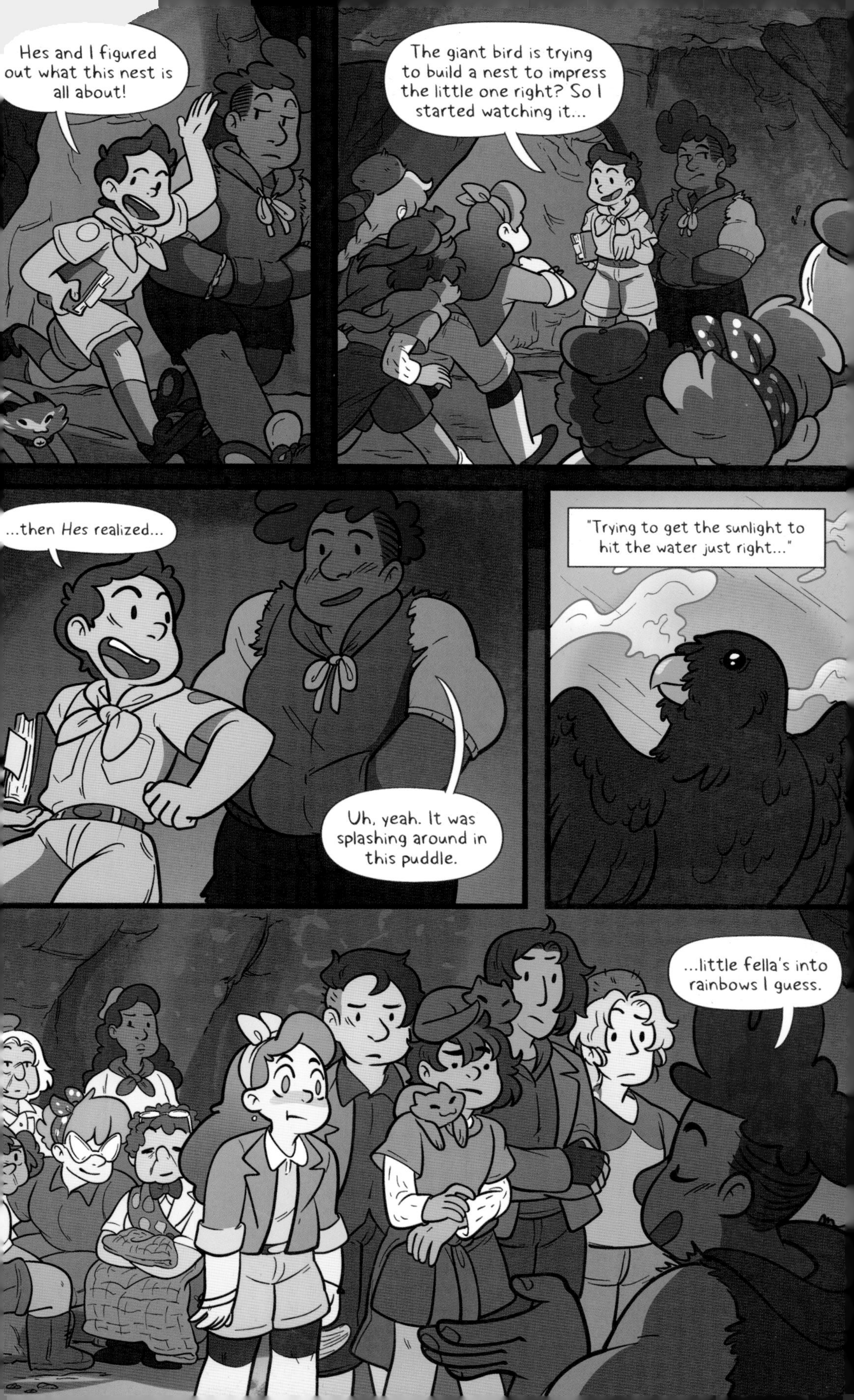
Hes and I figured out what this nest is all about!
The giant bird is trying to build a nest to impress the little one right? So I started watching it...
...then Hes realized...
Uh, yeah. It was splashing around in this puddle.
"Trying to get the sunlight to hit the water just right..."
...little fella's into rainbows I guess.

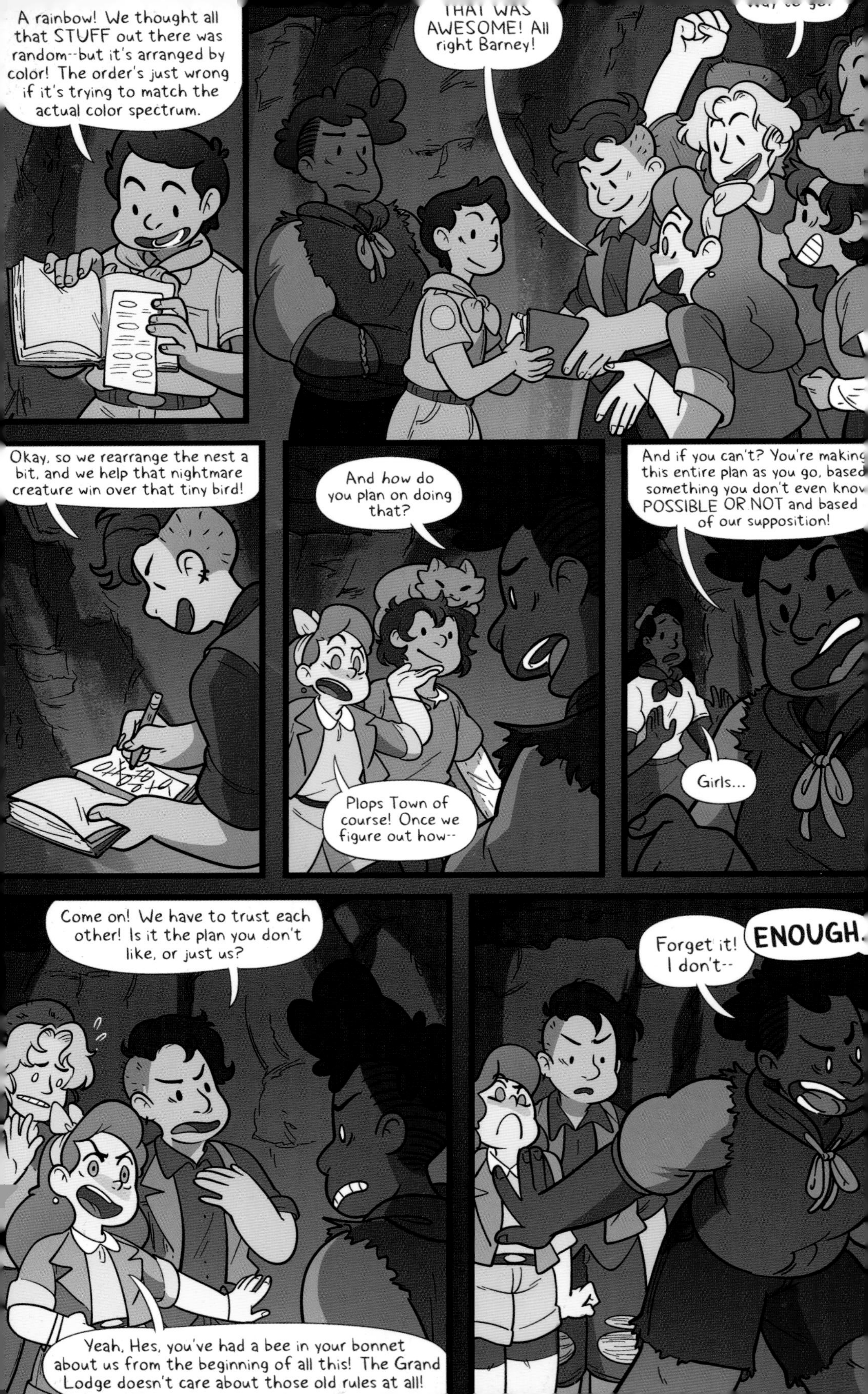
A rainbow! We thought all that STUFF out there was random--but it's arranged by color! The order's just wrong if it's trying to match the actual color spectrum.
THAT WAS AWESOME! All right Barney!
Okay, so we rearrange the nest a bit, and we help that nightmare creature win over that tiny bird!
And how do you plan on doing that?
Plops Town of course! Once we figure out how--
And if you can't? You're making this entire plan as you go, based something you don't even kno POSSIBLE OR NOT and based of our supposition!
Girls...
Come on! We have to trust each other! Is it the plan you don't like, or just us?
Yeah, Hes, you've had a bee in your bonnet about us from the beginning of all this! The Grand Lodge doesn't care about those old rules at all!
Forget it! I don't--
ENOUGH.

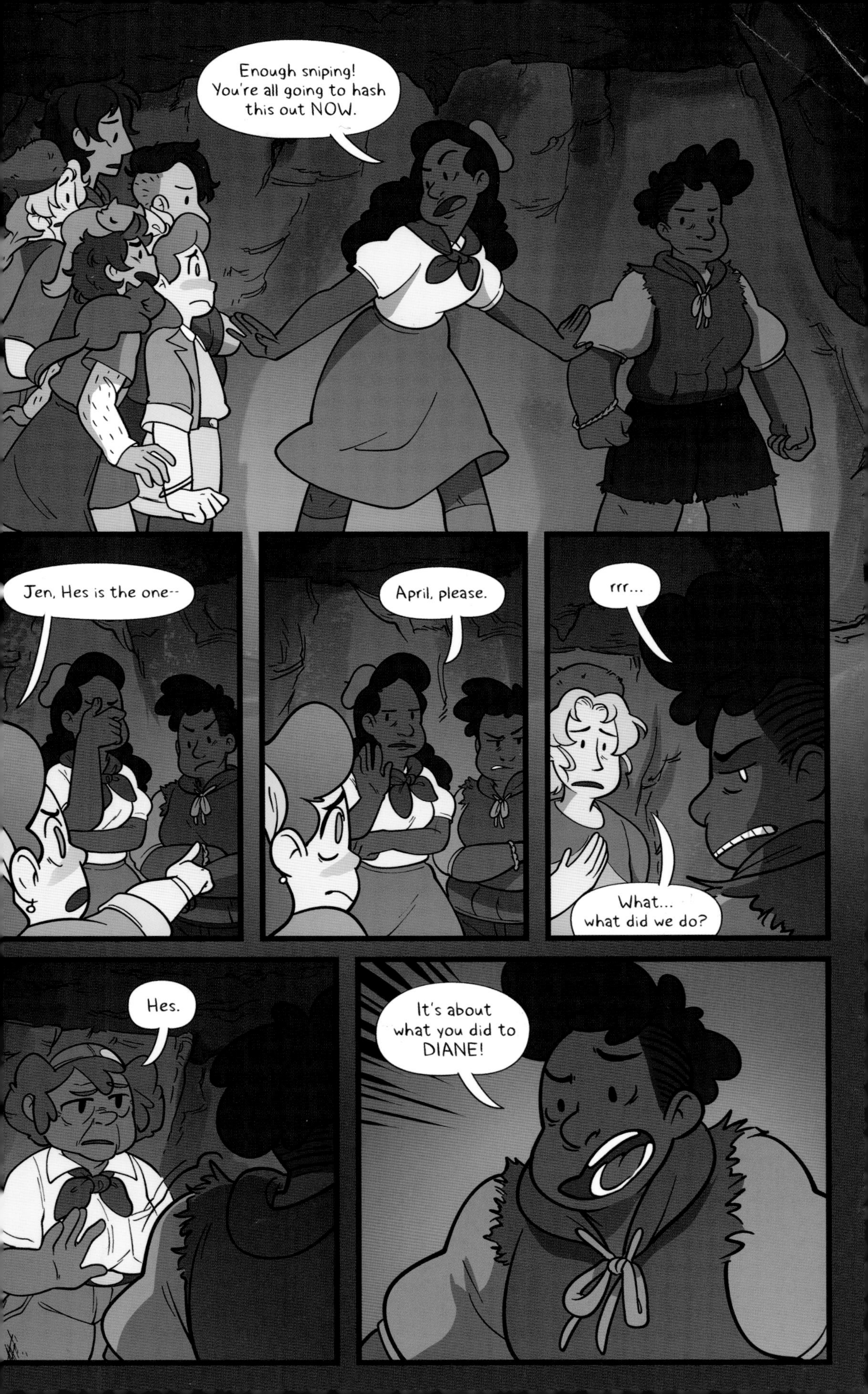
Enough sniping! You're all going to hash this out NOW.
Jen, Hes is the one--
April, please.
rrr...
What... what did we do?
Hes.
It's about what you did to DIANE!

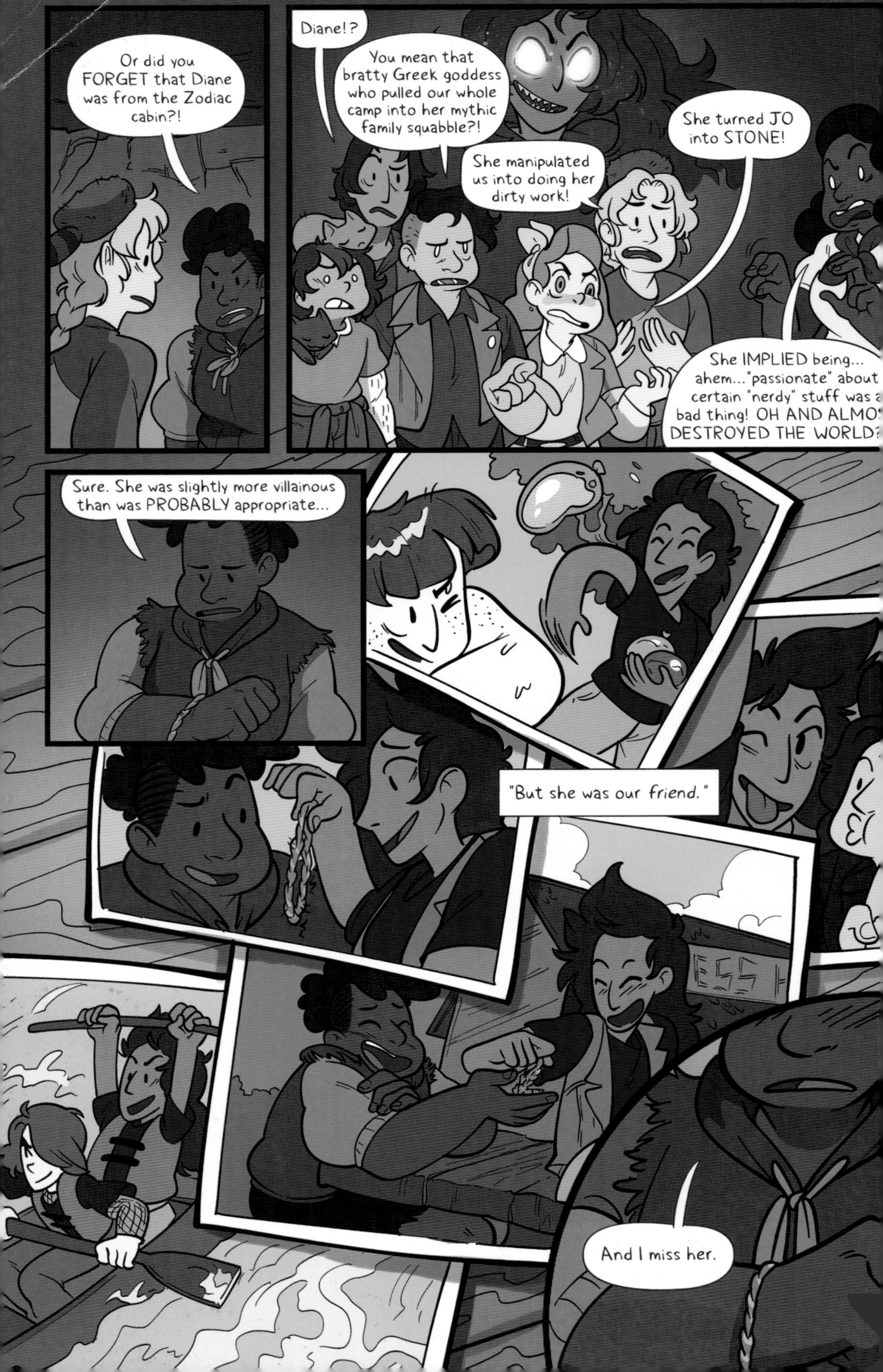
Or did you FORGET that Diane was from the Zodiac cabin?!
Diane!?
You mean that bratty Greek goddess who pulled our whole camp into her mythic family squabble?!
She manipulated us into doing her dirty work!
She turned JO into STONE!
She IMPLIED being... ahem..."passionate" about certain "nerdy" stuff was a bad thing! OH AND ALMO DESTROYED THE WORLD?
Sure. She was slightly more villainous than was PROBABLY appropriate...
"But she was our friend."
And I miss her.

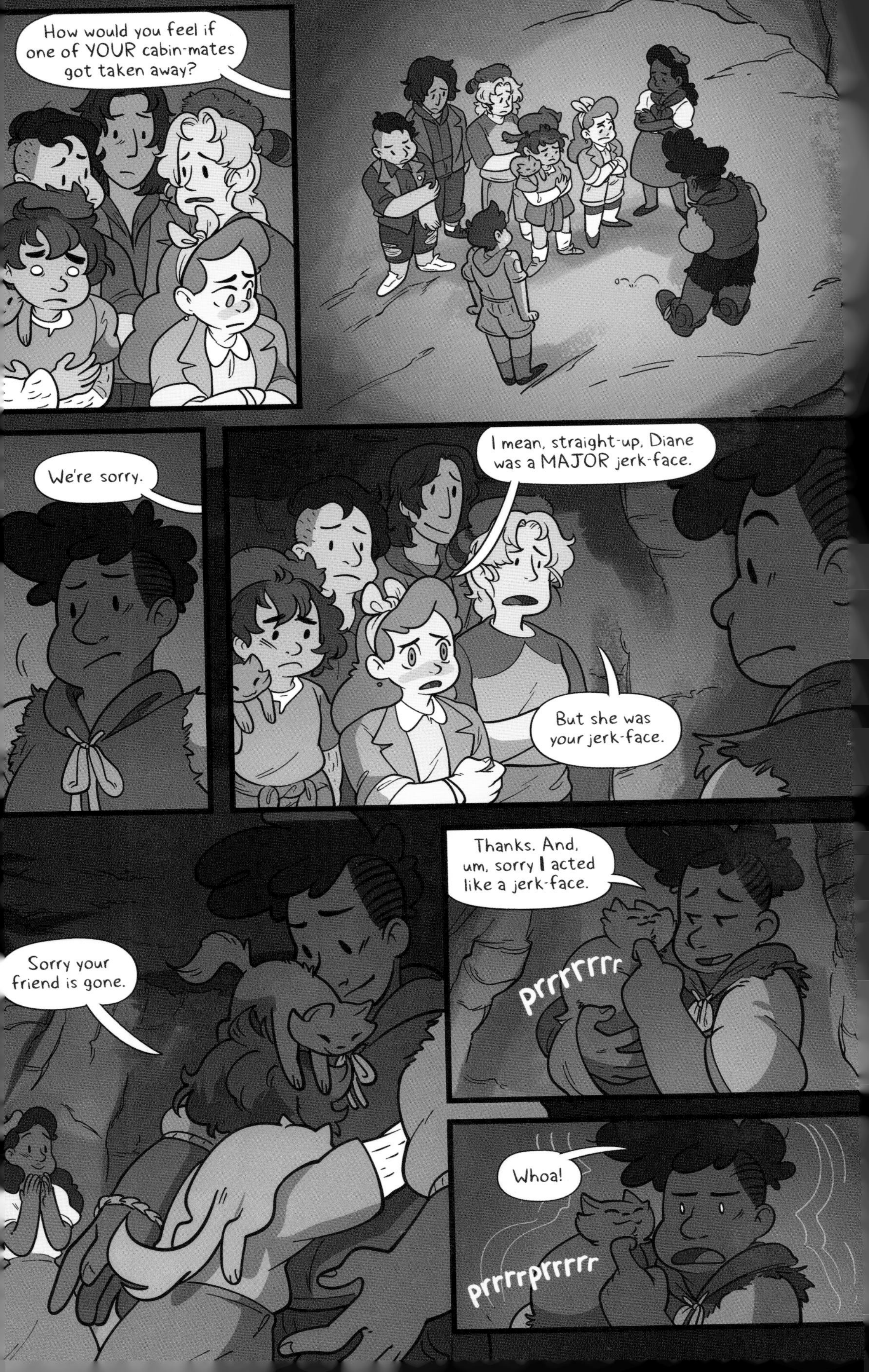
How would you feel if one of YOUR cabin-mates got taken away?
We're sorry.
I mean, straight-up, Diane was a MAJOR jerk-face.
But she was your jerk-face.
Sorry your friend is gone.
Thanks. And, um, sorry I acted like a jerk-face.
prrrrrrr
Whoa!
prrrrprrrrr

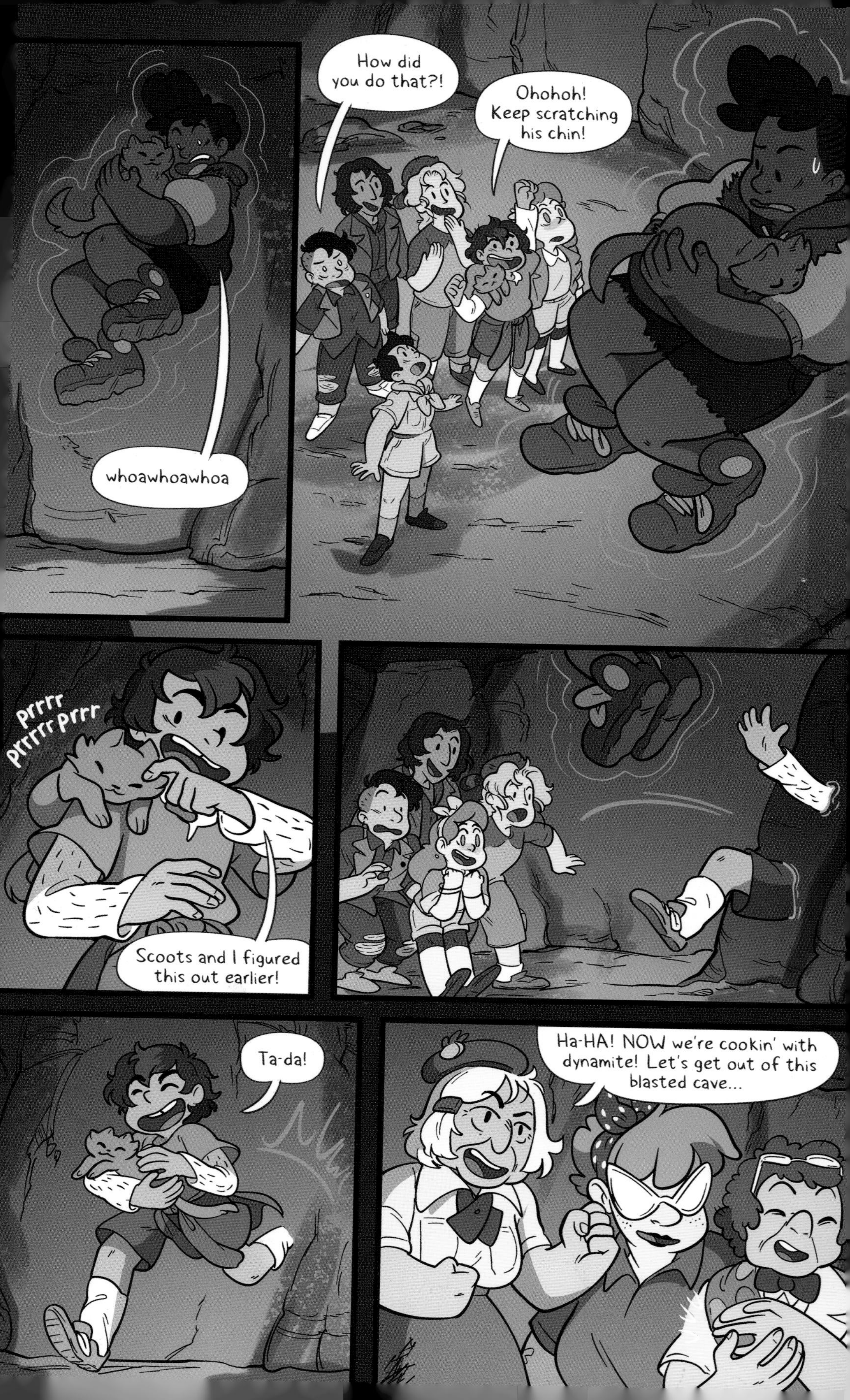
whoawhoawhoa
How did you do that?!
Ohohoh! Keep scratching his chin!
prrrr prrrrr prrr
Scoots and I figured this out earlier!
Ta-da!
Ha-HA! NOW we're cookin' with dynamite! Let's get out of this blasted cave...

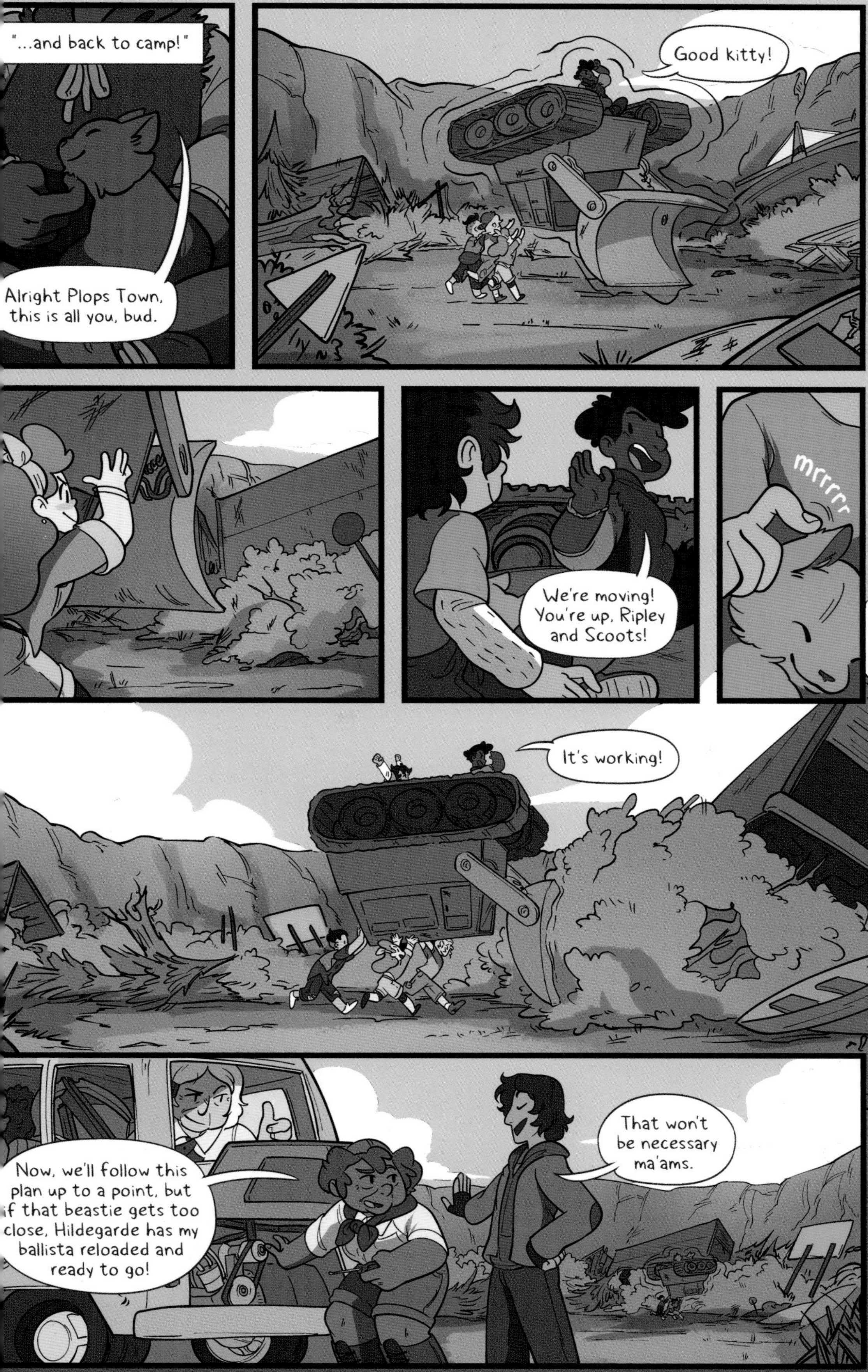
"...and back to camp!"
Alright Plops Town, this is all you, bud.
Good kitty!
We're moving! You're up, Ripley and Scoots!
mrrrrr
It's working!
Now, we'll follow this plan up to a point, but if that beastie gets too close, Hildegarde has my ballista reloaded and ready to go!
That won't be necessary ma'ams.

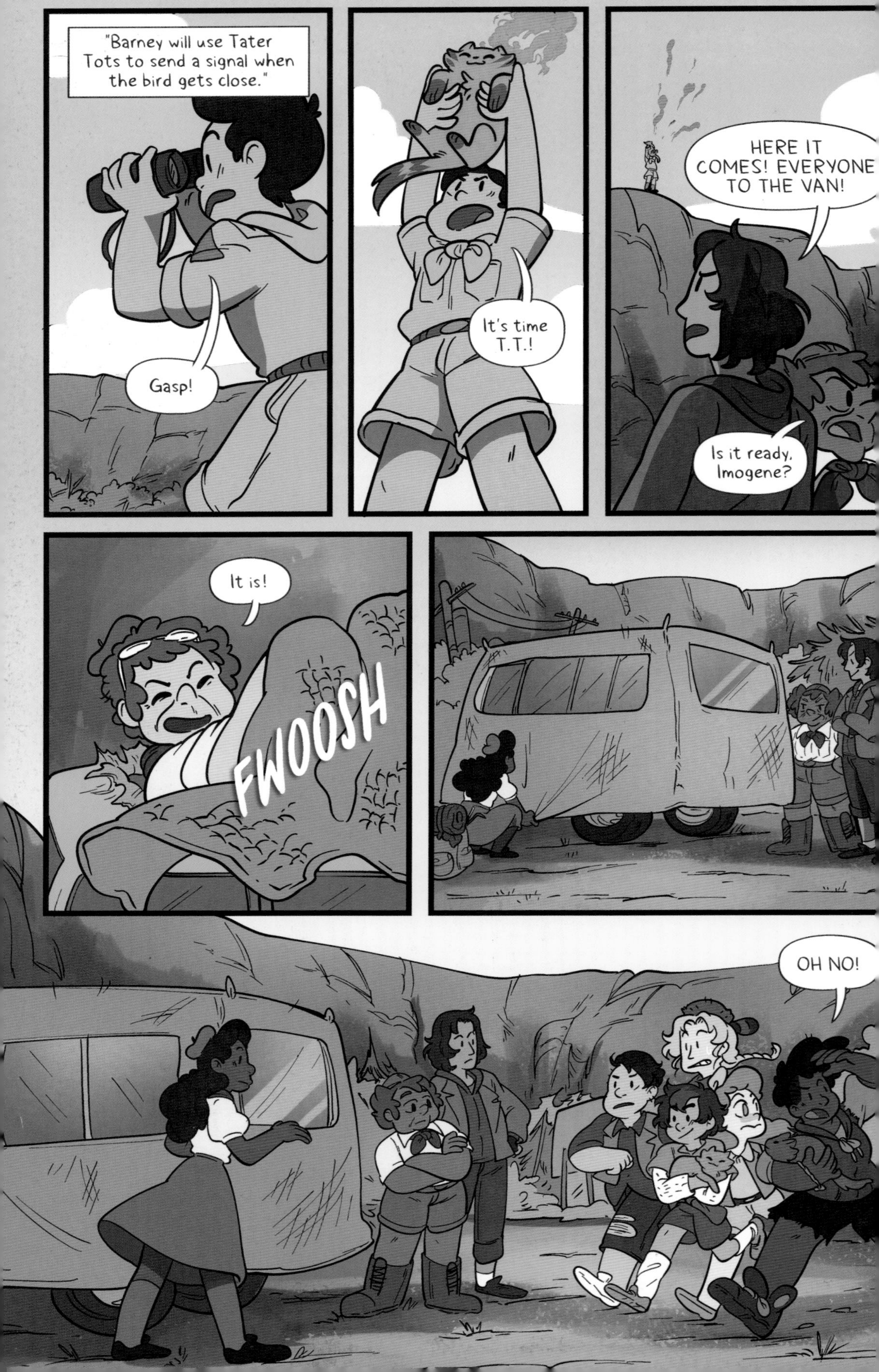
"Barney will use Tater Tots to send a signal when the bird gets close."
Gasp!
It's time T.T.!
HERE IT COMES! EVERYONE TO THE VAN!
Is it ready, Imogene?
It is!
FWOOSH
OH NO!

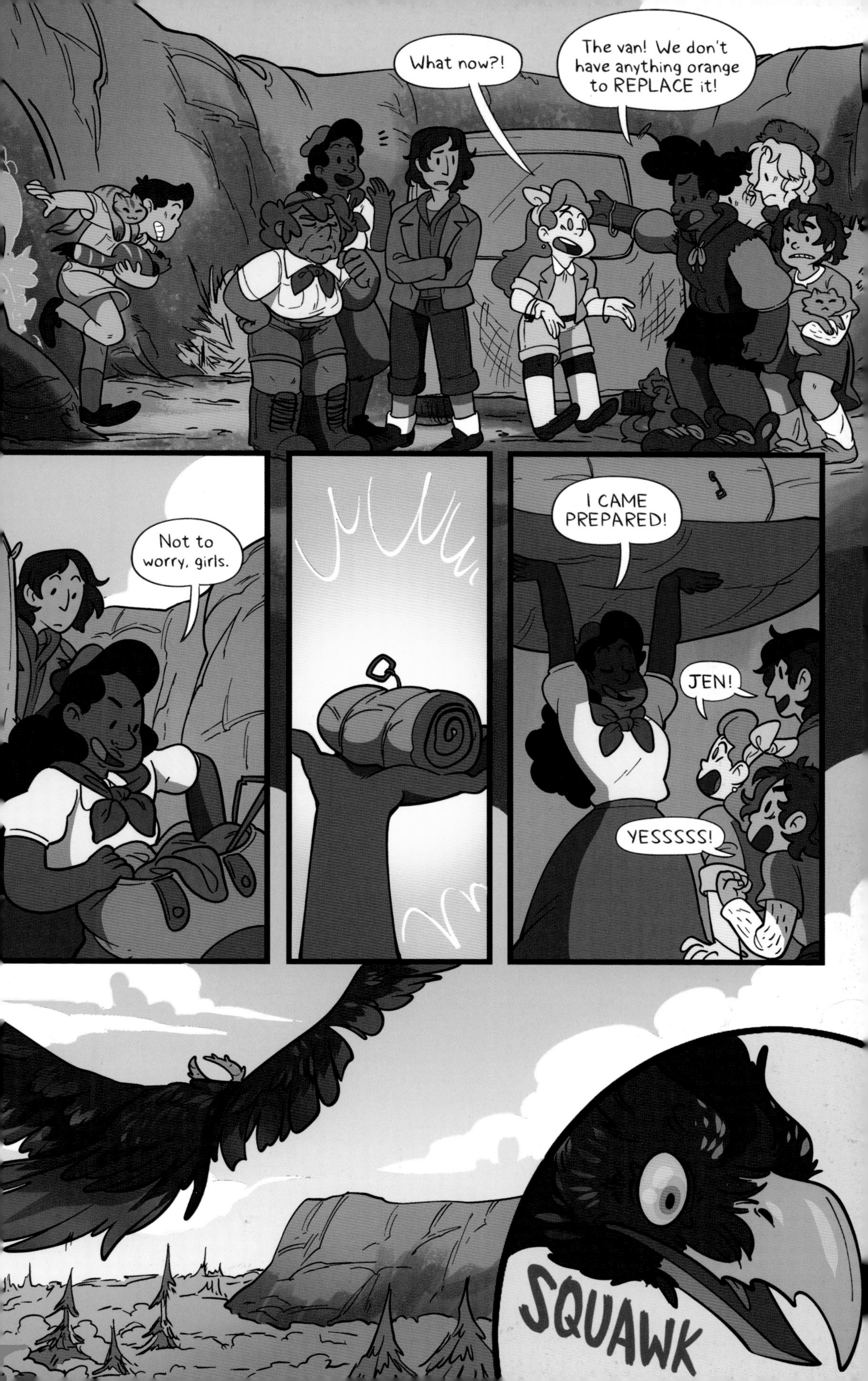

What now?!
The van! We don't have anything orange to REPLACE it!
Not to worry, girls.
I CAME PREPARED!
JEN!
YESSSSS!
SQUAWK

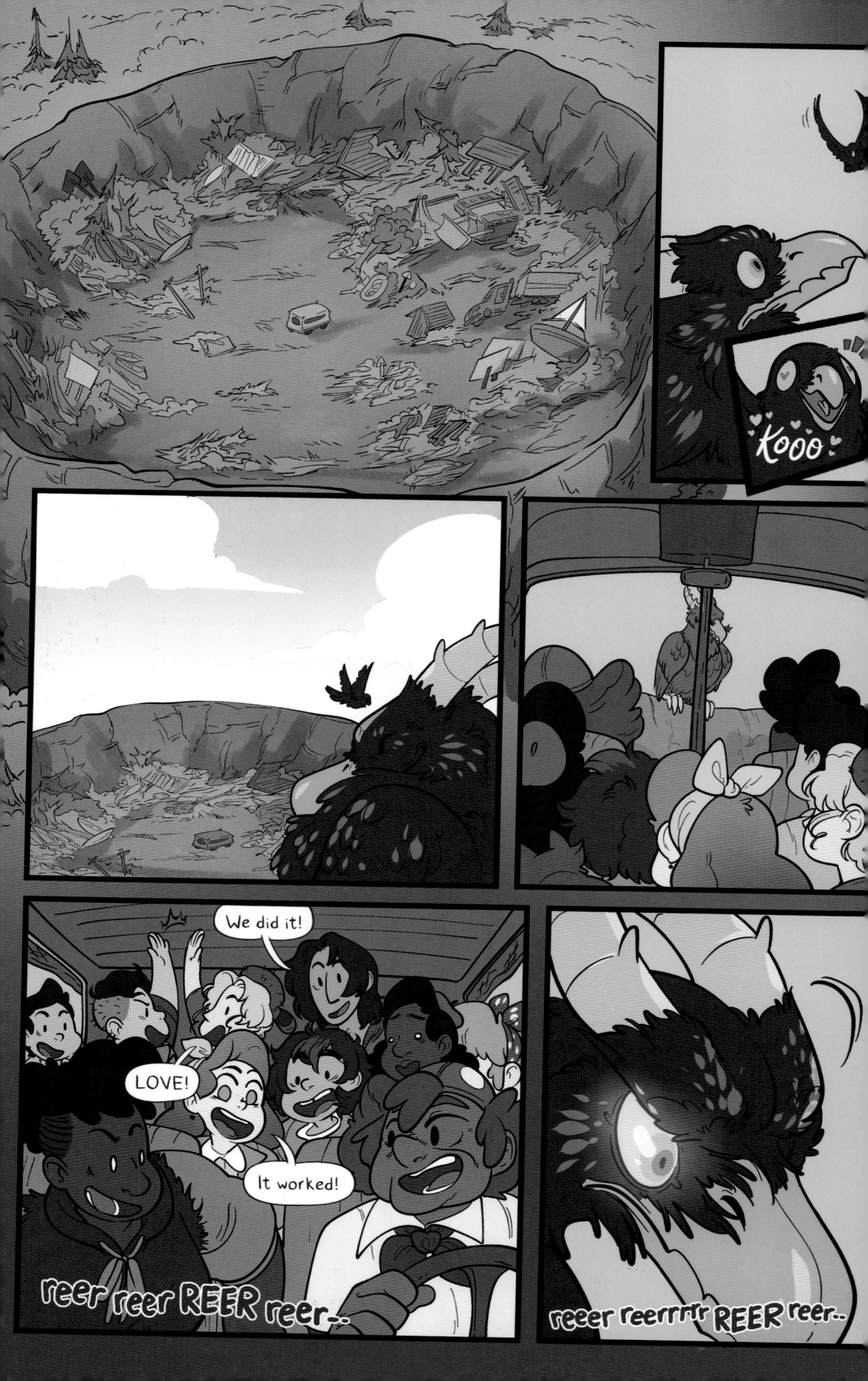

Kooo
We did it!
LOVE!
It worked!
reer reer REER reer..
reeer reerrrr REER reer..

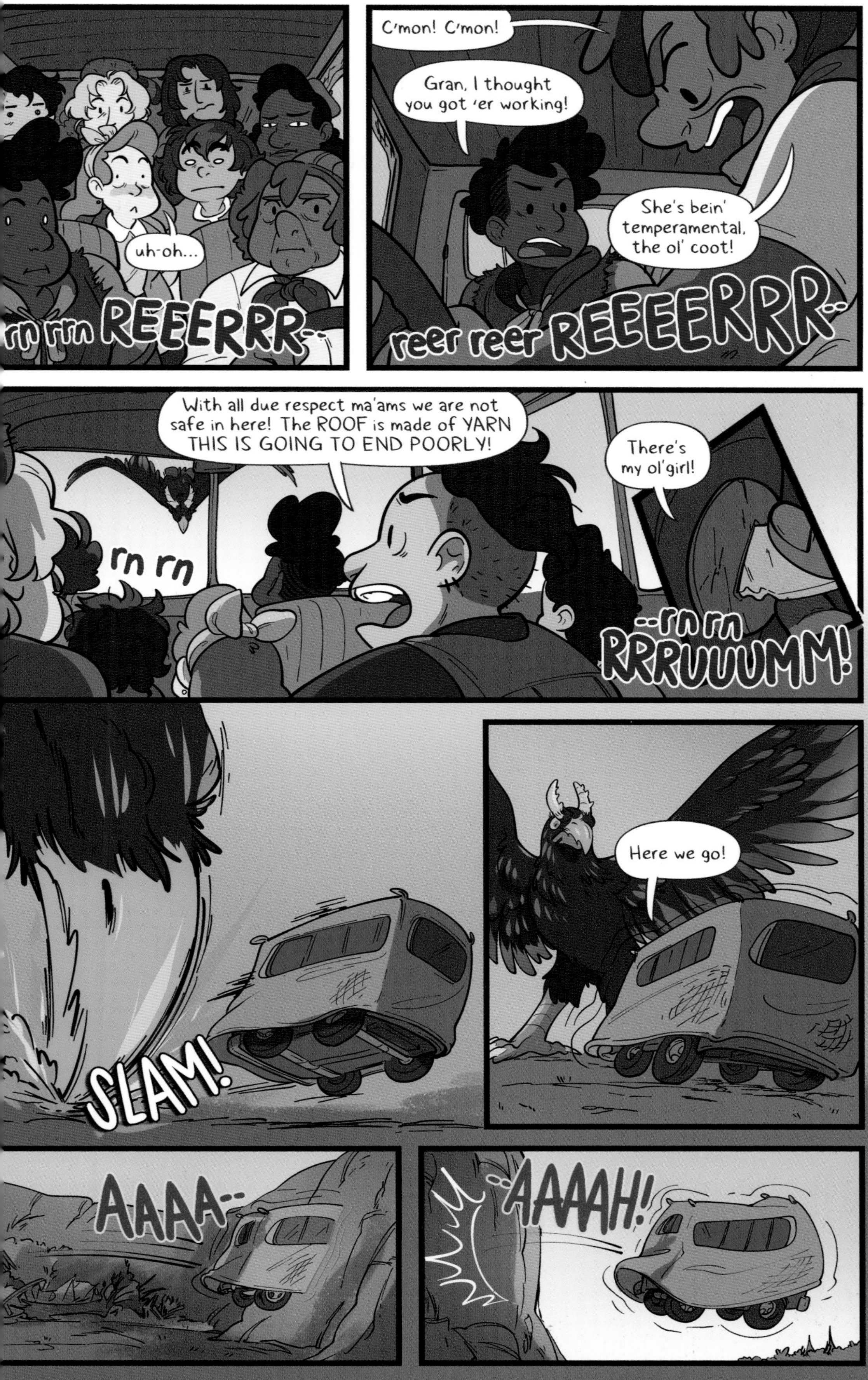
uh-oh...
rn rrn REEERRR--
C'mon! C'mon!
Gran, I thought you got 'er working!
She's bein' temperamental, the ol' coot!
reer reer REEEERRR--
With all due respect ma'ams we are not safe in here! The ROOF is made of YARN THIS IS GOING TO END POORLY!
rn rn
There's my ol'girl!
--rn rn RRRUUUMM!
SLAM!
Here we go!
AAAA--
--AAAAH!

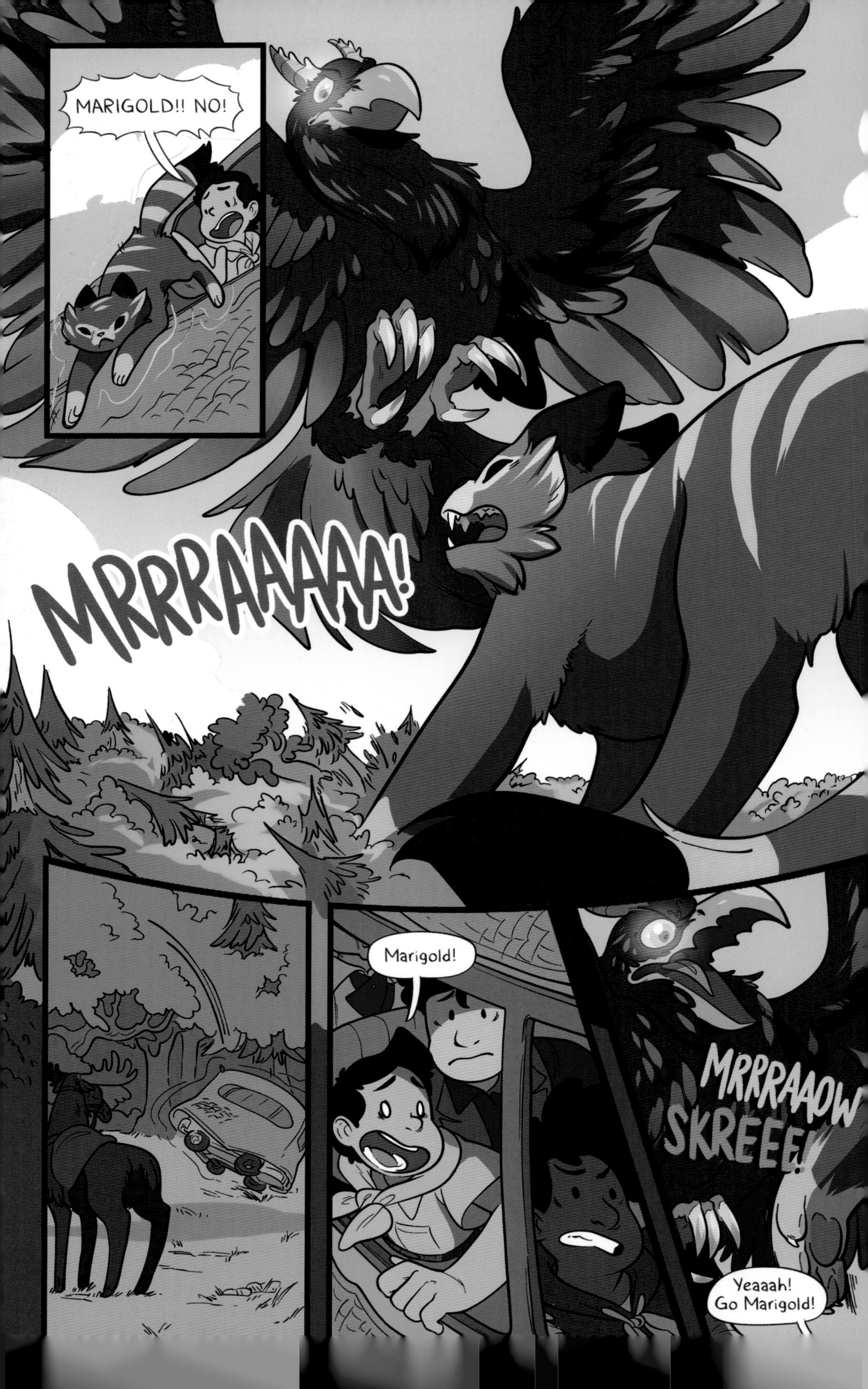
MARIGOLD!! NO!
MRRRAAAAA!
Marigold!
MRRRAAOW
SKREEE!
Yeaaah! Go Marigold!

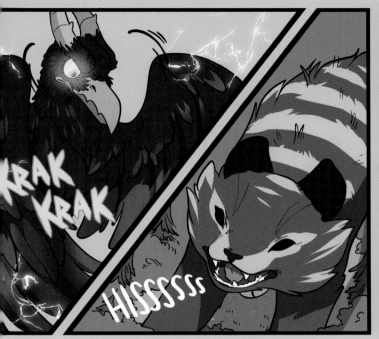

KRAK
KRAK

HISSSSSS

C'mere Jeremy!

HISSSSSS

Jee Jee!

HMPH!

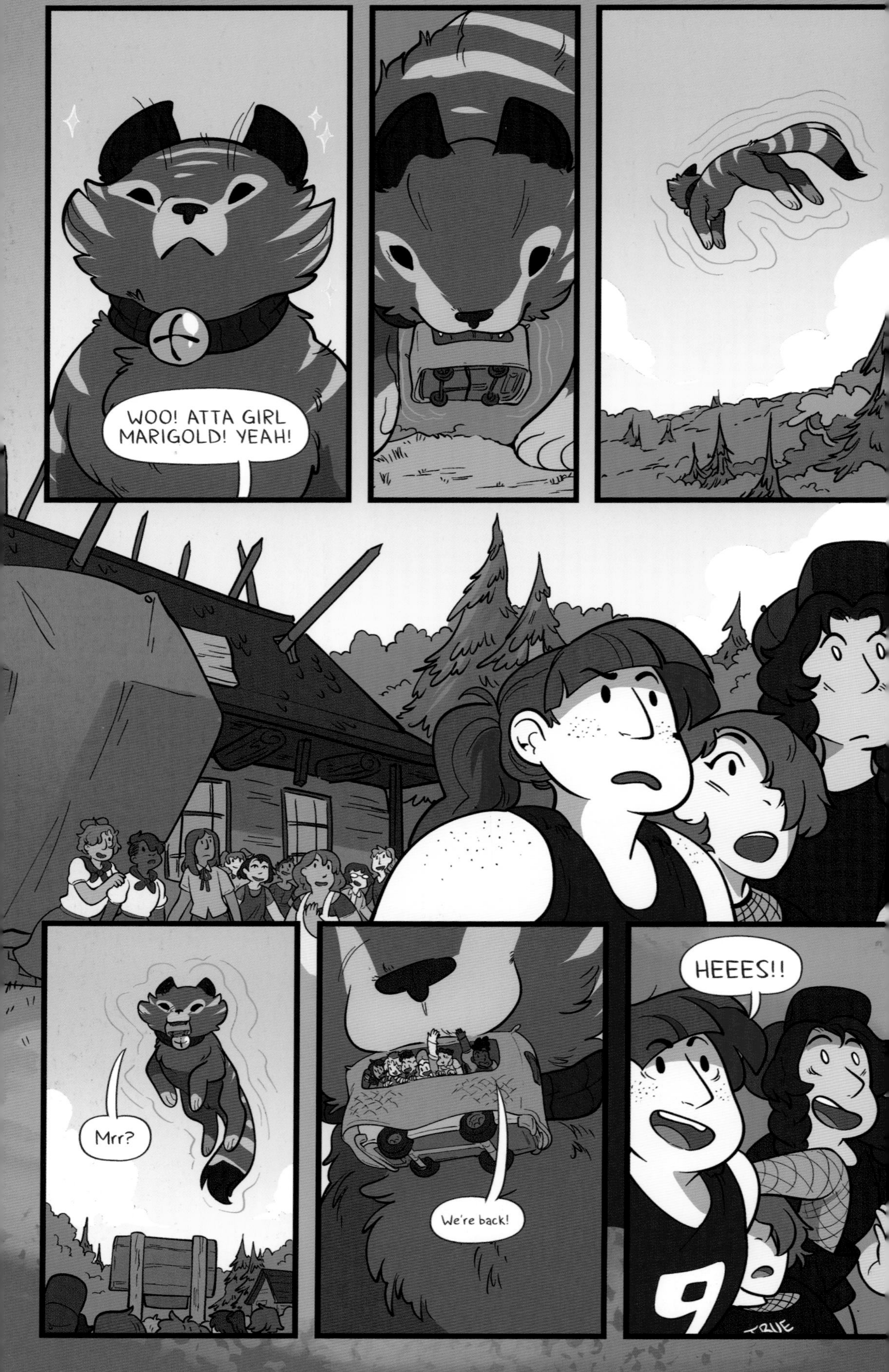
WOO! ATTA GIRL MARIGOLD! YEAH!
Mrr?
We're back!
HEEES!!

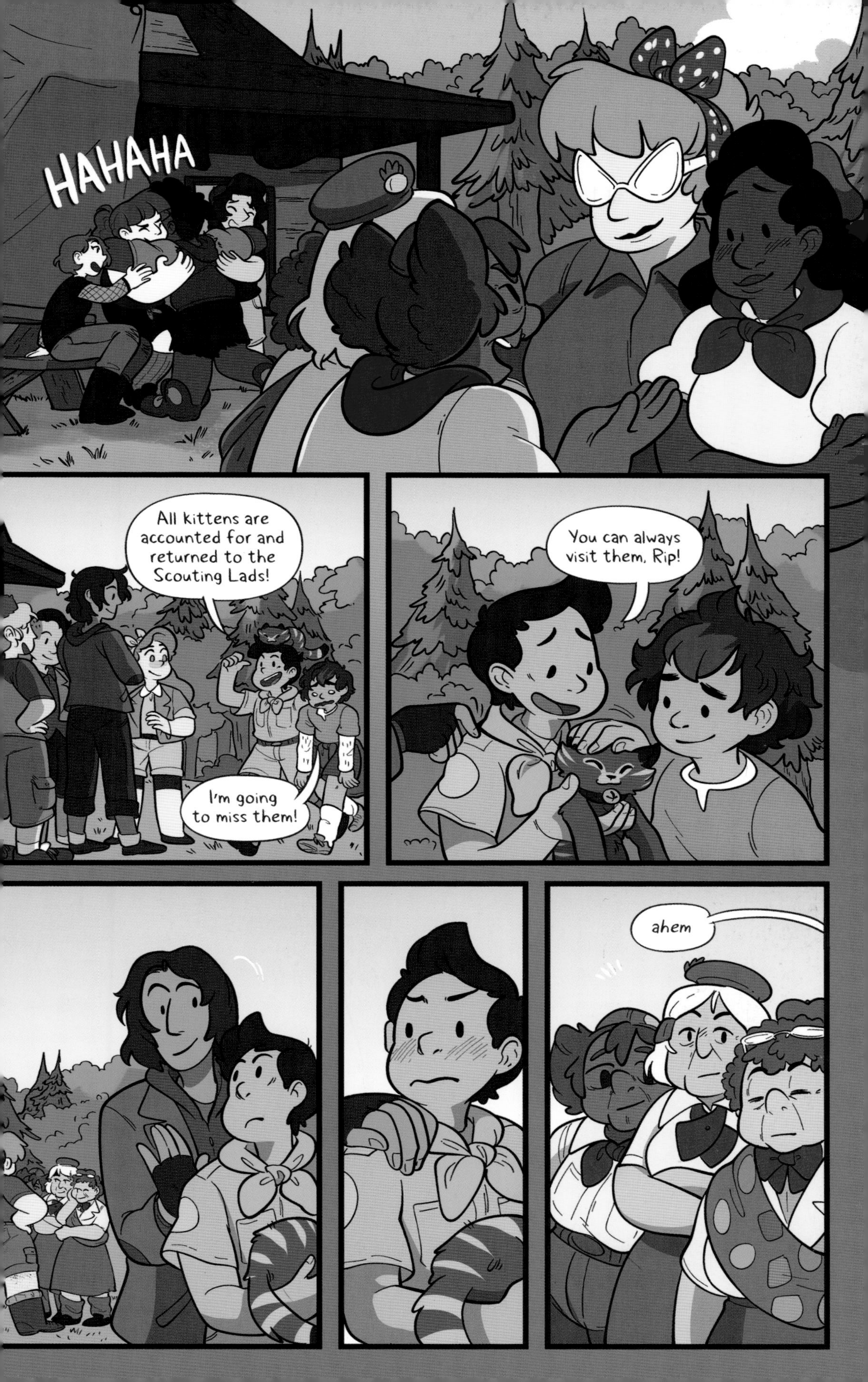
HAHAHA
All kittens are accounted for and returned to the Scouting Lads!
I'm going to miss them!
You can always visit them, Rip!
ahem

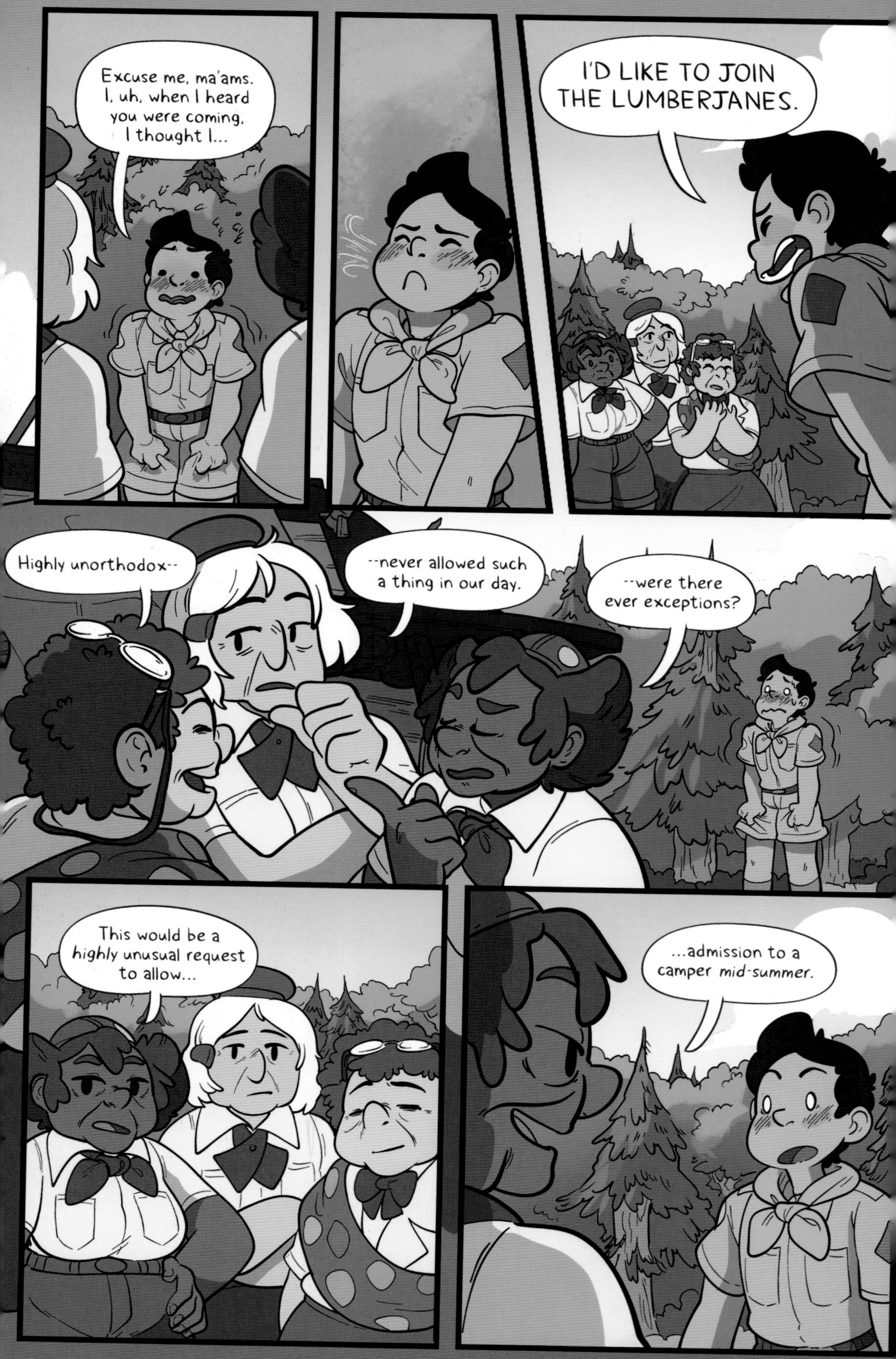
Excuse me, ma'ams. I, uh, when I heard you were coming, I thought I...
I'D LIKE TO JOIN THE LUMBERJANES.
Highly unorthodox--
--never allowed such a thing in our day.
--were there ever exceptions?
This would be a *highly* unusual request to allow...
...admission to a camper *mid-summer*.

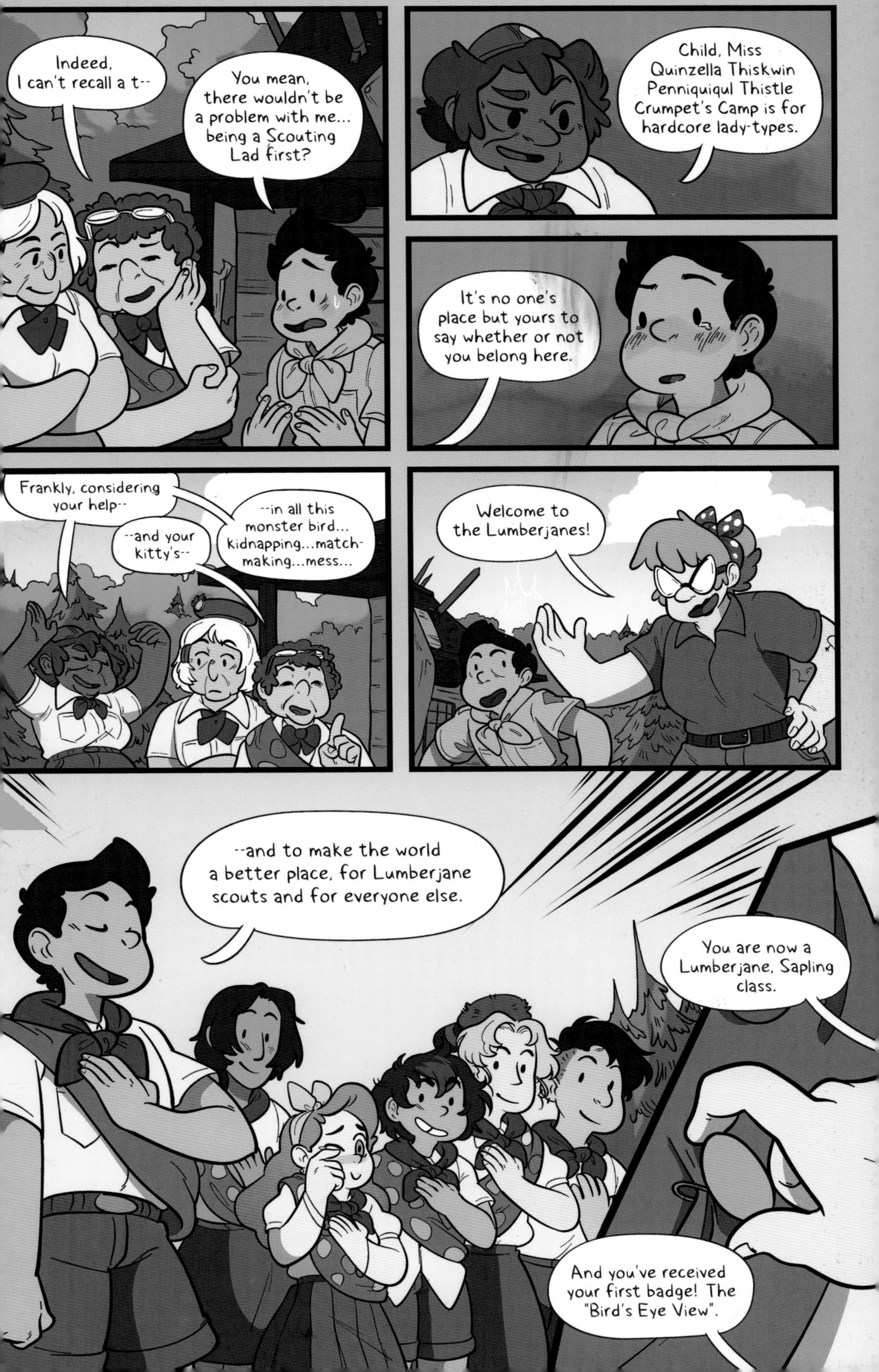
Indeed, I can't recall a t--
You mean, there wouldn't be a problem with me... being a Scouting Lad first?
Child, Miss Quinzella Thiskwin Penniquiqul Thistle Crumpet's Camp is for hardcore lady-types.
It's no one's place but yours to say whether or not you belong here.
Frankly, considering your help--
--and your kitty's--
--in all this monster bird... kidnapping...match-making...mess...
Welcome to the Lumberjanes!
--and to make the world a better place, for Lumberjane scouts and for everyone else.
You are now a Lumberjane, Sapling class.
And you've received your first badge! The "Bird's Eye View".

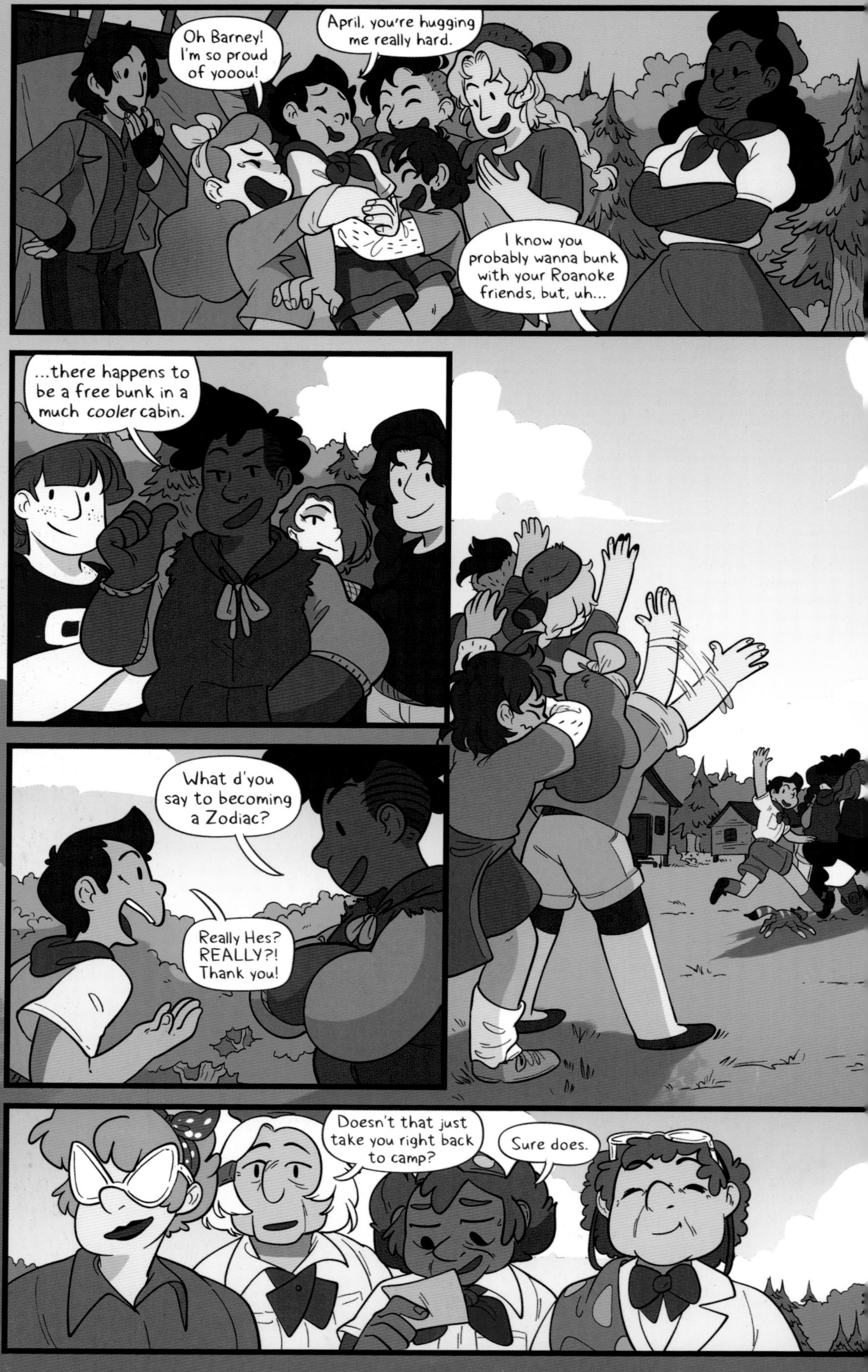
Oh Barney! I'm so proud of yooou!
April, you're hugging me really hard.
I know you probably wanna bunk with your Roanoke friends, but, uh...
...there happens to be a free bunk in a much *cooler* cabin.
What d'you say to becoming a Zodiac?
Really Hes? REALLY?! Thank you!
Doesn't that just take you right back to camp?
Sure does.

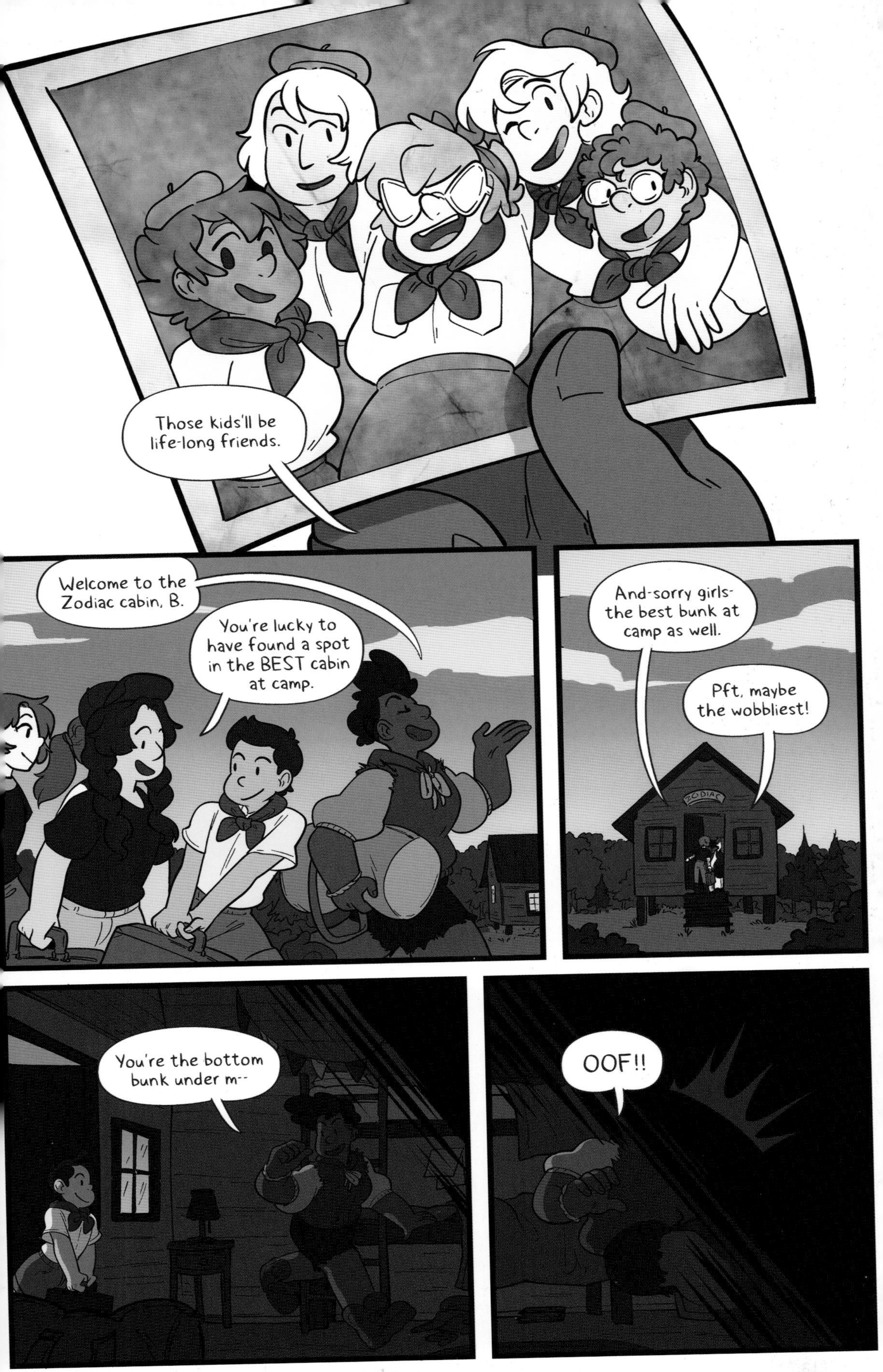
Those kids'll be life-long friends.
Welcome to the Zodiac cabin, B.
You're lucky to have found a spot in the BEST cabin at camp.
And-sorry girls- the best bunk at camp as well.
Pft, maybe the wobbliest!
ZODIAC
You're the bottom bunk under m--
OOF!!

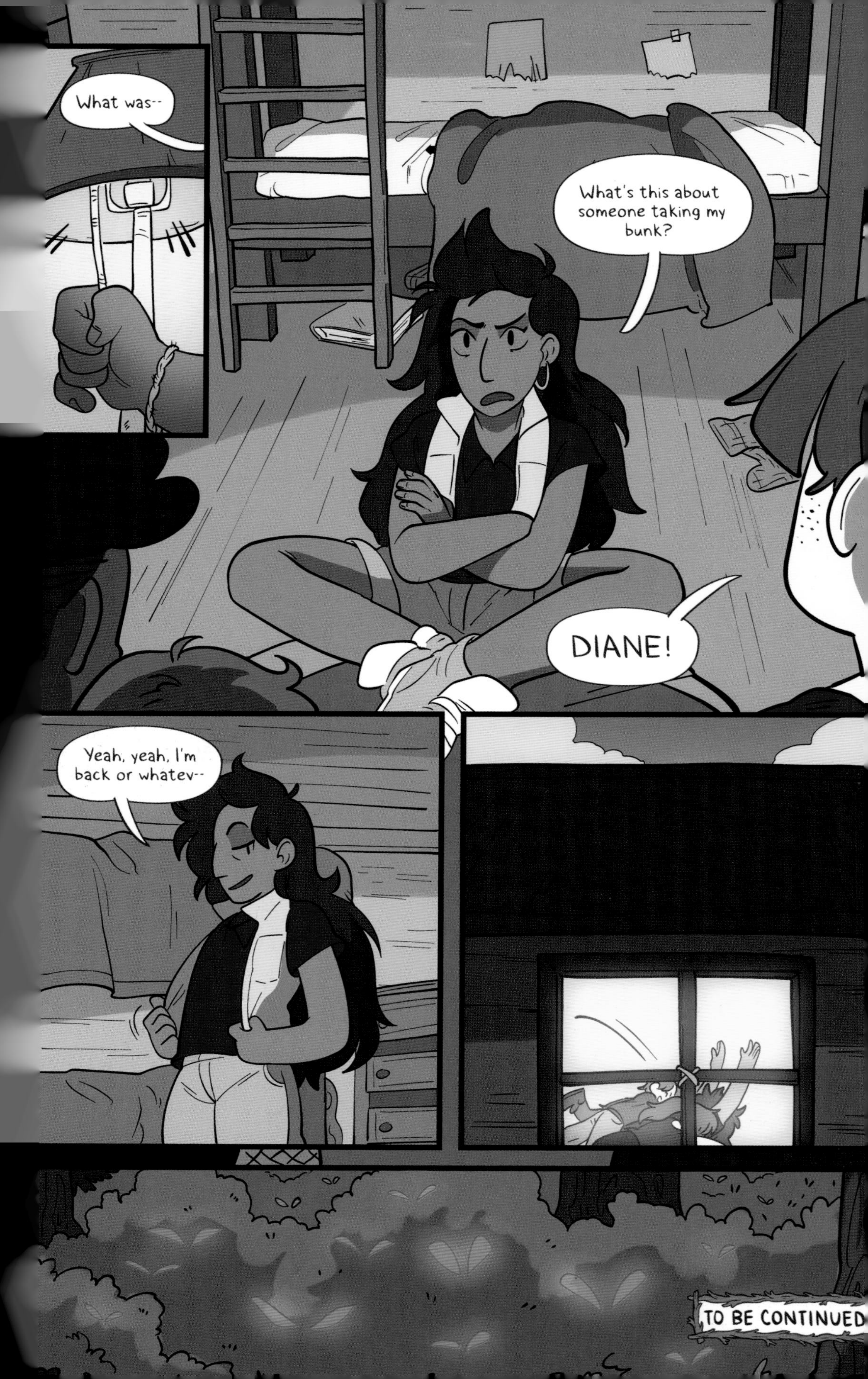
What was--
What's this about someone taking my bunk?
DIANE!
Yeah, yeah, I'm back or whatev--
TO BE CONTINUED

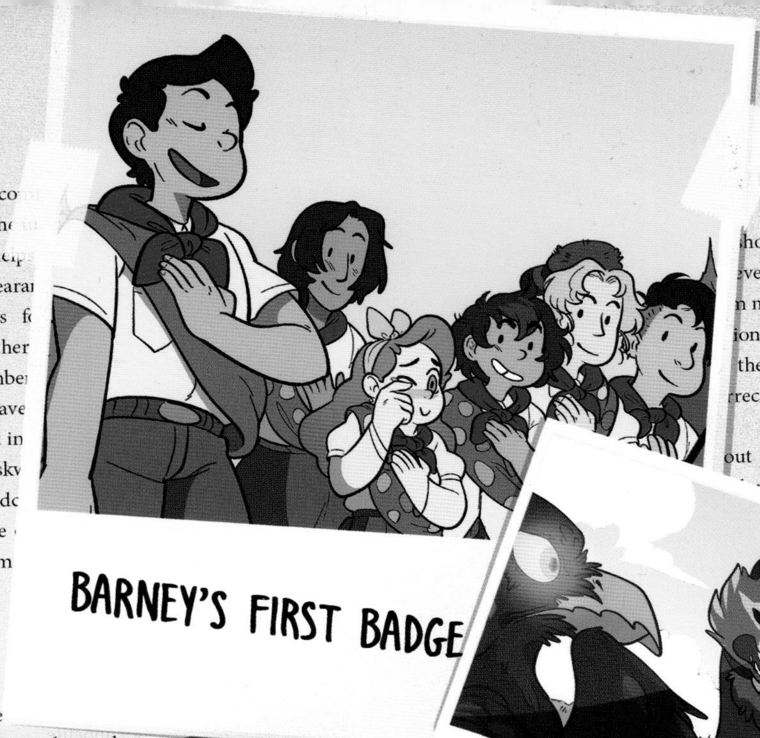
BARNEY'S FIRST BADGE

will co

The u

It helps

appearar

dress f

Further

Lumbe

to have

part in

Thiskv

Hardc

have

them

IE UNIFORM

should be worn at camp events when Lumberjanes n may also be worn at other ions. It should be worn as a the uniform dress with rrect shoes, and stocking or

out grows her uniform or ter Lumberjane. a she has her her

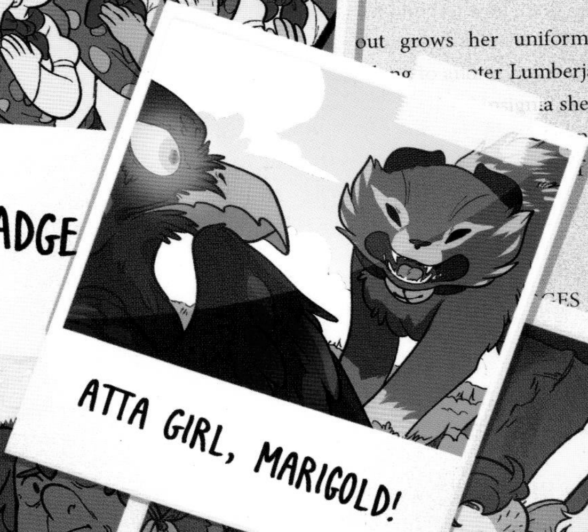
ATTA GIRL, MARIGOLD!

The

yellow, short sl

emb

the w

choose

slacks,

made o

out-of-do

green bere

the colla

Shoes ma

heels, rou

socks shou

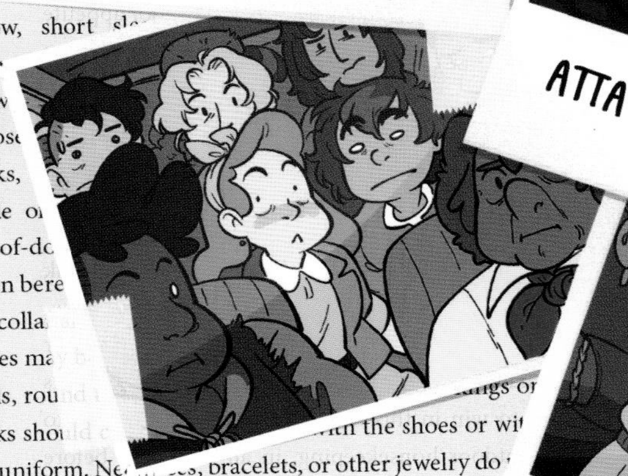

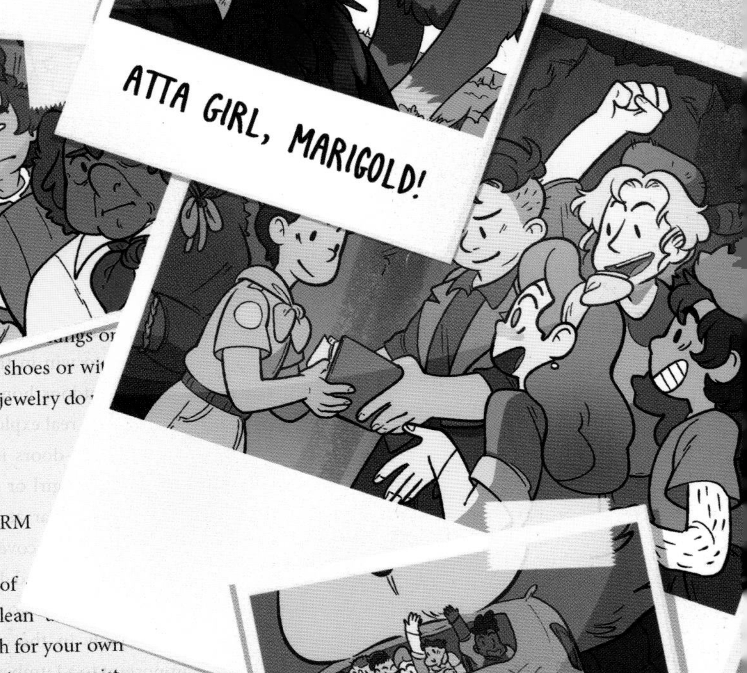

ngs or

with the shoes or wi

the uniform. Ne es, bracelets, or other jewelry do

belong with a Lumberjane uniform.

HOW TO WEAR THE UNIFORM

To look well in a uniform demans first of uniform be kept in good condition—clean pressed. See that the skirt is the right length for your own height and build, that the belt is adjusted to your waist, that your shoes and stockings are in keeping with the uniform, that you watch your posture and carry yourself with dignity and grace. If the beret is removed indoors, be sure that your hair is neat and kept in place with an insonspicuous clip or ribbon. When you wear a Lumberjane uniform you are identified as a member of this organization and you should be doubly careful to conduct yourself in a way that will show everyone that courtesy and thoughtfullness are part of being a Lumberjane. People are likely to judge a whole nation by the selfishness of a few individuals, to criticize a whole family because of the misconduct of one member, and to feel unkindly toward and organization because of the

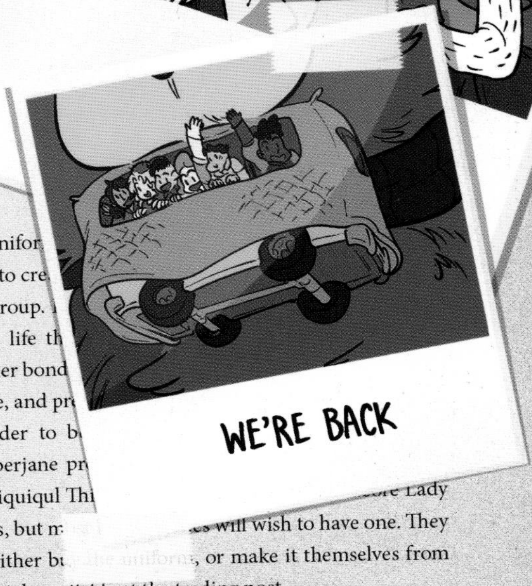
WE'RE BACK

The unifor

helps to cre

in a group.

active life th

another bond

future, and pr

in order to b

Lumberjane pr

Penniquiqul Thi ore Lady

Types, but m es will wish to have one. They

can either bu uniform, or make it themselves from

materials available at the trading post.

COVER GALLERY

Lumberjanes "Heart to Heart" Program Field

SPARROW A MOMENT BADGE

"Don't miss out on life's mysteries"

At camp, as in life, there is always much to do: games to be played, crafts to be crafted, badges to be earned. Barreling through your days at breakneck speed can be great fun, but it is important to take time and care, too. When a friend is struggling, you can make a world of difference just by taking the time to be by their side, or by offering a helping hand.

It can be difficult to put yourself in someone else's shoes, or to ever fully understand what the difficulties of someone else's life might be. Sometimes, all you can offer is a listening ear. But other times there maybe more that you can do, whether it's writing a kind letter, or helping to carry heavy boxes. Little things can add up to a lot!

The *Sparrow a Moment* badge is a badge that focuses on helping others, and taking the time out of your day to improve someone else's. Being considerate of others is a skill that we are all constantly learning, from the age that we first realize that playing with blocks or dolls becomes more fun when we can share with our friends.

When you were very small, something as simple as sharing a snack or a toy may have seemed impossible (And if you don't remember, perhaps you've noticed this stubborn trait in your younger siblings or cousins!). But now that you're older, you understand that making someone else happy will actually mean more fun for both of you, even if it means giving up something you care about for a brief time. As you get older, your ability to empathize broadens and deepens. Now that you're more mature, you can understand so many different ways to brighten someone's day and to offer help and love where it is needed, and to those who need it.

Try looking around your camp or cabin, and see if you can spy anyone who might benefit from a small surprise, or an offer of help. Listen when they tell you what will help them, since it will be different for every person, and try to focus on offering what they might need. Some might want a shoulder to cry on in a difficult moment, or advice on what to do. Others might prefer to take time away from what's troubling them, and do something fun with you. Both of these can be great helps, just as holding the door open for someone who has no hands free can be just as helpful as offering to split the load with them!

Always ask before you dive in, but you'll find that many of your friends will be happy to let you help! Some people will prefer to do things on their own, but they may still appreciate the offer, and in turn, they'll be there for you when you need it.

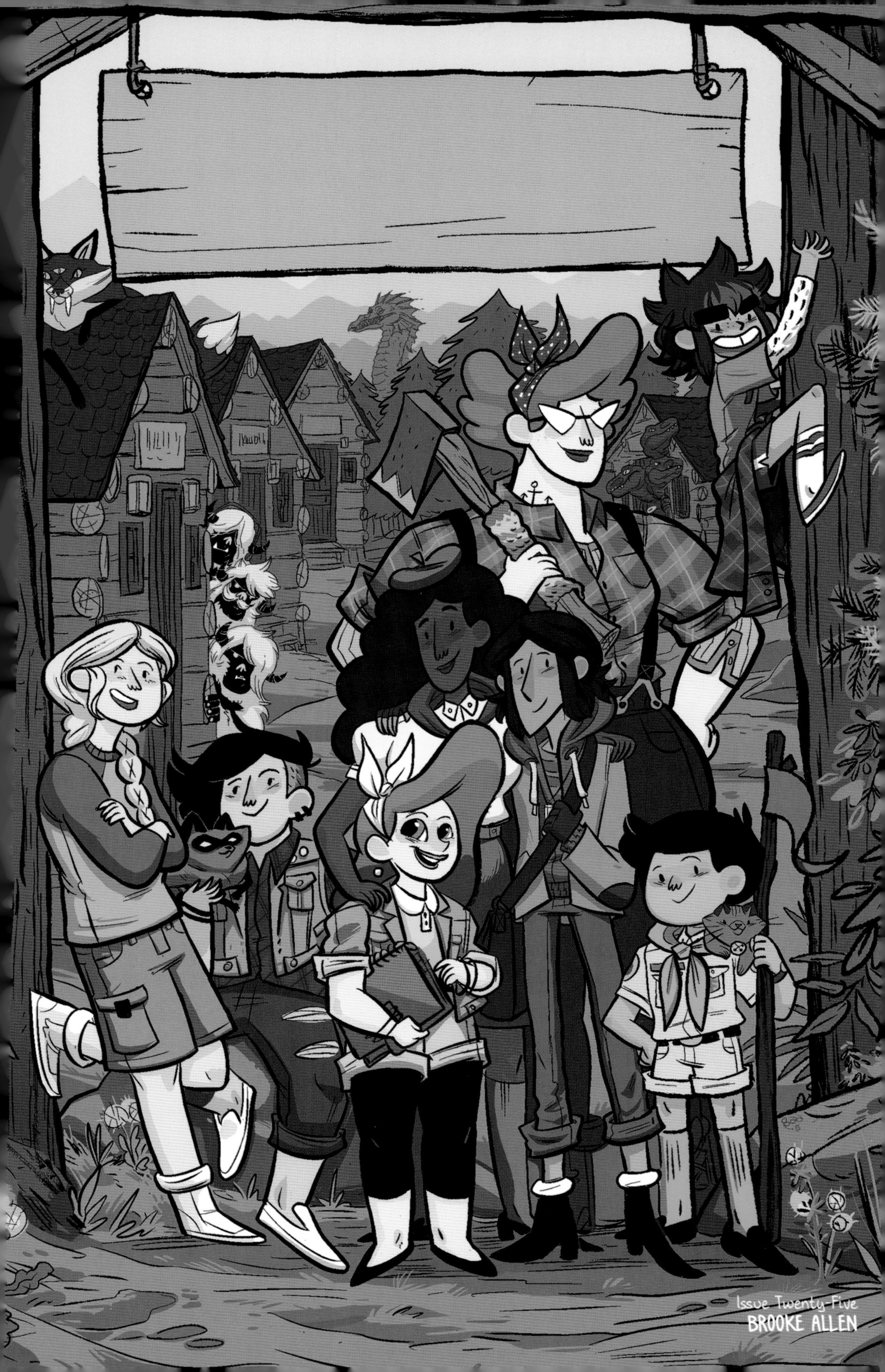
Issue Twenty-Five
BROOKE ALLEN

Issue Twenty-Five Variant
JONES WIEDLE

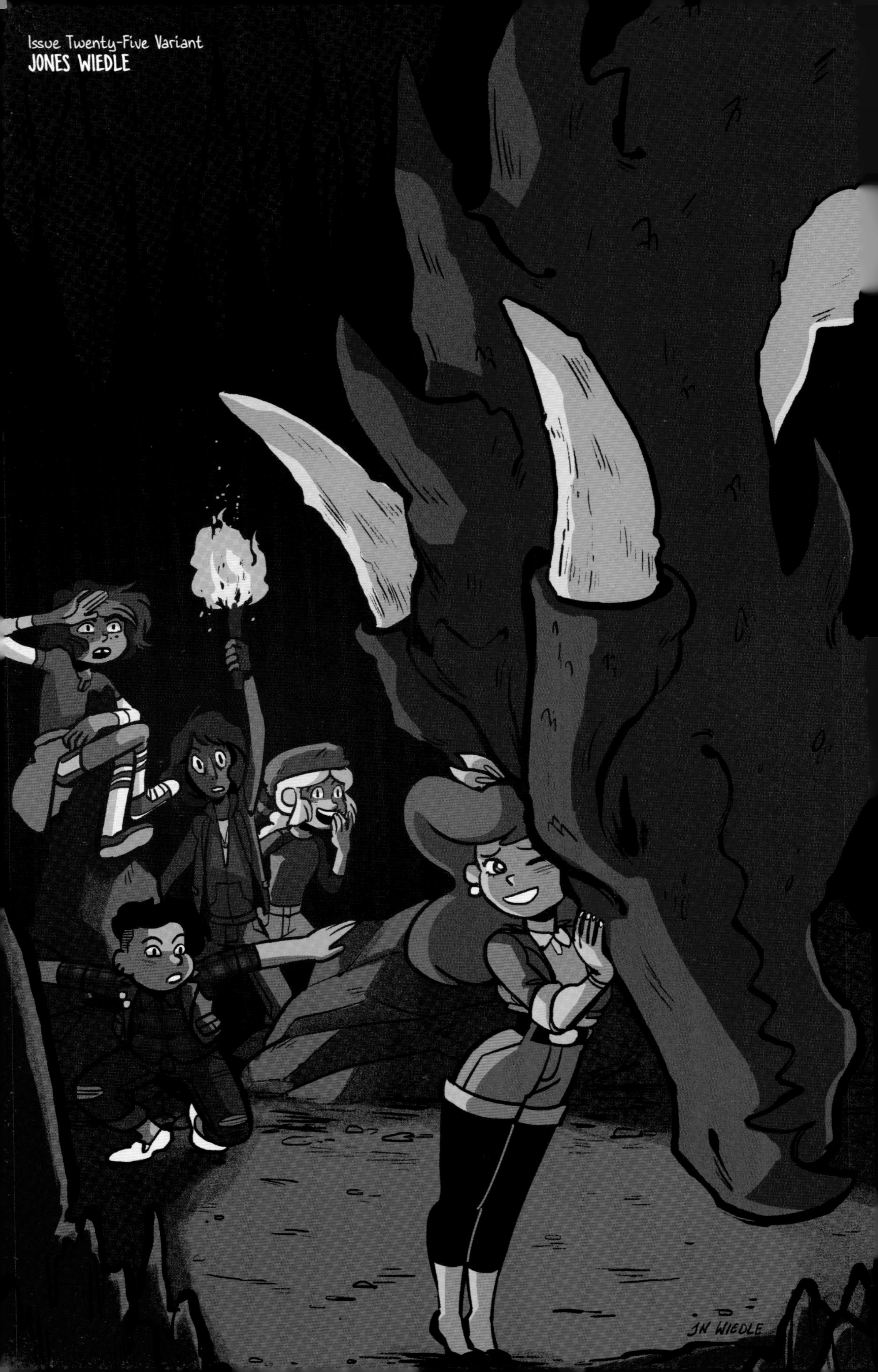
JN WIEDLE

Issue Twenty-Five FanMail
KAT LEYH

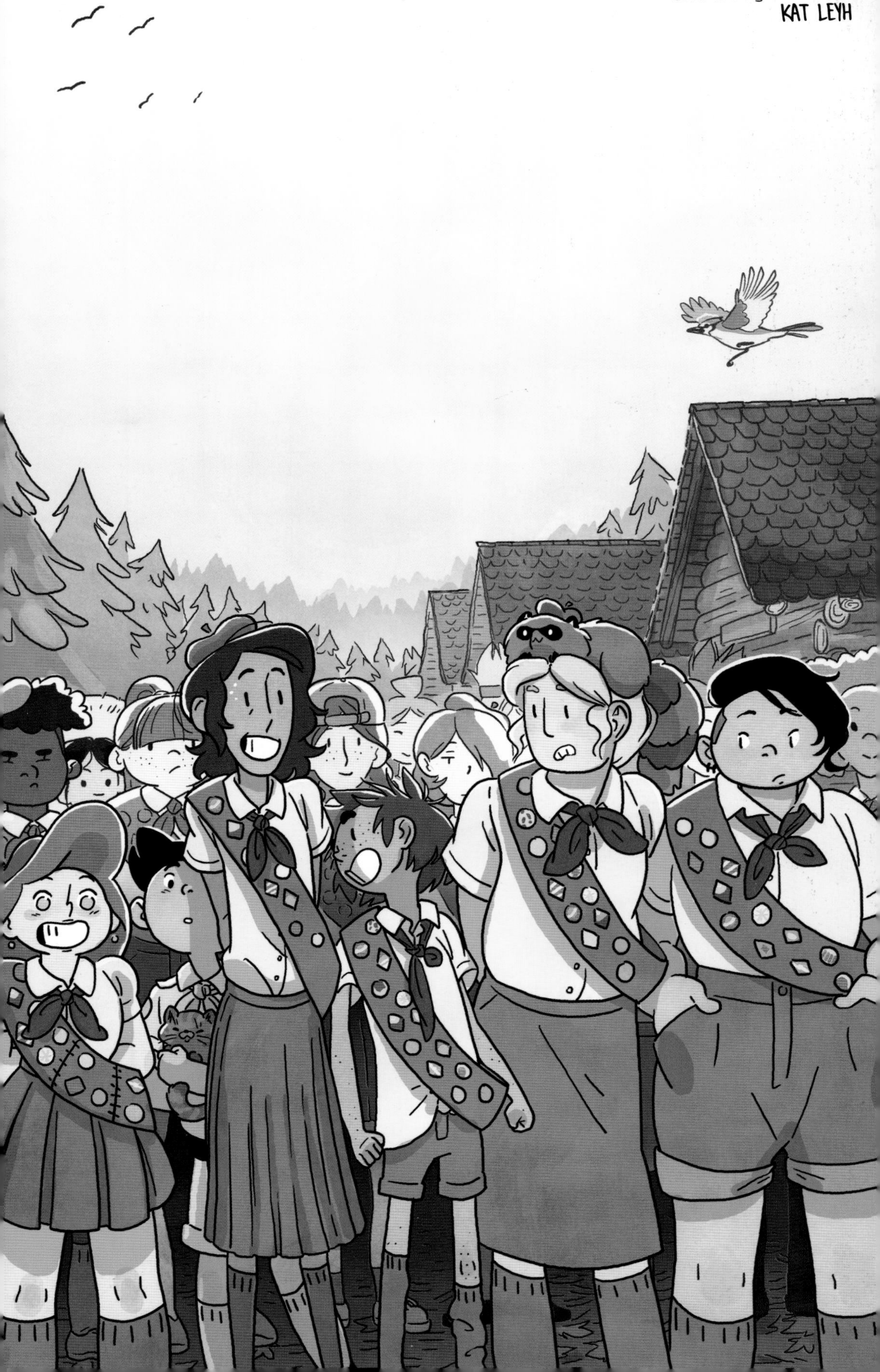

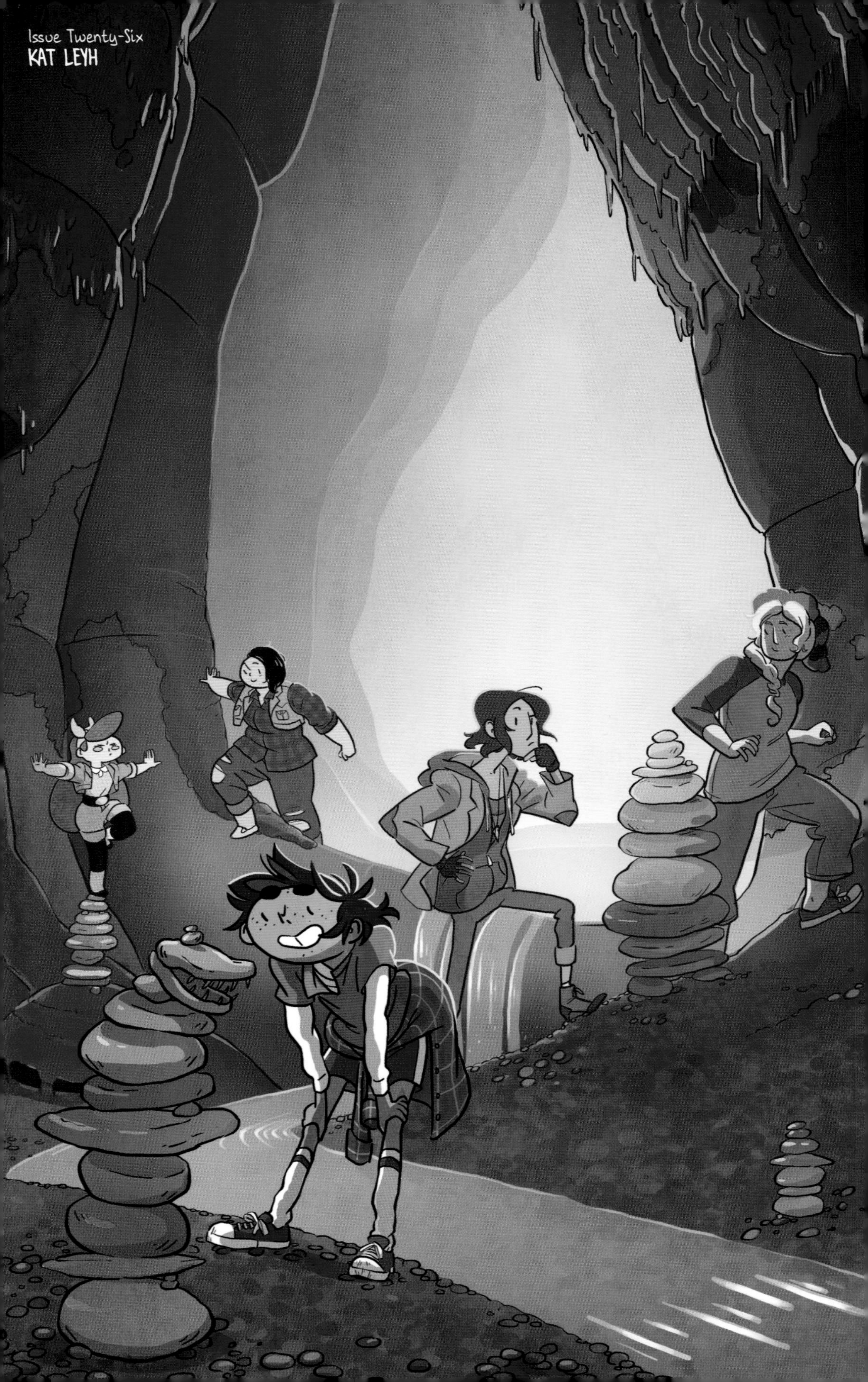
Issue Twenty-Six
KAT LEYH

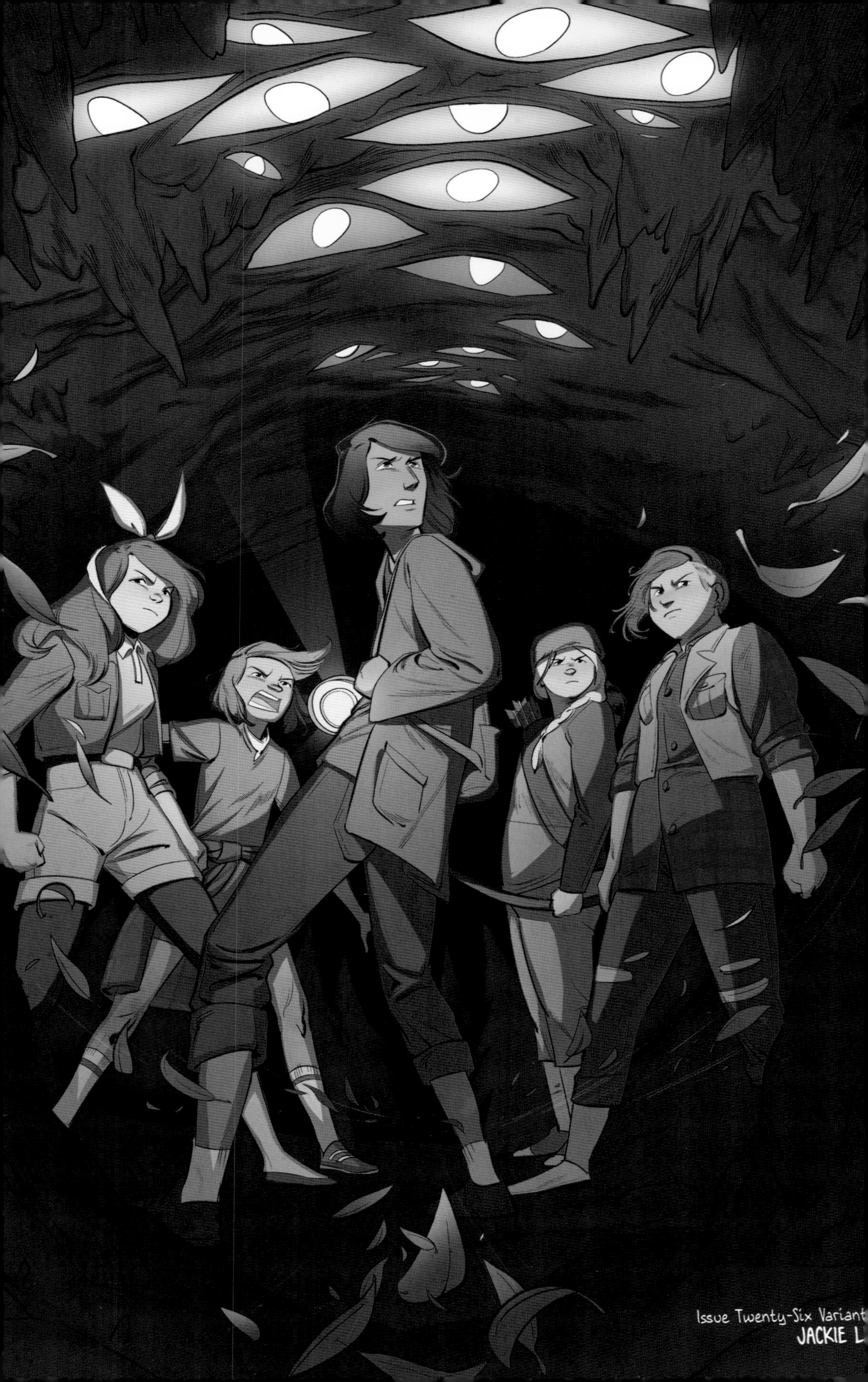

Issue Twenty-Six Variant
JACKIE L

Issue Twenty-Seven
KAT LEYH

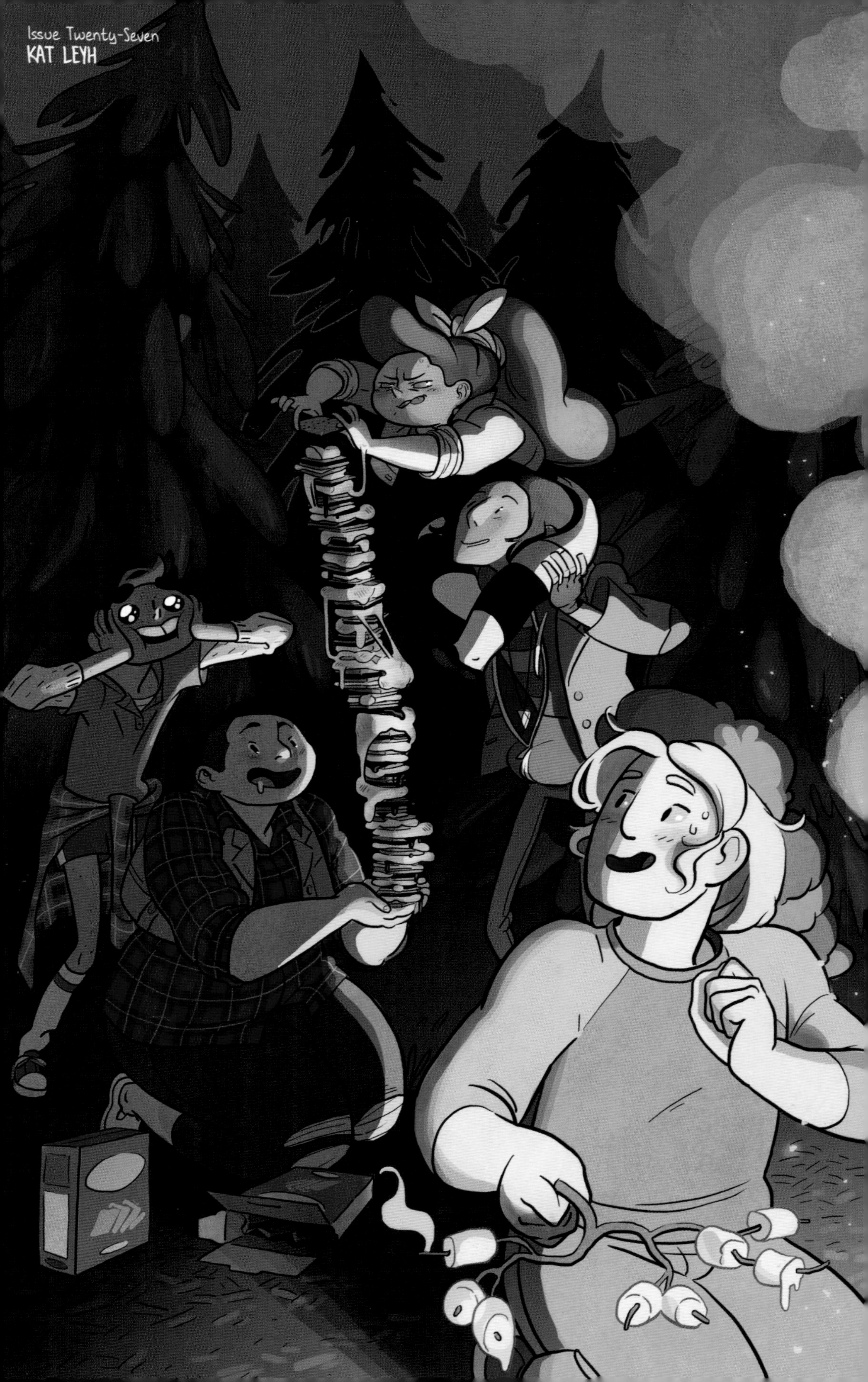